THE WINE-DARK OPAL

THE WINE-DARK OPAL

Virginia Coffman

G.K. Hall & Co. • **Chivers Press**
Thorndike, Maine USA   Bath, England

This Large Print edition is published by G.K. Hall & Co., USA and by Chivers Press, England.

Published in 1997 in the U.S. by arrangement with Chivers Press Limited.

Published in 1997 in the U.K. by arrangement with Severn House Publishers Ltd.

U.S. Hardcover   0-7838-8105-3   (Romance Collection Edition)
U.K. Hardcover   0-7540-1009-0   (Windsor Large Print)
U.K. Softcover   0-7451-8778-1   (Paragon Large Print)

The text of this Large Print edition is unabridged.
Other aspects of the book may vary from the original edition.

Set in 16 pt. Plantin by Rick Gundberg.

Printed in the United States on permanent paper.

British Library Cataloguing in Publication Data available

Library of Congress Cataloging in Publication Data

Coffman, Virginia.
    The wine-dark opal / Virginia Coffman.
        p.   cm. — (The jewels series ; bk. 2)
    ISBN 0-7838-8105-3 (lg. print : hc)
    1. Large type books. I. Title. II. Series: Coffman, Virginia.
Jewels series ; bk. 2.
[PS3553.O415W56 1997]
813'.54—dc21   97-7603

THE WINE-DARK OPAL

Chapter One

"Beautiful, isn't it?" Sybille Halloway remarked, turning her hand this way and that in the lamp-light. The multi-coloured opal glowed against the liver spots on the old actress's once flawless skin. She sighed. "But I read just last Sunday that opals are bad luck. I wonder. It might explain my recent money problems. Oh well . . ."

"Not bad luck if you can afford them," Roberta Fisher said, trying not to sound either tart or dry. "Shall I take the decanter upstairs to your bedroom?"

"No, dear. Leave it here on the sideboard. I might need just a drop or two before retiring. It's been a long day. So tiring, dredging up memories. You must always tell the truth just as I dictate it to you, Roberta. Don't make up things to sound worse — that is, more juicy than they are."

"Certainly not, Miss Halloway. I wouldn't dream of it."

She wasn't sure her quick agreement had pleased the actress. Besides, it would be very nearly impossible to make Sybille Halloway's memories of those 'Mad Sixties and Seventies' — her own description — sound more censorious than they were, according to Miss Halloway's 'confessions'. The risk, in the end, would not be that Roberta failed to tell the truth about Sybille Halloway, but that she accepted Sybille's dictation and caused both Sybille and herself to be sued for any number of lies about the sexual peccadillos of Continental royalty, British aristocracy, and international wheeler-dealers. Not to mention a few Hollywood glamour boys from the Golden Era whom Sybille claimed to remember fondly.

Then too, she had not been above dabbling in a bit of ladylike blackmail, pleading 'genteel poverty'.

Up went Sybille's hand again, the lights flashing from the opal as she studied the ring once more.

"My dear, the truth now. Do you really believe opals are bad luck to the wearer?"

Who cared? Sybille had obviously obtained the ring by threatening to expose a scandal about some hapless but important ex-lover. It was late and Roberta Fisher had a tiresome trip by Underground back to her flat at the other end of London from Miss Halloway's elegant old house within walking distance of Berkeley Square. But it struck her that the old lady might be really troubled, so she assured her as honestly as possible.

"Whoever gave it to you, Miss Halloway, gave it out of affection. That can't be bad luck." She yawned, hoping the old actress would take the hint, but her reply had been warmer than she intended.

"Well, in a sense. What a whiner he was! Said he'd planned to give it to his baby grandchild when the boy grew up to fit the ring. This was in the early Eighties. Boy must be a teenager by now. He won't need it. Teenagers have no use for real stones. Junk jewellery. That's their choice."

Roberta turned away, replacing the crystal decanter, but Sybille rambled on, busy reliving her glorious, scandalous past.

"Of course, if this ring came from one of my enemies —"

She caught Roberta's attention by that word. "Your enemies?" Sybille had boasted often enough that she made lovers out of enemies.

Miss Halloway was busy studying the lights reflected in the opal. "Two or three. Dead now. After all, the Sixties and Seventies were a long time —" She corrected herself. "A few years ago. My gentlemen have grown children now who think I am disgracing them with my poor little memoirs."

Roberta could understand that, but clearly, Sybille Halloway didn't. She looked at her ring again, then had a sudden notion. She reached for Roberta, holding her wrist momentarily.

"See those colours. Dark as the sea. Or wine, of course. You are so young, Roberta. You've your whole life before you. You could shake off bad luck and march on as though nothing had happened." She was putting the ring finger into her mouth and trying to force off the ring with her teeth. The manoeuvre worked and she took Roberta's hand again.

"There. Don't pull away. Ah! You see? It was practically made for you. It fits."

Unfortunately, it did. Open-mouthed and dumbfounded Roberta stared down at the heavy gold band and glowing darkness of the opal. She awoke to the gesture and tried to pull it off, protesting with a vigour that was more angry than shocked. The whole thing was absurd. Not the superstition. Roberta could take that or leave it. But she didn't like receiving expensive presents from people with whom she did not feel comfortable. Miss Halloway had been a 'user' of people, especially men, and while a good many might deserve it, that was Sybille Halloway's business. It had nothing to do with Roberta.

Roberta had been hired by the ex-actress to ghost her memoirs, and she was doing so. Sybille was originally an American actress, and Roberta was an American writer. It had seemed appropriate that Sybille's life story should be in the hands of someone who — as Miss Halloway put it — understood 'us Yankees'.

But it was not a subject that she was crazy about. It had come to mean that Roberta must work all the harder and at all hours, as she was tonight, on the advance she had received before flying to London to take on the job. That was almost three months ago. If she quit now, she would probably never get paid.

It occurred to her, not without some private

fears, that this ring might be a payment of sorts and wipe out Miss Halloway's debt to her. It was not a pretty arrangement.

Sybille waved away her protests. "We'll discuss it tomorrow." After a pause she added, "I really must have a few minutes to myself. To relax. Such a strenuous day. My dear Roberta, you have been very naughty you know, working me as you have these past weeks."

It wasn't the way Roberta Fisher would have described the woman's incessant additions to some pretty tall tales about the men in her life. There was not an unimportant male in the lot. And certainly, none of them had dropped her, according to her stories; it was the other way around.

Still, the old lady had made enemies and was making more with every word she dictated. Who were these enemies? There had been plenty of publicity about all her tawdry confessions.

Sybille Halloway's remark hadn't quite produced the denial hoped for, so Sybille added modestly, "But there. You really shouldn't dedicate yourself to an old woman like me at this hour."

Roberta was amused. "At nine o'clock?" Luckily, she remembered to add, "And no one could ever call you old."

"Dear child." Satisfied, Miss Halloway felt that she could pursue one more little request for a favour. "Before I let you run away, would you, after all, take upstairs that lovely cut-glass brandy decanter you mentioned, and of course, don't forget the disks we worked on this afternoon. Then you can be off to your precious tube station."

Roberta would have done as she was politely ordered but the ex-actress touched a strand of Roberta's lengthy and comparatively straight hair which was the colour of old, minted gold coins. "A bright, buttercup yellow rinse, my dear, and one of those kinky hairdos. It would make you so 'today'."

Roberta forced a grin. "How nice of you to care! What time will you want me tomorrow?"

"I hardly know, dear. Suppose you come at about nine-thirty and just be on hand whenever I want you. That should settle things nicely, don't you agree?"

"Very nicely."

"Good. I knew my opal would please you. I don't imagine they are too common in the States."

She had been a 'British treasure' so long, Miss Halloway had almost forgotten her birth in Scranton, Pennsylvania, seventy-five years ago.

The opal was a bribe. No question about it. But Roberta couldn't think of any way to return the opal without giving offence. Maybe tomorrow something would occur to her.

As Roberta crossed the polished dining-room floor with the careful ease of three months' practice, Sybille called to her.

"Oh, and dear, you will go through your own

tapes and disks of our interviews before you sleep, won't you? There just might be an idea." She laughed coyly. "Sometimes we get ideas in our dreams when we do that."

"Yes, Ma'am."

It was not often that Roberta Fisher was reduced to 'yes, Ma'am', and 'no, Ma'am', but she was afraid if she said anything else Miss Halloway would rattle on for another hour or two.

Joel Sawyer, Roberta's partner on a television series in Hollywood, hadn't said anything about the fifteen or twenty hours a day that the 'ghosting' job in London would involve. But Roberta had a very good notion now just why Joel had recommended her for the job after protesting regretfully to Sybille Halloway, the aged belle of London's 1960s, that an earlier commitment kept him from the great pleasure of immortalising her life between hard covers.

At the moment Roberta hated Joel Sawyer's guts.

It was time she moved on, beyond those of the industry, like Sawyer, who was teamed up as her senior writer on TV scripts as a repayment of old favours. Joel hadn't done more than a storyline on the last four shows of their series. When he wasn't in Palm Springs with his girlfriend he was soothing his wife's ruffled feathers with the latest 'feathers' from Rodeo Drive.

Roberta stifled a yawn at the top of the stairs, wondering where the time had gone since her twenty-first birthday four years ago, when, as a film student at the University of California at Los Angeles, her amateur movie — much of it done with old-fashioned hand-held cameras — had brought her to the attention of Hollywood and prestigious, though little known, awards.

At the first independent unit that employed her she had been asked, not for the first time, how she knew so much about 'LA-LA Land and the minnows floating around it'? She carefully explained that she had been born in Pasadena, perhaps only a few freeways away from Los Angeles, but almost a hundred years from 'that place'.

Since both Pasadena, and her father, despised Hollywood, and Hollywood was too busy to notice the affront, her explanations had fallen flat.

Roberta's father would have known. She sometimes thought he owned half of Pasadena, which might explain the two wives and a mistress he began to acquire three months after Roberta's mother died.

Without her mother, a confidante and friend, there was little to hold Roberta at home. Her father resented the idea of her attending UCLA; he had planned to introduce her proudly as the alumna of some prestigious women's college in the east. *Any* college.

Their relationship (post-UCLA) had faded to modest Christmas presents, chosen by her father's wives, and an occasional birthday card, remembered by wife number three.

"No more ghosting jobs," Roberta promised

herself as she stepped into the upper hall on which several bedrooms and an elegant salon opened. Almost everything in sight had been chosen in the fond hope that Sybille's guests would inquire about her ancestral past.

Roberta was still amused, a little sympathetically, by Sybille Halloway's choice of distinguished ancestors whose stony-faced portraits depressed the Regency hall.

No matter. They made the old lady happy and brought back a rich and imaginary past. More power to Sybille.

She was just going into Sybille's bedroom with the decanter when a knocking sound surprised her. She went back to the head of the stairs, listened, and decided that for some reason, the sound came from the tarnished lion-head knocker on the front door.

Miss Halloway's usual callers made arrangements with her in advance. She was still increasingly popular among some ageing male admirers. Not to mention those who came to protest over the horrifying possibility that her memoirs might see the light of day. Or more likely night. Yet even these men became surprisingly polite under the old lady's light flirtations. Roberta hoped she could get those charming qualities into the 'autobiography'.

Although Roberta had hinted once or twice that the victims of all these dubious memories just might take offence, Sybille had been shocked at such *lèse majesté*.

"But Roberta, my dear, they will be pleased. Honoured, in fact. Wait and see. Long ago somebody wrote a few dreadful truths about a Yankee mayor and the dear boy was far from insulted. He said they made him famous."

There might be some truth in that, Roberta thought wryly.

Only two or three of Sybille's one-time lovers had left her house near Berkeley Square still angry. Roberta hoped tonight's persistent knocker-on-doors wasn't one of them.

Miss Halloway had started toward the vestibule, then called out, "Mrs Allegretti, the door."

But the cook and her niece, one of the two maids in Miss Halloway's service, had been gone at least an hour and the chauffeur was probably in his little mews apartment somewhere behind the Halloway house.

Roberta returned to the banister above the main staircase and called down, "Shall I answer it, Miss Halloway?"

"Never mind, my dear." Miss Halloway's voice reached her from the front foyer. "I think I recognise . . . Well now, good evening. I never expected to see you, of all people."

Obviously, the visitor was known to her. Roberta descended the stairs but decided Miss Halloway could handle the caller, so started back up again. After a couple of seconds things below the stairs did not sound as pleasant as they might. She could make out a man's voice that sounded educated but deep pitched. She couldn't make

16

out the words. Apparently, Miss Halloway had no difficulty.

"How dare you! I owed your father nothing, and certainly not you or your family. You will all get just what he deserved. And no more. You may be sure of that."

This time Roberta, now a little nervous, heard the male voice further away and was impressed by its timbre.

"I won't argue the matter. You may find the courts less accommodating."

He must have left then, because Miss Halloway screamed after him, her voice floating out rather coarsely over the street.

"Go ahead and sue. I might have dealt with your father, poor dear. But from what I've heard about you, I'm not giving you the time of day. You'll only make yourself a laughing stock for your trouble."

She was certainly yelling at the top of her lungs as if he had already gone beyond her range. She slammed the door so hard even Roberta on the stairs was a bit shaken. She took two steps down and asked, "Is anything wrong, Miss Halloway? Did he threaten you?"

To her surprise Miss Halloway laughed her light, genuinely amused chuckle.

"Lord no, dear! Just a tradesman. Overcharged us, as usual. I'm always telling Allegretti to question some of their absurd prices. She's too easily taken in. Leave the decanter by the bed, dear. Don't forget."

As if I'm likely to forget, Roberta silently answered her. She passed the haughty, bloodless portraits on the landing that Sybille Halloway had chosen as her ancestors and marvelled that anybody should imagine those eviscerated characters giving birth.

Suddenly, she was stunned by a shriek, followed by a heavy, thumping noise, somewhere on the lower floor. Then there was nothing. Only stillness, and an eerie silence.

Horrified, she rushed back to the staircase and leaned over the banister rail. The glow from the lamp on the square newel post at the foot of the stairs showed nothing that moved, no sounds of life at all. She ran down the stairs.

Across the hall the double doors of the dining room remained open. Then she saw Sybille Halloway sprawled on the floor in front of the sideboard with its row of other cut-glass decanters just out of reach. She lay on her side, one foot doubled up under her.

Roberta ran to her, slipping over the glossy floor as Sybille must have done. Shaking badly, she saw the white roots of dishevelled golden hair over the old lady's left temple were dark with blood.

Trying to regain her balance as she bent over the silent, motionless body, Roberta reached out a hand, her fingers closing around the sharp corner of the sideboard. They brought away sticky smudges of blood. These followed a trail around the band of the ring Sybille Halloway had given her, not half an hour ago.

Chapter Two

Reaching for the telephone, Roberta Fisher had never believed she would thank God for the dead woman's brisk, businesslike cook, but the only name she could think of to call was Mrs Allegretti who was nothing if not efficient. And point-blank.

Was Roberta sure the old lady had actually died?

Yes. Roberta was sure. She had seen a dead woman before. She remembered all too well the awful stillness, the gradual chilling of her beloved mother's body in the last moments during which her heart gave up its struggle and Roberta waited for Kate Fisher's doctor.

Over the telephone she could imagine diminutive Mrs Allegretti nodding her head with its heavy, dark, yet attractive black hair.

"Good." (Nothing good about it!) "I'll call the proper gents. Her doctor and the District lads. We'll see to it. She's got no blood heirs. Told me once in her cups that she'd left it all to some indigent actors' charity."

After that, there were the comings and goings, the questions by polite gentlemen in topcoats, one of them wearing a hat that might have been worn in a late-night mystery movie.

True to her promise, Mrs Allegretti handled

everything except Roberta's actual recollections of the moments before Miss Halloway's death.

The first questioning was suspended sometime after midnight, but it resumed the next day. Roberta returned under 'request' and told them about Miss Halloway's last visitor the night before. They didn't receive this with any alarm but they did make her go over the minute details of what she had heard, what the 'tradesman' sounded like, and how long he was gone before Sybille Halloway went into the dining room, reached for a whisky decanter, slipped on the polished floor and struck her head.

Roberta suggested that they read the notes and listen to the tapes she had made of Miss Halloway's vivid past, where she certainly must have made a few enemies, however she might have shrugged them off. Her offer was accepted along with the attaché case which contained the notes.

Afterward, Mrs Allegretti shook her head, reminding Roberta, "The less you say to them boys, the better."

But four days later Roberta received a call at her bedsitting room saying she might pick up the attaché case at Miss Halloway's house, which relieved her considerably as it must mean that her part in Miss Halloway's death was done.

There was only one more delay. Another telephone call came as she was about to leave on her way to Miss Halloway's house a few steps from Berkeley Square. This was a breathy, friendly female voice.

"Miss Fisher? This is Sir Arthur Laidlaw's office. He wonders if you would be so good as to stop off today . . . Say, within the hour? That would get you here before dark."

"What about?" The name of Arthur Laidlaw was vaguely familiar. A man of some importance in the legal profession, she believed.

The woman was jovial, but not very communicative. "Oh, my dear, nothing important. Just putting 'paid' — as my father used to say — to the matter of Miss Halloway's case."

So now it was a 'case'.

Roberta was ready to leave the house anyway, and would like to have taken a taxi, but she hadn't yet been paid for her three months' work and it was highly unlikely she would be paid now.

Or was that why Sir Arthur wanted to see her?

Too much to hope for. Better take the tube.

She was in a foreign country, out of a job, and she had to get home. An Atlantic flight, not the Concorde this time, and the US flight to Los Angeles. Once she got back to her Hollywood apartment, to tide her over she could borrow for the first weeks from her Studio Employees Fund at a decent rate of interest. She didn't like to do it, but that was preferable to borrowing from her father with his cool, superior "I knew you couldn't make it alone".

The spatter of raindrops had begun to blur the windows of Sir Arthur Laidlaw's ante-room when Roberta arrived, making it more difficult to see the noisy matinee traffic homeward-bound in the street below. Roberta had expected that a man of Sir Arthur's distinction would have crowds of supplicants waiting to see him but when she arrived in the room, although the corridor door was unlocked, she found herself alone in the waiting room.

Standing by the nearest window, Roberta was annoyed to see on the news placard outside, the nickname 'Ghost' that the London press had given her in their brief mention of her concerning her employer's death.

MALE THREAT HEARD BY SYBILLE'S YANKEE 'GHOST'.

"Yankee Ghost. That's me," she thought. It was all ridiculous. She was a fully-fledged screenwriter. The Screen Writers' Guild said so, as did the companies, independent and otherwise, who had employed her. 'Ghostwriters' were not supernatural. There was nothing supernatural about her, nor about Sybille Halloway's death. Why had she even mentioned to the police the visit of the man with whom Sybille argued only minutes before she tripped and fell? It had nothing to do with a ghastly but simple household accident.

Sorry as Roberta was for the unfortunate Sybille, she knew the hints of foul play by the press wouldn't do much for her own reputation when she returned home.

Why hadn't she kept her mouth shut when that

polite plain-clothes gentleman asked her all those questions? Above all, he had wanted to know if she recalled anything else about Sybille's wild shriek. Roberta tried to be helpful, but she had heard only that cry. It seemed to her, and eventually to the police, that the old lady reached for the whisky on the sideboard and slipped, striking the delicate part of her head against the sideboard. Roberta had repeated this honestly, wincing as she relived Sybille Halloway's last moment.

In Sir Arthur Laidlaw's office Roberta glanced again at the placard on the Strand corner. Then she backed away from the window and sat down in the straight, uncomfortable office chair before looking around again at her shabby surroundings.

These were curious offices for a celebrated English barrister who should surely reign either glamorously, or like a Dickensian figure huddled in cluttered rooms and surrounded by dusty legal tomes and the wax masks of former — and hanged? — clients.

"Why does Sir Arthur want to see me?" she asked herself for perhaps the hundredth time, not at all comfortable with the possibilities that presented themselves. "How did I get into this mess?"

Looking back on the last three months, Roberta realised there were many moments when she liked the chattery egotist who had employed her, found the woman amusing, and certainly sympathetic in that last hour of her life, as well as surprisingly generous over the opal.

23

Unless you were superstitious.

Roberta looked down at the gold band of the ring. She studied it now, turning her hand this way and that as Sybille Halloway had done. The delicate beauty of the rare harlequin opal seemed to have taken on new lights. Or was Sybille Halloway's absurd fear contagious? Roberta started to ease the ring off but then decided not to give in to superstition.

She considered the stone again. Absurd or not, Sybille Halloway had believed in its evil and now Sybille was dead. One of the detectives had smiled at the reason why Sybille Halloway had given her the ring. When Roberta asked what she ought to do about it, he said, "I should think the poor lady wanted you to keep it."

She wondered now if she had been summoned to Sir Arthur Laidlaw's office on some technicality about the ring. She shivered and turned the opal stone into her palm. Maybe the beautiful thing actually was accursed.

The door to Sir Arthur Laidlaw's private office opened and Roberta dropped her hand into her lap quickly, trying to assume a confidence she was far from feeling. A moment later Sir Arthur's secretary (or was it his law clerk?) strode into the ante-room. Her smile greatly relieved her features as she held out a hand in welcome. Roberta was surprised, but only for an instant, before she accepted this welcoming gesture.

"Sorry no one was here to meet you, my dear. I was the one who rang you. Gerda Peavis, Sir

24

Arthur's confidential secretary. Sir Arthur will be here shortly, but it was necessary to speak with a client — that is, a friend — before he saw you."

What was that all about? Roberta murmured that she understood, which she didn't, and seated herself in the stiff, ladder-back chair indicated by Mrs Peavis.

She was puzzled again when Mrs Peavis glanced back at a small landscape in oils hung between the windows, close to where Roberta had earlier been sitting.

"You have been admiring the village, Miss Fisher? It was painted by Sir Arthur's friend, Nicholas Demian, the gentleman he had lunch with today. Edenbrook village is Demian property. It's been there for centuries. Sir Arthur stays there occasionally. Mr Nick, by the way, does those horrid political cartoons in the press and magazines."

Roberta looked around, then saw the curious, almost primitive painting that showed a tiny rural village at twilight, or perhaps just as the quaint street lamps went on. An odd, deserted-looking place, it contained merely a square of Dickensian cottages beside a quiet brook, and a few other cottages, framed by a thick, almost primeval wooded area.

Mrs Peavis was all enthusiasm. "The place is heaven. Sheer heaven. I've been there myself. Nick Demian and Sir Arthur have been friends from childhood, and Sir Arthur is determined to find a new mistress for Demian House. Mr

Nick's wife has been dead for years and years. It's Miss Sheila, Mr Nick's sister, who is mistress of the house at the moment. Much nicer than her brother." She confided in a conspiratorial tone, "He loves women and then deserts them. A nasty piece of work in my opinion."

"Is your Mr Nick against marriage on principle? Or just too fussy?"

Mrs Peavis shrugged. "I suppose he was stung once and doesn't intend to make the same mistake twice. That doesn't stop dear Sir Arthur. He sometimes takes glamorous young ladies on visits but there's always a problem. The last one didn't think the food was appetising enough and the natives, including Mr Demian, were unfriendly."

"Restless natives, in fact?" Roberta asked, playing the part for humour.

"Oh well, Mr Nick is an artist, as I say. Quite different from Sir Arthur, but I believe artists are."

Roberta laughed. "Some of them. All my Hollywood friends call themselves artists."

Mrs Peavis looked faintly annoyed. "That really isn't what we — I mean Sir Arthur — had in mind. You'd be the last person on earth who would get on with Mr Nick. He's terribly opinionated."

Roberta wondered if she herself had been labelled as 'opinionated' because of her quotes in the press.

"Then what did you have in mind? Why am I here? By any chance, is it a job?"

Mrs Peavis hurried on. "Actually, it was my notion yesterday when the inspector told Sir Arthur about you. Your training and background. We need a writer; a sympathetic one. Of course, we knew someone was working on those dreadful memoirs, but we thought she was quite a different sort. But the inspector told us you made quite an impression on him."

"Don't tell me this Sir Arthur wants his life spiced up!" Roberta found herself only half-joking.

Mrs Peavis's mouth pursed momentarily, but she did not take offence.

"No, dear. Not precisely. Sir Arthur wouldn't dream of having any part in a sordid affair like Sybille Halloway's memoirs. Now, this is very hush-hush, you understand."

"What is?" No use in mincing words. Something was brewing here. It might even be a job. Something that paid without her client dropping dead.

"Sir Arthur, and a few others who shall be nameless at the moment, would like to have the story of Edenbrook written up. It's a task that can't be delayed too long. It should be done before the end comes for poor Edenbrook."

What were they expecting? An earthquake? A national disaster? "You expect the end to come pretty soon?"

"Well, by the end of the century it will be gone. Bound to be."

Roberta gave the strange, isolated picture on

the wall a second, longer look.

"Edenbrook. But you said it has lasted for centuries."

Mrs Peavis looked at her oddly, as if she had been about to contradict her. Then she back-tracked. "I mean to say, the poor old village deserves some sort of tribute before the next century. That's not very long from now."

Roberta had taken other assignments which interested her very little. It then became a chal-lenge to make them interesting to television view-ers. So far, she had succeeded modestly. Had they actually been more intriguing than a centu-ries-old village that was remote and, as Mrs Peavis described it, just a tad mysterious?

And there was the prospective fee to be con-sidered. Roberta certainly needed the work.

She said, "I would wish to do justice to a place with Edenbrook's history. It must be very col-ourful."

This wasn't entirely true. There was something too enclosed, too lonely about the painting which promised long weeks of boredom in a village hidden from the world by those deep woods, and probably full of hostile locals.

But it could hardly be worse than borrowing from the studio, or going home to Pasadena to act as a buffer between her father and his spend-thrift third wife.

Mrs Peavis considered. "Colourful? Well, yes. I suppose one might call it that. Like wandering backward in time. Back when the leases were signed it must have been charming; everyone so happy, pitching in to rebuild. Around the turn of the century Edenbrook had pretty much reverted to uncultivated countryside, almost a wilderness. And then, along came families, and life again; thanks to the Demians, you could say. Not that —"

"Then why not a story of these Demians who revitalised everything, as you say?"

Mrs Peavis examined her cream-polished fingernails absently. "Well, there aren't many of the family left. Only Mr Nick and his boy, Jamie, and of course, Mr Nick's sister, Sheila. Sir Arthur was always very taken with her. I mean, since his own wife divorced him, at his request. American, you know. Oh — I'm sorry. But the lady was what you might call 'taken in adultery'."

"Shocking. I can see how it was, though. Being American, and all."

Mrs Peavis eyed her, as if doubting her sincerity, but Roberta looked back at her blandly, and she went on, "Miss Sheila is a bit of an old maid, but I must say, we like her." Obviously, she and her employer might be said to think as one.

Roberta asked, "Then who wants me to write about Edenbrook?"

"Mr Nick's tenants, of course. They want to present what they and their ancestors have done to cultivate the property, make it worth so much more, so they may be able to keep the property their whole lives are bound up in. It's all owned by Mr Nick and then his son. Mr Nick's sister

29

Sheila inherited a tidy little fortune. In stocks and bonds, not property. If it weren't for them, then it would go to the tenants, I suppose, if they had good lawyers. But let's not think of that sort of dreadful solution."

Why couldn't Sir Arthur himself take on the problem? Or was he afraid of losing this Nick Demian's friendship? If so, the idea of suggesting that Roberta Fisher handle the matter was more than a little underhanded.

Roberta saw at once that she couldn't help the Edenbrook tenants. She knew nothing whatever about British entailment laws and laws of primogeniture. Or laws of possession and tenant rights.

She heard voices in the hall and doors being opened and closed. Mrs Peavis looked behind her in panic.

"Oh, they've come back. Don't say a word before Mr Nick, will you? He doesn't know about — what we discussed."

I should think not, Roberta told herself.

She heard two male voices now in the next room but couldn't make out what was being said. The door that had been ajar was pushed fully open. Mrs Peavis hurried toward the voices.

A good deal of her feeling about her employer was clear to Roberta when Sir Arthur, a fair-haired, graceful gentleman, stood aside at the doorway, waving his friend, Nicholas Demian, into the ante-room.

Sir Arthur said pleasantly, "Well, Nick, we are in time. You remember Mrs Peavis of course, the lodestar of these chambers." Mrs Peavis tried to look both humble and proud.

A dark man, of slightly above average height, caught Roberta's interest. He might be the gentleman-ogre Mrs Peavis indicated, but he seemed to have manners. Perhaps something else stirred beneath the sallow complexion, the high, pronounced cheekbones, and especially the deep-set eyes which seemed to give Mrs Peavis so much trouble as she took his hand but avoided his eyes. All the same, at first glance, he seemed harmless.

Roberta made out the faint amusement in his voice as he said, "Certainly. I haven't forgotten Mrs Peavis and her husband. They were obliging enough to pose for me. A sketch, wasn't it?"

Mrs Peavis raised her chin and tried to look imperious, but Sir Arthur Laidlaw smiled.

"Well, Nick, I don't think we need dwell on that. Your sketches are pretty sharp, as I myself know too well. Now then, Mrs Peavis, I see you have persuaded Miss Fisher to visit us and satisfy her natural curiosity."

"Curiosity?" Roberta repeated, remembering her annoyance at having to make this unwarranted call on a man, or men, whom she didn't know or care about.

Mrs Peavis turned quickly to oblige her employer. "Oh, yes, indeed, Sir Arthur." She waved a hand in introduction. "She has really obliged us. Miss Roberta Fisher, may I present Sir Arthur Laidlaw." She added, almost as an afterthought, "And Mr Demian."

31

Roberta became aware of the dark man's survey which was complete, a head-to-toe affair. She would have liked to believe this was due to his artistic profession, but there was nothing flattering about his interest, nor his ever-so-faint smile that seemed edged with contempt. Maybe she was imagining it. She hoped so. What had she done to this fellow to make him dislike her on first acquaintance?

Unless, of course, Mrs Peavis's own dislike was based on solid knowledge and the man simply made himself disliked by everyone.

"Of course, we musn't forget the young lady," he said, reaching for her hand. She hadn't held it out. No one bothered to 'shake' where she came from, but he found her hand, took it painfully in his cool, hard fingers. He added, "A pleasure to meet the young lady, naturally."

There were some perfectly proper compliments that could be ruined by their inflection. This seemed to be one of them.

She was not the only one who felt it. Sir Arthur cleared his throat, almost in warning, either to Mr Demian or to Roberta. Her hackles rose, along with her tawny eyebrows, but she replied sweetly, "How nice of you to say so, Mr Demian. But then, I was happily prepared for your charming manners."

Mrs Peavis gasped, then giggled as she saw that her employer, though surprised, also seemed amused.

"That should teach you, Nick. A sound dose

of your 'manners', right back at you."

Nicholas Demian waved this away as a n
sequitur. "Yes, yes. But this is getting us i
where, and I have to meet my son this eveni
Jamie is on his way home from that Swiss scho
Quite a traveller. He wants to come from P:
by train, by Channel Tunnel."

"Oh, how exciting!" Mrs Peavis cri
"Through what they call the Chunnel. I m
talk to your son sometime soon. My husb:
and I want to spend a weekend in Paris, and
insists on taking the Channel train."

No one paid much attention to her. It
quite evident to Roberta that both men
something else in mind, and she herself was t
target. This idea didn't boost her confidenc
the pleasure of the next few minutes before
walked out on both men!

"And now, we come to the crux of our I
matter," Sir Arthur said, addressing Mrs Pe
in his friendly way. "It must be nearing teati
Peavis. Would you do the honours?"

"Oh yes, Sir Arthur. Only a minute. A te
second."

Mrs Peavis leaped to obey, disappearing
her employer's office, ignoring Nich
Demian's impatient, "Must we?"

Roberta was not about to be put down by
graceless behaviour. "I'm afraid I can't stay,
Arthur. I have an engagement." As Den
looked at her, she amended firmly, "Several
gagements." She was surprised to see that

though he did not smile, Demian's dark eyes certainly appeared to be amused.

Sir Arthur shrugged. He did not trouble to call his secretary, who a minute later brought in a tea tray with pot, cups, napkins and something that looked like currant buns. They were very tempting but she would not give Nicholas Demian the satisfaction of staying a minute longer in this company than he chose to stay in hers.

"None for me," Demian dismissed this social gesture, leaving poor Mrs Peavis with a full tray and nowhere to put it. Seeing her helpless position, Roberta moved forward, but Sir Arthur obligingly took the tray and set it on the end table beneath the little daub of Edenbrook.

She was pleased by his good manners, but Nicholas Demian said abruptly, "Since your time is valuable, Miss Fisher, let me get to the heart of this little matter. . . . You don't recognise me, do you?"

Roberta couldn't figure out what this was leading to. She certainly would remember Nicholas Demian if she had ever met him before.

"Certainly not. We've never met." That ought to hold him.

Sir Arthur corrected her in his pleasant way. "Not met, precisely, Miss Fisher. But you have heard him."

It came to her then. Something in the timbre of the man's voice. Not unattractive. Educated. In other circumstances arresting in its depth and

quality. But angry. Well, that figured, being Nicholas Demian.

Miss Halloway had dismissed him to Roberta as a 'tradesman' with whom she shouted insults on her doorstep. In fact, he must be the last person who had seen Sybille Halloway alive.

Chapter Three

Roberta would love to have said something witty and cutting at this revelation, but she did almost as well without intention, by flinching. The idea that this man had been so near Sybille Halloway in her last moments was a nasty thought. Roberta's accidental reaction was offensive enough to the three watching her, she had no doubt, but though Sir Arthur Laidlaw tried to cover it by clearing his throat, Nicholas Demian received it calmly enough. Maybe he was used to arousing these responses in strangers.

"What did I tell you, Arthur? You realise now why I had to mention the visit to your friend, the inspector. This young lady finds me a sinister fellow. Probably a murderer."

"I don't think we need go that far," Sir Arthur murmured, trying to soothe both his guests.

Having pulled herself together, Roberta gave Mr Demian a gamine grin.

"Oh, but I'm sure you wouldn't try anything with two witnesses present."

She wondered if he had coloured just a trifle, or was it merely the bad lighting in the ante-room? Of one thing she was sure: he didn't think there was anything humorous in her remark. Obviously, he appreciated only his own humour.

"All this is irrelevant," he began, but she cut him off.

"If you've said everything you want to say, gentlemen, I'll be off. I do have a pressing engagement tonight."

She picked up the worn but impressive Hermès bag and slung it over her shoulder while Sir Arthur Laidlaw and Mrs Peavis were still protesting.

She had already started across the thick, slightly faded Persian carpet when Demian interrupted his friend Sir Arthur.

"For God's sake, let her go. She may say anything she cares to. At least the authorities know I have nothing to hide."

"Certainly not, sir," Mrs Peavis babbled, cutting into her employer's calm reassurance with a fib. "Miss Fisher told me she would be happy to return the notes the Halloway woman dictated."

Now it all made sense. They didn't care about explaining Nicholas Demian's quarrel with Miss Halloway the night she was killed. They wanted something, undoubtedly the disks, notes and audio tapes of Sybille's past. Just in case Demian's precious family was named in the memoirs.

As a matter of fact, if they were there, they were heavily disguised and it would take some detecting on Roberta's part to ferret them out.

Why hadn't the two men been honest and come out with their problem at once? Or, since the police held the notes at present, why hadn't Laidlaw and Demian obtained them from their acquaintance, the inspector?

Sir Arthur had started forward to open the door for Roberta but she had got there first. Just as she reached the hall she heard Sir Arthur say in the office behind her, "Nick, are you a complete fool?"

"Very possibly." The idea didn't seem to trouble him. Maybe he was used to playing the fool!

Sir Arthur evidently hoped to change the subject. "I've been wanting to ask you how Sheila is. I would love to bring her up to the City for a play and perhaps a late supper."

"You'll have to ask Sheila about that. God knows, she is her own mistress."

Sir Arthur chuckled. "Being one's own master seems to run in your family."

Roberta heard the lift and ran for it along the old, creaking corridor. By the time she reached the street, night had brought on both fog and mist. She was grateful for her newly purchased Burberry and hurried along the busy pavement to the nearest Underground with her hair lashing damply at her cheeks. Lights were everywhere but their use was handicapped by the thickness of the weather, shrouding early theatre crowds as they hunched over against the autumn mist.

Roberta didn't want to return tonight to Sybille's house but she had left her hand recorder and so much other property there that if she didn't recover it now, the unpleasant visit would hang over her.

The tube was crowded, which might be expected at this hour, but now that she had made up her mind about the call she preferred to carry it off. Why dread the business for days ahead when it could all be handled now in a few minutes?

She hadn't thought this simple ride could make her nervous, but as she kept track of stations and stops on her short trip, her imagination worked overtime. Somebody in the carriage was looking at her. Watching her. She raised her head.

Not a soul in the carriage seemed to be interested in her. Men and women, even two children, appeared either tired and bored or reading a tabloid, or in the case of two teenaged girls, filing their nails.

She knew she had allowed her uneasiness the last few days to play havoc with her common sense, but right now, when she should be getting ready for her stop, something flashed into her mind.

As a child she had played a game with classmates in which the person who was 'it' had to count to ten and then turn around. If she caught one of the other players moving, she was out of the doghouse and that player was 'it'. How often she had missed catching someone moving! The eerie part was knowing that all of them shuffled around while her eyes were closed and yet she couldn't catch one of them.

Was this going on in the tube?

Angry over her susceptibility, she thought in disgust, I ought to have my head examined.

She was very glad to get off at her stop and make her way up and out onto the street, then in the semi-darkness beyond the Square, to Sybille Halloway's slender, two-and-a-half storey house that had been old in Victorian days.

The lights were on in the back of the house where Mrs Allegretti was cleaning the kitchen, pantries, floor and ceiling for the new theatrical owners. The presence of that stout-bodied, rough-voiced little woman would help a lot.

Unfortunately, when the cook came to answer the quaint and noisy knocker Sybille had installed, Roberta saw that she was ready to leave, heavily shrouded against the drizzling rain, and carrying a sturdy black umbrella, probably belonging to her husband. The ivory handle was heavy enough alone.

"It's all yours, Miss," she announced, opening the door wide. "My keys is on the bureau like the lawyer fellow said. Good luck to you, Miss."

"And to you, Mrs Allegretti."

The cook remembered something and added casually, "One of the Metropolitan laddies from the other night left a big brown envelope for you. It's on the sideboard in the dining room. You know. That thing that killed poor old Miss Halloway."

How thoughtful to leave the tapes and notes just there, Roberta thought, but realised that the police had left the envelope in Mrs Allegretti's hands, and it was she who had placed it in that particular place. No matter. Poor Sybille was dead now and need never know these little nasty moments again.

Roberta watched the cook stride along the pavement, flat-footed but definitely unafraid. Then, ashamed of her own ridiculous fears, Roberta stepped into the house.

The minute she found herself in the vestibule, Roberta noticed that Sybille's heavy, sweet perfume, Bellodgia, clung to everything. There was no escaping it. Mrs Allegretti had probably 'borrowed' some — nothing wrong with that, except that the scent remaining was so overpowering Roberta found herself hurrying across what Sybille had called her 'drawing room', a small room with long windows facing a street that gave a partial view of the not too distant Square.

At the back of this room was the stately dining room with its slippery floor where the Toast of the Sixties had entertained. The furnishings were heavily decorated with curlicues on every mahogany piece, except the sideboard, whose sharp, unadorned corner had proved so deadly.

The manila envelope was large and overflowing with the material compiled and dictated for the dead woman's memoirs. Roberta took up the awkward pile, carried it to the dining-room table and left it there to be picked up when she finished collecting the odds and ends she had left in the upstairs study. She gave the living room and dining room a glance. She wanted to be certain no prowler, or one of Sybille's 'dailies', was hanging around, to be come upon suddenly. Then she went up the stairs, across the hall, oppressed by the memory of the old woman's last living moments.

She marvelled, now and then, at the inexplicable noises one could hear in an empty house at night. Especially when poor Sybille hadn't wanted to die and would have fought hard with the Grim Reaper if she'd had a chance. That damned polished floor!

Upstairs at the end of the hall of portraits too tacky to be called a 'gallery', Roberta went into the study that was crowded with cheap, aged furniture, probably unwanted after serving a long term on the lower floor. She pulled out the bottom drawer of an old-fashioned chiffonier where she kept copies of her disks, tapes and shorthand notebooks pertaining to Sybille, not the originals she had given to the police. These were often first drafts and worth very little in themselves except for the facts they contained. The drawer was much too easy to pull out, as if it were empty.

It *was* empty!

Who the devil — ?

A faint scent clung to the drawer, as if a human breath had exhaled some cooking scent. Or was it a liqueur scent? Anisette probably. She had never liked anisette and certainly hadn't touched the drawer with anisette-scented hands. Well, at least, it wasn't thick perfume. Was it the police?

They probably thought Roberta had held out on them. She hoped they enjoyed all Sybille's sexual shenanigans, or at any rate, the way Sybille had recalled them. For the most part, they had been tracted from the formal memoirs because they were more likely to be grounds for lawsuits.

She opened each of the other drawers. All empty, except the top one where something rattled around and proved to be a safety razor. She hadn't seen one in some time and was curious. But then she realised that one of Sybille Halloway's visitors might very possibly still use safety razors. Or even worse, cut-throat razors.

At least no one had removed Roberta's favourite Spanish bolero jacket. She retrieved it from the wardrobe and put it on under her Burberry, which still felt a trifle damp. No matter. Better to wear it than to carry it. She was glad she had taken her light laptop processor home two nights ago to her bedsitting room. She had always thought it possible the machine could be stolen by one of Sybille's guests.

There was a rather fetching little black beret on a shelf in the wardrobe. She had almost forgotten it. She pulled it on over the right side of her head. It gave her the jaunty, independent look she preferred.

What else? Better check in case she had forgotten anything.

The house squeaked and creaked and made all kinds of unwarranted noises, but she was getting used to them. After looking around Sybille's own frilly bedroom with its absurd half-tester, also frilled, she decided everything upstairs was as it should be and came slowly down the stairs to the ground floor to see if she could find any hint of what had happened to the copies of her notes and disks.

Under all this last-minute cleaning up, she was still puzzling over Sir Arthur Laidlaw and his unpleasant friend, Nicholas Demian.

She hadn't become aware that there were so many creaks and cracks everywhere, although she had been here often enough. But of course, Sybille had been in the house as well. She told herself these were typical sounds of a lonely old house. Annoyed by her imagination, she decided she would head for the kitchen area. This had been the domain of Mrs Allegretti and her young hired relatives who served Sybille's guests at her frequent dinner parties for two. They could probably give very interesting twists to the private life of their employer. But they were hardly likely to be in the house now.

Meanwhile, another more immediate concern began to trouble her again. Something had to be done about her own expenses in getting home to California, and for the first unpaid weeks afterward. The bedsitting room in London was hers for ten more days. After that, she would owe the next month's rent.

She stepped onto the worn but expensive carpet in the hallway at the foot of the stairs and heard something crackle under her shoes. The vestibule light to her left made one of her computer disks clearly visible as she shifted her foot. She had scratched and cracked the disk. No good now, even if she had intended to use it. But she couldn't remember dropping it.

She might not use the material itself, but she violently resented anyone else having it. Besides, there was the less selfish side to it: she knew that using it would bring harm or ridicule, even perhaps personal problems to the living if all Miss Halloway's material was published.

I was willing to publish it, she reminded herself. But that was before the old lady had died so unexpectedly, so cruelly.

She looked around and saw more items in the dim light beyond the vestibule. Half an hour ago this carpet was clean. No disks, no shorthand notebooks, no audio tapes . . .

All these had been jammed into a big manila envelope. Now the notebook covers were hacked by a sharp blade, more paper notes so torn they would make no sense, and several disks appeared to have been deliberately scratched and mutilated, again by a sharp blade.

And all this mess, obviously taken out of the manila envelope she had left in the dining room, was scattered here for her to find, between the time she went up the stairs and this moment when she came down. Had whoever it was already been upstairs and taken the other notes and tapes? Or had that been done earlier and by someone else? The thought was chilling.

They were worthless to her, but they might not be worthless to someone mentioned in them. Nicholas Demian was obviously too young, probably under thirty-five, but he would be interested in anything written that would place his father, for instance, in a derogatory light. She couldn't remember any mention of a 'Demian' but obviously Sybille had been wise enough to conceal some of the more flagrant associations. Certainly, Roberta had warned her to.

She had intended to destroy all the evidence of Sybille's foolish tongue, but this gratuitous violence to her property infuriated Roberta.

Would someone take a sharp weapon to her as well as her property?

There was no place here in the hall, or dining room beyond, where the person who had possibly ravaged Roberta's own property might be hiding at this moment — was there? She swung around. No one was in the dining room, and there were no signs of any disturbance except the remnants of her notes and tapes on the floor at her feet.

What about the odd noises she had heard that seemed to come from the back of the house a few minutes ago?

There was one again, in the kitchen area. Possibly a window being pushed up. Since she had no weapon at hand, she moved silently along the back hall, aware, as the seconds passed, that the intruder was either very quiet, or more likely gone by now.

The front vestibule and hall lights illuminated

most of the big kitchen, which was deserted. Beyond it the old-fashioned still room opened onto an alley that looked as if it had once been part of a mews. The single sash window was open and night air poured in. Roberta heard running footsteps on the cobbles beyond, but looking out she could not see anyone in the misty dark of the alley.

She closed the window which was impossible to fasten now and left the kitchen. In the hall at the foot of the staircase she picked up the useless mass of papers, disks and tapes, and shoved them and the manila envelope into her shoulder bag. They were all that remained of three months' work.

There was a chance that Miss Halloway's telephone had not yet been cut off, or that the new owners had reconnected it. She didn't want to get involved with Scotland Yard, or some other police, and as for the remains of her work, she didn't intend to use it now. Still, the whole business was highly sinister.

Sir Arthur Laidlaw might take care of the business. Breaking and entering were still criminal offences. Sir Arthur's profession entailed involvement with the police.

There was a telephone extension on the end table behind her in the hall. She reached for it.

Dead. Not surprising.

She picked up her bag again and walked to the vestibule hoping she did not appear as outwardly shaken as she felt.

At the front door she looked back before switching off the overhead light. Nothing. In the open front doorway she studied the little street. A deep blue or black Mercedes was parked half-way up the street on the opposite side but it was too dark to tell whether anyone was at the wheel. Two couples strolled past the car but aroused no interest inside it as they walked toward the welcome lamps of Berkeley Square.

Roberta closed the door of Miss Halloway's house, heard the lock click, and walked rapidly toward the brighter lights. Across the street the two men glanced over at her, saw she wasn't dangerous, and went on chattering to their companions.

Roberta took a long breath when she passed the Square, then headed for the nearest Underground station. She wanted to get away from this district as rapidly as possible, elegant though it might be when one was not alone.

A car engine started up somewhere behind her but she was rapidly approaching a well-lit area and would not give in to yet another of her cowardly fears!

Chapter Four

Behind her a car, probably the Mercedes, was rumbling along at so slow a pace the driver had to be following her. Roberta picked up speed, hoping to lose herself in a noisy, drunken group piling out of a taxi in front of an old but stylish Regency house.

They were too fast for her, however, and by the time she reached the front of one of those close-packed, subtly elegant buildings, the party crowd had poured inside, leaving her alone. The Mercedes, meanwhile, had edged across the street and was crawling along beside her. She had hoped to ignore the Mercedes stalker but now the car was so close she had to leap out of the way when the car door was suddenly pushed open.

Aware that she was about to be pulled into the car, for whatever unsavoury purpose the owner of the Mercedes had in mind, she recoiled, missing the car door but colliding with a lean, fairly well-groomed hand inside the vehicle. A male hand.

He was probably drunk and certainly not acting his age, but there was force in his fingers as she discovered when she wriggled her own fingers to free herself.

She said, as calmly as she could, "Either let me go or drive on. I have excellent lung-power."

"I believe you." His grip relaxed a little but he turned her fingers over in his palm. "Has anyone ever told you that opals are bad luck?"

She knew him by this time, even before the street lamp illuminated his face as he leaned toward her. Here he was in all his evil splendour, that bad-tempered creature who had been the last to see Sybille Halloway alive. Nicholas Demian.

She said the first thing that occurred to her, something she thought might shut him up.

"I never look a gift horse in the mouth."

"I'm sure you don't." It was coldly said and she thought its inference was as nasty as possible. This annoyed her, because in spite of herself, she felt embarrassed over receiving the ring. His hand had released its hold on hers and she was stepping back onto the curb when he issued an order.

"Get in. I've no interest in kidnapping you, if that's what you are afraid of. I am trying, with more than my usual patience, to strike a bargain with you."

Having read too many bad movie and television scripts, Roberta bristled for a couple of seconds before she suspected that what he was after was far from the virtue of a Yankee scriptwriter. But if he was talking about Miss Halloway and her memoirs, two points gave her pause: he couldn't have personally ruined the notes and tapes, and he certainly hadn't crawled through a kitchen window and escaped down an alley to avoid her. Such juvenile activity was not his style. Maybe he had been waiting for the report of some athletic hired burglar.

However, she hesitated now, considering the alternatives, and that gave him the upper hand.

"I'll make it worth your while, so jump in and we'll discuss it. If you insist, I can get Arthur Laidlaw to act for both of us. At least, you trust him I suppose?"

Seeing her about to get in and ignoring his helping hand, he slid back under the wheel, slapped the seat beside him, and watched her slip gracefully into the car. When she glanced at him out of some curiosity, she was surprised to see that with a little effort, he might almost be said to have smiled.

She did enjoy the knowledge that the tapes and notes he wanted so much were practically shredded and currently in her shoulder bag, so close to him they dug into his hip.

"You can drop me off at the nearest Underground station," she informed him pleasantly.

He said nothing to that and she added, "I wouldn't have guessed it, but you do really get your kicks out of crawling through the windows of kitchen pantries."

He almost pulled up to a stop but recovered quickly enough to answer her with the same intonation.

"Not since my college days. What pantry win-

51

dows do you have in mind? And how do they concern me?"

"They don't. Not any more. Miss Halloway's memoirs were shredded within the last half hour."

"What!"

"By someone who then climbed out of the Halloway pantry window beyond the kitchen while I was upstairs. Meanwhile, you were probably parked out in the street waiting to accuse me. Possibly even waiting for your thieving partner in crime. Well, Mr Demian," she finished, "if you were, he's double-crossed you."

This time he did stop. Luckily, they were at a crossing. His fingers closed tighter on the wheel. She was relieved that he hadn't used that hard a grip on her.

"Are you lying to me?"

She bit her lip, forcing herself to smile. "You think so?" She tore open the zip of the shoulder bag and dumped its contents all over his expensive sports jacket.

"Help yourself. If you examine it carefully, I think you will find everything there. No effort was made to destroy page numbers. It's still faintly legible." She added, "If you like crossword puzzles."

He took up a handful of papers of assorted sizes, plus a broken disk which cut his palm, Roberta was happy to note. It was hard to argue against the condition of this mess. He tacitly admitted it.

"If all the notes are here concerning my idiot father, it seems I may owe you an apology." He flipped through the pile.

She explained, "Most of the names are phoney, and I don't recall seeing a 'Demian' among them."

"Unless, of course," he added with a nasty hint of humour, "you may have hidden other copies for future use."

It was too much.

"Oh, for God's sake, let me get out of here!"

She was fed up. There must be a million things she cared more about than Sybille's lying, smarmy memoirs. She said so aloud as she reached for the door.

He didn't put his hand out to stop her, which was a relief. She didn't want to wrestle her way out, and he left her momentarily speechless by his unexpected apology — at least what passed for one.

"All right. I'll take your word for it. I can't see any point in your giving me this mess and then demanding a ransom for the copies." His sudden smile came as a complete surprise. "I enjoyed your eloquent description of Sybille Halloway. I must remember that. Do you have many 'smarmy' employers in Hollywood?"

"I assure you, I find just as many over here!" she snapped.

When he offered her his hand this time she could sense that he meant something quite different from his early physical violence.

"I was wrong. I admit it, something I seldom do, Miss Fisher." He hesitated. "But don't disappoint me."

He still wasn't entirely convinced. Thank heaven, she would soon be rid of him!

"This is my station. My dear Mr Demian, will you do me an enormous favour?"

"My dear Miss Fisher, I'm afraid to ask what favour?"

"Keep your skeletons in your family close. And whatever you do, don't bore me with them!"

"I'll do my best."

He reached across her body and pushed open the door. She got out, headed for the Underground steps at a leggy pace, and did not look back. Even her scriptwriting partner, Joel Sawyer, in Hollywood, began to seem more palatable after these recent experiences with London's upper crust.

But she was most angry because she had let herself behave so stupidly with Nicholas Demian who owed her something. She should have accepted some payment from him, certainly enough to get back to Hollywood and new assignments.

Crowding into the Underground carriage after a mad rush down the steps she mulled over various possibilities that would get her home as cheaply as possible. The obvious move left to her would be to put the matter before Sir Arthur Laidlaw, although it had been Nicholas Demian who accepted the pile of chewed-up and stomped-on notes that had not been paid for and were, therefore, still her property. She didn't want them or the tapes and disks but at least she ought to be paid for the work of typing and taping.

Still, her pride and that indignant farewell performance she had put on made it impossible to reverse her stand. She should have pointed out that the property she gave him, ruined or not, was hers and should be paid for.

On the whole, the sensible thing would be to phone Joel Sawyer and tell him to send her the money for her flight home. After all, it was his fault that she had taken the assignment. In return, she could give him a screen treatment of Sybille's memoirs, changed here and there to protect the guilty. Make Sybille an old Hollywood star, for instance. Her mind worked over this idea as it often did when she was approaching a new assignment.

When Roberta came up out of the Underground at her stop, the reasonably clean, quiet street held no unpleasant surprises. A hurrying young female in tight denims and a T-shirt that advised the readers 'You Call It' brushed past her and hurried into the Underground.

A male with his coat collar pulled up to shroud half his face and hair stood against a lamp-post down the street and ground a dying cigarette into the pavement. He did not look at her. His only interest seemed to be in the ashes of the cigarette. Everything was much as usual except that Roberta had not stopped off at a café for her evening meal and would have to make do with the remains of some tomato soup heated on the single burner, and the bottom half of a cinnamon roll.

She crossed the street and went up the steps to the door of a three-storey house that was old, well-kept and respectable, but a good deal less welcoming than the Spanish motif 'Villa Riviera' in which she lived below the Hollywood Hills.

The way things had gone on this assignment, she would be relieved to get back to the Villa Riviera and the Culver City television studio. The door was still unlocked and she went into the clean, lower hall with its rose-papered walls presided over by a framed watercolour of St Paul's Cathedral. There was a pervasive smell of boiling food, probably sprouts and potatoes, so Mrs Sloan, the widowed landlady and owner was not entertaining her Bridge Club tonight.

The minute Roberta closed the street door behind her Mrs Sloan's door on the ground floor gently clicked shut.

"Nosy old bag!" she thought. The woman had grown consistently less sociable and more suspicious each day since Miss Halloway's accident. She probably pictured Roberta as one of those nasty murderesses from the crime-ridden USA.

Roberta went upstairs to her room, which looked untouched, immaculate and unlived-in. It was obvious that Mrs Sloan had chosen this afternoon to give the place a thorough cleaning. And maybe a search? There had been talk the last day or so that "With that dreadful Halloway woman dead I imagine you will be leaving for the States rather soon. I would appreciate knowing as soon as possible, so your apartment can be let to someone more permanent. You do understand, Miss Fisher?"

Did she ever! She meant someone who was not working for a woman with a sordid past who, according to a hint in the papers yesterday, just might have been murdered . . .

Roberta allowed herself ten minutes before going down quietly to the telephone in the ground-floor hall, near the bathroom.

It was too much to hope that Sir Arthur Laidlaw would still be in his offices at a time when most Londoners of his importance were at dinner, at banquets, or out drinking at their clubs.

Someone did answer but it wasn't even Mrs Peavis. A charwoman obliged, reporting impatiently, that Sir Arthur was at dinner with friends.

"Oh, yes, of course," Roberta bluffed it out. "He mentioned that when we were chatting this afternoon, dinner with Mr —"

"Mr Demian and the gentleman's young son. He's just come home from school in Switzerland. I'll be leaving your message, Miss. Sir Arthur, he often rings through to find out what calls were left for him. Takes pains with his clients, so he does."

"Thank heaven for that! His clients are fortunate."

The woman sounded a little huffy. Roberta

couldn't blame her. Probably anxious to get on with and through with her work.

"It's always been his habit, Miss. Never one to take it easy. Name, please."

"Just tell him that Miss Fisher reported a forced entry of Miss Halloway's house and some papers destroyed. Say that Miss Fisher hopes to see him about an entry of her own apartment."

The charwoman obviously pricked up her ears.

"What? You'll not be saying — what number, please?"

"Just the message, if you don't mind."

She didn't want her landlady, Mrs Sloan, listening to everything and probably telling half the neighbourhood.

The phone went dead and Roberta consoled herself with the realisation that, aside from calling some authority or other, there was nothing else for her to do. She would at least tell Sir Arthur she had given Demian the papers freely, if Demian pretended he had forced her to do so.

As she went back along the hall to the stairs past Mrs Sloan's door, she noted that it was ajar again, as she expected. She had been surrounded tonight by doors ajar and people watching her, besides committing theft and destroying her property. It gave her an uneasy feeling.

She noticed that her hand shook a little as she tried to put her key into the lock. She wasn't used to this cowardice and once she stepped into the room she locked the door from the inside and sat down in the one armchair the room provided, to think out her own position in all this burglary mess.

She saw her reflection in the mirror of the chipped and scarred old maple dressing table. It was about five feet across the room from the armchair but she could see her pale, no — peaked face. Her eyes, usually among her best features, were anxious-looking, and her hair was unruly.

She was staring blindly into the future, when her scattered thoughts coalesced on an idiosyncrasy which had been hers from birth. She was left-handed, and always set her hairbrush on the left side of the dresser. But not tonight. Tonight it was carefully placed on the right, near the box of tissues and her little tablets of aspirin for the headaches Sybille had given her on occasion.

Simple enough. Mrs Sloan had cleaned her room today and maybe done some snooping of her own. Roberta got up and went to the dresser.

She found one curious little item: a piece of shorthand notebook paper no more than an inch wide. Beside the dresser, in the wastepaper basket were a few more pieces of torn paper, all of them perfectly blank.

It made no sense, but so far tonight, very little did. It seemed more than odd, downright ridiculous, that Mrs Sloan had torn up a blank sheet of paper, and the pieces gave no sign whatever of having invisible writing or anything else on them. The only thing it accomplished was to let her know someone had searched her room.

One more thing to tell Sir Arthur tomorrow.

She might even hint that she suspected his friend Nicholas Demian of having prowled around her room looking for Sybille Halloway's unsavoury memoirs. But if that had been true, why would he, or anyone else, go to such pains to leave evidence so she would know at once that the place had been searched?

Chapter Five

An office boy turned Roberta over to Mrs Peavis who escorted her across the ante-room to the barrister's office.

"My dear," Mrs Peavis informed Roberta proudly, "I'm delighted that you called for the appointment. Otherwise, we would have been forced to call you. Sir Arthur agrees with my idea. But then, I knew he would." She lowered her voice to a stage whisper. "He always does. He says I excite his mental faculties."

Whatever that meant. "Really?" How nice for you!

"Oh, yes. We've already put it to work. A pinprick here, a pinprick there, thanks to the press. And it's going to — to pay off. As you might say."

Entirely at sea, Roberta murmured, "Delightful."

She was trying to sound enthusiastic, but a night interrupted by creaking noises in the darkness and once, a definite turning of the knob of her locked door had worn down her nerves. It had also stocked up resentment over her own involvement in Miss Halloway's troublemaking.

She had known before she met Sybille Halloway that there would be problems in transcribing the memories of a woman who had lived what anyone could call 'a high-old-life'. Truth was usually the least of it. There were always exaggerations, half-truths, wishful thinking, and plain lies. But Roberta had done her best to disguise the 'injured parties', if any.

The ghost-writing job had cost more than a few hours of sleep in the last three months and she was angry that such matters should still cause someone (or more than one?) to dog her footsteps.

The barrister's door was closed but Roberta doubted if closed doors and a barely audible knuckle rap ever stopped the dauntless Mrs Peavis, who pushed the door open. Roberta caught a glimpse of Sir Arthur Laidlaw at a far window, his sandy gold hair glistening in the watery sunlight, as she remembered him before. He was frowning as though a problem occupied all his thoughts.

When Sir Arthur heard the women behind him he turned, hesitated a moment but smiled and inclined his head in recognition, and then crossed the room, extending a hand to Roberta. His manner, though correct, was friendly, and he seemed to offer a genuine welcome.

"How good of you to come, Miss Fisher! You have been exceedingly gracious about this whole troublesome affair. And then, you have all your work torn up, destroyed — we shall be fortunate if you don't go straight home with a very bad opinion of us all."

She couldn't resist that warmth and kindness.

Her spirits began to climb. She ventured to bring up the matter about which she had come to see him.

"Thank you, Sir. I almost wish you hadn't been so kind about everything because I'm afraid last night I walked into another mystery."

"Really? But you did turn over all the notes and tapes to Mr Demian, such as they are?"

In spite of his words she sensed the doubt in them. For all his friendly manner, he was quick to think the worst of her, just as Demian had.

"I gave him what was left. All I had."

He nodded. "So he assured me. You musn't notice his manner with women, Miss Fisher. Poor Nick may be what I believe they refer to as a misogynist."

"Hates women," Mrs Peavis put in knowingly but unnecessarily.

Sir Arthur brushed this away. "Not entirely. His marriage was not a success, I believe, and he doesn't seem to have found the right woman since."

So he takes it out on all women, Roberta thought.

"How unfortunate that he can't find a perfect woman!" she said, heavy with sarcasm.

Mrs Peavis sniggered, but the barrister merely reminded both women a trifle severely, "A number of women seem to have looked upon him as having the Midas touch and pursued him for that reason only."

"What other reason?" Mrs Peavis asked herself

in a low but audible voice. Her employer and Roberta wisely ignored this.

Sir Arthur continued, "A solicitor friend of mine helped him piece your tapes and manuscript together. The tapes seemed to be of help." He shrugged. "Not that it was important. The Halloway woman's bawdy life would hardly be of importance after fifteen or twenty years, except as amusing gossip, but my friend Demian found it a 'confounded nuisance' so long as it was floating around in just anyone's hands."

I suppose I am 'just anyone', she thought and asked aloud, "Then why this hullabaloo?" After all the trouble she had been put to last night she didn't think much of the way he dismissed the matter so cavalierly.

Mrs Peavis put in, as if her beloved boss had been attacked, "Oh, that's just Mr Demian. He isn't very popular, as you may imagine. And he thinks everyone is his enemy."

"Peavis!" A little of the lawyer idiom had come into the way that single name was snapped out by Sir Arthur.

Turning to Roberta he went on, a little confused, "I thought you were referring to the torn manuscript."

"No, Sir Arthur. Not that torn paper. Between the time I left my accommodation to come to your offices yesterday evening and the time I reached home last night someone tore up papers in my room. They had nothing to do with Miss Halloway's memoirs."

That startled him. He opened his mouth to say something but was interrupted by Mrs Peavis.

"Good heavens! Could it have been Mr Demian looking for the manuscript?"

Sir Arthur said repressively, "Certainly not, Mrs Peavis." He was about to explain his reasoning to Roberta but she cut him short.

"I doubt it, Sir Arthur. Nothing was taken, and the blank sheets were torn out of my unused shorthand book."

That puzzled him. "Blank! Then why?"

Roberta was rather proud of her reasoning, though she knew that there was always a stronger possibility that Mrs Sloan had been prying while she cleaned her room. On the other hand, what if the landlady was innocent in all this?

"Someone wanted me to know he — or she — had been there. Sort of a warning. Scare tactics perhaps."

"Now, why should anyone want to do that?"

Sir Arthur motioned his secretary to sit down. As she did so, somewhat abashed, he offered Roberta the highbacked and well-cushioned armchair he apparently reserved for clients.

"Do sit down, Miss Fisher. I don't quite see the connection between this matter and the dead woman." He seated himself in his own chair and leaned across the desk, his elbows brushing aside several leather folders and longer legal briefs. "Now, Miss Fisher, why do you believe someone wishes to warn you? A friend? Or otherwise? What harm can you do this hypothetical burglar?"

She didn't appreciate what sounded like heavy sarcasm, a denial of her fears and a dismissal of the whole 'burglary'. On the other hand she had known all along that there was the ever-curious Mrs Sloan to consider.

"You may be right. My landlady has looked through my things on occasion. 'Straightening up', she calls it. My shorthand notebook was lying on my dresser. She could have knocked it off while dusting, but why she would tear out the pages I can't imagine unless they had been crushed or ripped when the book fell and she got rid of them. Tidying up, you might say."

"Highly possible," he agreed, evidently liking the explanation. "I think we are giving too much importance to a matter with a trivial explanation." He gazed directly at Roberta. "Among us all, we seem to have treated you rather shabbily. However, this entire Halloway affair has led me to pursue an idea. To your advantage, I hope. I am going to ask you a delicate question. The answer will go no further than this room; I give you my word. Unless you yourself speak of it."

Delicate? she wondered. Could it be about money? If he knew how nearly broke she was! Since it wasn't her fault — Miss Halloway being a great procrastinator with the world's best excuses — Roberta had no hesitation in letting the whole world know, when it came to that. She had a definite claim on Miss Halloway's estate.

"Fire away. I'm prepared. What is the fatal question?"

He had a letter opener in his fingers. The steel blade shone and seemed to be sharply efficient. The hilt was another matter. It bore the sinister-looking head and hunched shoulders of a Notre Dame gargoyle. With the point Sir Arthur traced the irregular shape of an ink blot on the old-fashioned green desk blotter.

He looked up. "Miss Fisher, many of those in the village of Edenbrook seem to believe you have little sympathy for Nicholas Demian. We may blame the press which has exaggerated your mention of Nick's quarrel with the Halloway woman the night she died. Do you mind?"

Aside from sounding pompous, the question was ridiculous. What difference would it make? People she didn't know and didn't want to know probably guessed she had no interest in a man she had met twice for ten minutes and had no intention of ever meeting again. Who cared?

Trying not to sound derisive again, she said calmly, "No. I don't mind. I'm not really crazy about all that arrogance. Not to mention the chip he carries on his shoulder."

Mrs Peavis giggled but subsided as her employer stabbed the letter opener into the ink spot without looking at her.

Then, in his mild, persuasive voice Sir Arthur reminded Roberta, "Nick is beginning to blame individuals and not the usual trials of life, for . . . everything unpleasant that happens. To me, he is a lifelong friend. But to his tenants at Edenbrook, I'm afraid he is becoming an ogre. He insists he will not renew the Demian lease which has controlled his land for at least a century. It was once a Crown gift, I believe. But that's of no concern now. The tenants hope to present a case of their own to fight for their homes and property when the lease runs out. That will be before the new century."

She couldn't see where she would fit in. She was not a legal expert and said so.

He disagreed. "You have everything to do with it. What is wanted is a good and sympathetic writer, not a legal mind. His tenants want to present their side, the innumerable ways they have improved the property through scores of years. This includes their cottages, shops, a public house, et cetera."

It was a medieval idea that landlords could still hold property for scores of years, property on which the tenants had made the improvements of an entire village. She was still digesting this when he shook her by saying, "After you left yesterday I had a telephone call from two of Nick's tenants whom I know from my visits to Edenbrook. One was a fellow named Brinkby, a gardener. He has the land at Edenbrook in his charge. Jovial, sporting lad, but worried, like most villagers about losing their homes and their land in two more years."

"Just think," Mrs Peavis put in. "All their years of work, their homes, everything, will then revert to Mister Nick and his son."

Sir Arthur nodded. "Quite true. I've always

dismissed their complaints. But I feel a little more inclined to do something constructive this time, if only to protect that hard-headed friend of mine."

"I doubt if anything would penetrate there."

His eyebrows went up but he admitted, "I am inclined to agree. The tenants who called me had read about you in the news. They knew you had spoken to the police against Nick. They thought that you might see their side of —"

"Don't get me mixed up in this. I only mentioned the truth and the police brushed aside Mr Demian's visit. I have nothing more to say on the matter."

He brushed this aside. "The point is, these tenants at Edenbrook thought you might put together a resumé of their physical labour and the moneys spent on these improvements through scores of years."

"They don't need you or me for that."

"You still don't understand. This information is verified in their files: the payments, cheque records, and individual work by the villagers. They have the facts but they want them presented with sympathy. Readable and persuasive. Not what a friend of mine calls 'legalese'. Bring out the inhumanity of having to destroy or give up a centuries-old village. Almost the destruction of centuries-old lives. Names. Dates. Some of the people known to history in small ways. All they've built up can be torn down in days. The Demians, or if necessary, the courts, will hear that correctly. It may open some eyes."

"Has the land belonged to the Demians always?"

"Since time out of mind. But during the last century tenants whose families signed with the Demians around 1900 have poured all those scores of years into that little territory."

Mrs Peavis burst in anxiously, "The tenants want to show all they have done to build on and repair what once belonged to the Demians. They do have a point, Miss Fisher but Mr Demian simply refuses to listen."

"Perfectly true," Sir Arthur admitted. "Nick grows more set in his ways every day."

I can believe that, Roberta thought. What a detestable man Nicholas Demian was! And yet — did anyone know his side of it? Was there a side to it that they didn't know?

Mrs Peavis pointed out, "Mr Brinkby said he had read you were a Hollywood writer and they always —" Roberta wrinkled her nose but Mrs Peavis ignored this. "They always warm up their grievances, so to speak."

Sir Arthur added, "These are perfectly respectable country yeomen. Nothing sinister about them. I'm afraid that's Nick's overactive imagination."

"It sounds promising to everyone but me."

They both looked at her with more than a little disappointment. They were genuinely surprised.

Mrs Peavis tried once more. "Only for a couple of weeks. The money would be very good. Sir

Arthur says it would match whatever you were to receive from Sybille Halloway."

"I hope we can do better than that," Sir Arthur agreed. "In fact, I am very much of the opinion that the villagers would find you most helpful. Naturally, if anything strikes you as a danger to Nick, which is most unlikely, I'm sure you will report it to me at once."

"In other words, go into the Demians' enemy camp and spy for him." She smiled tightly. "And if I do, will I wake up with my throat cut?"

The barrister reacted to this as to a pleasantry, but Mrs Peavis murmured, "Really, my dear, this is England. Not the States."

Sir Arthur shook his head. "Peavis, I don't think insulting Miss Fisher's country will do the trick."

Roberta decided nothing but brutal frankness would do. "Forgive me, but in your legal capacity, Sir Arthur, you would be far more suitable to this job than I am, and I'm sure you know it."

Mrs Peavis hurried into the breach, "Oh, but he couldn't do that. The Demians are such close friends. And besides, what would Miss Sheila say? She might never forgive —"

"Peavis!"

She shut up.

After a tense little silence, Roberta got up to go. "I'm sorry. I really am. But I was mixed up in one death and I'd just as soon not be mixed up in a spying job. I'm sure you will find someone else more suited. But don't think it hasn't been — fun." She reached across the desk and shook hands with the barrister, then with the stunned Peavis. "See you in Hollywood."

Chapter Six

On the way back to her bedsitting room Roberta faced her next step — in fact, the only step: calling Joel Sawyer. She had always suspected Joel of trying to curry favour with her father by reporting all her activities, especially any monetary foul-ups. 'Artistic Failures' in television were not recognised or worth discussing, but money was something he understood all too well and would enjoy reminding Roberta that both her gender and her mother's genes had shown her up again. She might as well come home where she was needed and help 'poor Daniele' (his hard-drinking present wife) take care of his household and social calendar.

The whole London Affair had disappointed Roberta more than she had previously admitted. What now?

She might have bailed herself out of the Halloway mess by looking into the job Sir Arthur had suggested, but there were no guarantees even here, and it sounded like one of two things: acting the spy for the arrogant Nicholas Demian against his unfortunate tenants, or just as bad, playing the Edenbrook citizens' game and trying to build up a case against Demian.

She didn't really believe the latter was Sir Arthur's motive. After all, he appeared to be sincere in his friendship for the dark, scowling curmudgeon, but she didn't want to feed Demian's ego by reporting everything his tenants did or said. If Sir Arthur's hints were based on fact, Demian probably deserved to lose a lawsuit to the centuries-old families of his tenants. He sounded like a real Scrooge.

So, if Roberta was ever going to get back to Hollywood, it looked as if Joel Sawyer was the answer. Damn him!

By the time she arrived on Mrs Sloan's doorstep she was not in the mood to cater to her landlady. This time Mrs Sloan was not hiding behind doors left coyly ajar. She stepped out into the lower hall, almost in Roberta's face.

"Ah, Miss Fisher. I've been awaiting your return."

Roberta had a little difficulty putting her thoughts together. She had been boiling down the phrases to use in her transatlantic telephone call to Joel Sawyer, and had to shift now into a more polite manner. Polite but reserved. She certainly didn't want her landlady to think she was in trouble, financial or worse, in connection with Sybille Halloway's death.

Ever since the day after the accident Mrs Sloan had seemed to feel that this foreigner from sinful Hollywood just might be more involved in death — or even murder — than the police had yet admitted.

Roberta said, just short of being haughty, "Yes,

Mrs Sloan? How may I help you?"

She blinked. Roberta was sure it hadn't occurred to her that her tenant with dubious credentials could help her in any way except, maybe, to depart the premises quietly.

"Well, I shouldn't say — that is, with Miss Halloway's unfortunate passing, I assume you will be returning to the States?" Her carefully drawn eyebrows arched and her lips pursed expectantly while she waited for Roberta's excuses and final agreement.

But Roberta brushed by her, remarking as she did so, "Oh, no. Not, at least, until Sir Arthur Laidlaw, a friend you know, gives me his legal opinion."

Mrs Sloan was quietly triumphant. "Dear me, I assume his legal opinion on what you witnessed the other night?"

"Heavens, no!" Roberta stopped momentarily on the stairs. "On the person or persons who rifled the property upstairs in my room."

That shook her up. "Rifled the — ? Surely, not in my house!"

Roberta tried to be all charm and regret. "I should have reported it to you first. But I thought perhaps you had moved my things. Thrown away papers, et cetera, as a favour to me."

Mrs Sloan's mouth fell open. She reddened, which made her pale rose complexion look mottled. She forgot herself long enough to lose the imperious propertied-lady manner.

"Never touched the stuff. As if I'd twiddle

about with that silly business. Not me, and you best tell Sir Arthur so or I'll have you up for false — well — false —"

Roberta assured her, "Oh, I believe you, Mrs Sloan. I only hope Sir Arthur does."

She went on up to her room at the head of the stairs, leaving her landlady staring up at her with a forehead deeply wrinkled in thought.

In her room, with the door locked, Roberta dropped down abruptly on the sofa and considered her situation.

With this latest skirmish she hadn't accomplished anything except to make it easier for Mrs Sloan to throw her out on some pretext or other. There were only nine days before her next month's rent was due, and there was no putting it off. She would have to call Joel Sawyer without delay.

Well, no time like the present. She took a much-used credit card out of her handbag, unlocked the door and went down to make her dreaded call. She made no attempt to silence her shoes on the polished but uncarpeted stairs, so she knew Mrs Sloan would be nearby. In this case, justifiably, once she found the call would be across an ocean and a continent.

By the time Roberta reached the telephone on the table in the front hall she heard the betraying click of Mrs Sloan's bolt lock and was prepared.

She explained several times to the operator before finally getting to the USA code. By this time Mrs Sloan was out in the hall breathing fire from her mouth and her narrow, pinched nostrils.

"Nobody here is paying for that call, Miss."

Roberta flipped her card up for the landlady to read. She seemed to understand, but remained there, obviously wanting to hear for herself what went on over a transatlantic phone call and especially who would want to receive the call from a young woman mixed up in a most unsavoury way with a dead, ex-chorus girl.

Roberta calculated the time difference — it would be the early hours out on the West Coast. No matter. She was reasonably sure of catching Joel at his apartment now. At any other time he would be wherever the winds, women and sometimes location jobs of patch-up dialogue carried him.

She waited nervously, trying not to drum her fingers, which Mrs Sloan would certainly see as uneasiness. She wouldn't be far wrong, either. After an agony of waiting, Roberta heard a squawking, clicking sound. She pictured Joel's shaky hand crawling across his bed and fumbling for the phone. She wasn't able to enjoy her relief very long, however.

The sleepy sound answering from Joel's Wilshire Boulevard apartment was his current girlfriend's breathy, childish voice.

"Roberta? You sound just like you were right next door. Oh, sweetie, you missed Joelly by a mile. Didn't he tell you? They sent him on location. Well, it was a patch job. Mostly love stuff.

They asked for you first, but of course that was just about the time you chose the London job, so you weren't available. Good money, too."

Roberta felt icy all over. That rat, Joel! He had deliberately tied her up with Sybille Halloway so she wouldn't be able to take this job that meant 'good money'.

"Remarkable coincidence." Roberta took a deep breath and thought quickly. "All right. But he owes me over four thousand dollars from the Hawaiian location job. The money hasn't arrived yet. Contact him and tell him it's got to be wired by tomorrow or I'll get that bastard so deeply involved with the Guild he'll never climb out."

Roberta heard a little stir in Mrs Sloan's hall; the woman had shifted her weight from her right to her left foot.

Meanwhile, on the phone, Joel's girl assured Roberta almost tearfully, "I haven't managed to reach the Criterion Company for weeks. They're in the heart of the jungle. Well, Sri Lanka. Or is it Ceylon?"

"Same thing. Get hold of —" Roberta knew that if Joel Sawyer was on a 'difficult location' like Sri Lanka, and didn't want to take a message, nothing but the Third World War would do the job. Besides, there had been civil strife recently in Sri Lanka. He would have a hundred excuses.

Out of the corner of her eye she saw Mrs Sloan, leaning a little forward, eager to find out if Roberta's unsavoury methods succeeded. There was only one thing left, at least in regard to Mrs Sloan.

Roberta's transformation surprised even herself. She practically gushed over the phone.

"How lovely, my dear! You shouldn't have teased me like that. You're sure it's in the works now? Settled with my London account?"

"But sweetie —" came the girlfriend's plaintive cry. "You misunderstood me. I —"

"Same to you, dear. And many of them. Direct to my Barclay's account in London."

She cut the connection while Joel's girlfriend continued to protest. Roberta stood there looking at the phone for a minute. She had used her two credit cards to make the London trip and during the last two months Sybille Halloway had haphazardly, or shrewdly, given her what she called 'a little retainer' of four hundred pounds when they first agreed on the contents of the book, but this hadn't lasted long, even including the withdrawals on her credit cards. Roberta's hints had flowed over the ex-celebrity's head and off into the ether. Only Miss Halloway's death had prevented Roberta from a confrontation on the subject for which she was building up her grievances. However, chivvying money out of old ladies was not something Roberta did every day and it had been one of those things she just naturally put off, hoping it wouldn't be necessary.

Damn the woman! Why did she have to go and die?

Roberta managed a triumphant smile as she

passed Mrs Sloan on her way back upstairs. She knew she would have to start thinking up other ways of raising money.

She spent the next half hour making lists, looking up phone numbers and crossing them out. She was wondering how much more she could put on her American Express card without embarrassing questions being asked. Her last month's rent had cut close to the bone already.

Her acrylic writing board was covered with notes and figures when Mrs Sloan, just a tad more polite than she had been, knocked on her door and called to her.

"Telephone, Miss Fisher."

Maybe a miracle had happened. The girlfriend had made contact with Joel Sawyer in Sri Lanka and the money was coming.

Probably not. Still —

She unlocked the door, thanked Mrs Sloan on the way down the stairs, and took up the phone. It was Mrs Peavis. Wouldn't you know it!

The woman was her usual, gossipy, eager self. "So glad I got you, dear. I know how busy you must be, making plans to leave and all . . ."

"Yes. It will be very soon now. I'm waiting for a confirmation."

"But not today."

"No" Unfortunately not. She softened, wondering if she could borrow from Peavis's adored boss.

"Good," that enthusiastic lady went on. "Because my luncheon date — a horrid client of Sir Arthur's, trying to put over a dreadful merger, a female too — had to cancel and I've got the reservation open at the Savoy Grill Room. What do you say?"

It would be hard to refuse that. A good lunch at one of Roberta's favourite places, and it would save her buying dinner tonight. She might even hint at her problem in getting home. After all, the dead woman's estate owed her the money. Sir Arthur could collect from that. If a lawyer couldn't, who could?

"I'd love to, Mrs Peavis. How good of you to think of me! What time?"

"Shall we say twelve-thirty? That'll give us just time for a drink."

When she left the phone this time, though no nearer to home than ever, Roberta's spirits were up. The invitation must be a good omen. She hurried upstairs after giving the madly curious Mrs Sloan a big smile and studied herself in the mirror of the old dressing table. She had dressed to impress Sir Arthur this morning, wanting him to know that she was not some fly-by-night girl from Hollywood trying to make trouble with talk about a torn shorthand notebook.

With fresh make-up she would look her best. The rest was up to her, to charm Mrs Peavis into using her influence on her employer.

It was annoying to have to pay for a taxi but she wanted to arrive in style at the Savoy.

Just as well. Mrs Peavis was already there and was waiting for her in the elegant, male-domi-nated lobby.

Mrs Peavis twittered, "I'm delighted that you could come. I might have cancelled, I suppose, but I never know quite what to say to young people —"

"Young people?"

"Well, to tell the truth, I fibbed a little about that luncheon date. It's actually a trifle different. And you, being nearer his age, would help me entertain him through the luncheon."

"Entertain who?" Roberta demanded, more sharply than was diplomatic in the circumstances. Surely not Nicholas Demian! No. Sir Arthur would handle that. But she knew she had been tricked and was not too pleased with the idea.

She would have to put off hinting about the money. Meanwhile, Mrs Peavis, following her friend, the head waiter, was ushering Roberta toward the Grill Room. The warm glowing room, combining an ambiance of business with pleasure, was masculine but a number of tables were occupied at this hour by women in hats, which seemed to add a touch of old-fashioned elegance to the obvious business that was being conducted.

Mrs Peavis was heading to a table for four where a tall, sandy-haired boy about fourteen or fifteen was seated. Odd. She couldn't imagine anything she had in common with a boy his age. He stood up as the head waiter led the women to the table.

The boy had a sprinkle of light freckles across

his nose and a boyish mouth that seemed vulnerable and sensitive. Still, he smiled now, and she was won over even before she saw that he put most of his weight on his left leg. His right leg stuck out straight from hip to ankle, in a dated steel brace under his trouser leg, which balanced his stance.

Mrs Peavis said nervously, "Miss Fisher, may we call you Roberta — such a quaint name — may I present one of my favourite people, James Demian. We call him Jamie or Jem." Seeing Roberta's start as she took the thin, sharp-boned hand the boy extended, Mrs Peavis added, "He wants to write for the screen, you know. And he was delighted at the possibility of meeting a real professional."

The boy flushed a little and Roberta had no doubt Mrs Peavis's remarks embarrassed him. Roberta tried to put him at his ease. Everything about him seemed vulnerable and young, except his eyes. They were not at all like his father's but grey-blue and older than his general appearance. They were the eyes of a child who has suffered and thus grown up too fast.

The pity she felt instinctively was lost in a warmth — and even affection — to match his own friendliness.

"I don't suppose I can do much," she admitted, "but I certainly can encourage you." It was always dynamite to promise anything to would-be writers but she couldn't help feeling that Jamie Demian was an exception.

When the women ordered drinks, gin and tonic for Mrs Peavis and Scotch whisky and water for Roberta, Mrs Peavis laughed at Roberta's order. Even Jamie grinned a little.

When Roberta frowned Mrs Peavis explained. "You needn't specify *Scotch* whisky here, my dear. They understand that you want Scotch, unless you specify otherwise."

"Chauvinists," Roberta said but she smiled.

She couldn't be angry with the boy, just because Mrs Peavis may (or may not) have chosen another sneaky inducement to make her take the Edenbrook job.

When their drinks came she addressed Jamie, ignoring Mrs Peavis. "So you want to write for the movies. What kind of thing?"

His grey eyes lit up. "Something that's a mystery. And yet — you know — an education, and historical." He added hurriedly, "but interesting enough for the chaps I know to sit through it."

He had certainly amazed her. "Good heavens! That's a tall order. You talk as if you had it all planned out."

He seemed surprised that she should doubt his ability. That, at least, was like Nicholas Demian. A sublime confidence in himself. Although she resented it in his father, perversely, she admired it in Jamie.

"It is. I had the idea in Switzerland at the academy. An ancient man was found in the snow. Really. Thousands of years old. Italy and Germany both claimed the body."

"Yes. I remember." She wondered if his crippled condition had given him the chance, or drive, to work on such a subject when most boys were playing cricket or joining destructive 'gangs'.

"I think it's a wonderful idea. I hope you don't let anyone discourage you. You want to tell about the man himself?"

"His life. How he got there. Why he died. Make him human . . . which he was! Nobody's going to discourage me. And I have experience at writing plays. I do them for the Old Mill — our village players — when I'm home at Edenbrook. You get lots of practice that way."

"Yes. You do. You're going about it in the right way. I'll certainly scavenge among my acquaintances, such as they are, to find some connections for you. Who knows? Something might work out."

He looked so pleased, and rather proud of himself, that she wondered again how he could be related to that other Demian.

Mrs Peavis, meanwhile, was looking like the cat that swallowed the canary. It was clear that she thought young Jamie could win her over to visit Edenbrook, even if she and Sir Arthur had failed.

Wrong. The mere fact that Joel Sawyer had gone off with an assignment that should have been hers, was enough to make her itch to fight him on Hollywood turf where she knew she was valued more than he was. Besides, there was no future to a two-week run at a godforsaken place called Edenbrook!

Whenever the conversation lagged, Mrs Peavis was right there to promote some remark from either Jamie or Roberta. The boy seemed to be innocent of any ulterior motives and Roberta enjoyed talking to him, but she didn't like being manoeuvred and Peavis was a champion at it.

Jamie was halfway through his ice cream, and Roberta growing uneasy about the loan she needed, when Mrs Peavis startled both of them by her squeaky little cry, "Oh, no!"

Jamie, who seemed to know Mrs Peavis very well, asked with amused sympathy, "Not the bad tooth again?" Then he looked behind him where Mrs Peavis was staring and dropped his spoon.

"Father!"

Sure enough. Roberta saw two men crossing the room, deep in conversation, one a heavy-set, bald man with jowls shaking as he laughed. The other, a sardonic, dark man, seemed to be responsible for the fat man's enjoyment — naturally, he would be Nicholas Demian. He went on talking, moving his hand expressively.

Roberta watched him — the life and soul of the party! Such a brilliant wit, he didn't have to laugh at his own jokes. She was surprised that he could be so attractive when he was in a good humour.

But all this didn't erase the crime of her hostess. Roberta nudged her. "Sorry, Mrs Peavis. He would be the last man to persuade me."

For some reason Mrs Peavis was upset. "You don't understand, dear. Sir Arthur told me not to let you two meet. Mr Demian was supposed to be at the Hilton today, lunching with the publisher of his political cartoons. That's the man. Sir Archibald Underwood." From her obvious panic she must be telling the truth. This in no way changed Roberta's mind, but she was amused.

Clearly not a party to Mrs Peavis's little machinations, Jamie cleared his throat a bit anxiously and called, "Father! Over here."

Roberta was in no mood to meet Jamie's arrogant father at this hour, especially if he was a party to this idea of using her to spy on his tenants. Unfortunately, she had no say in the matter.

Upon hearing his son's voice above the buzz from other tables, Nicholas Demian excused himself to his publisher friend and came at once to Mrs Peavis's table. Roberta gave him full credit for one thing — he had a good relationship with his son.

When he reached the table, inclining his head politely to Mrs Peavis and Roberta, he said, "Hello, Jamie. Out with the ladies, I see. Lucky man." Gently pushing his son by one shoulder, he eased him back into his chair and leaned nearer to ask the boy something inaudible to the others.

Jamie said eagerly, "Oh, plenty. No problem. You couldn't join us, I suppose?"

"I wish I could, Jamie. Believe me. But we'll have a good dinner tonight. At that Elizabethan place you like near the river. Well, Miss Fisher, Art tells me we won't have the pleasure of seeing you again, this trip. Is it off to the wilds of California?"

"Unless I change my mind."

She objected to having her life laid out for her even if it was what she planned. No matter how kind he was to his son, she found his smile and the expression in his dark eyes unenlightening. They might mean anything.

She was sure now that she had at least aroused his curiosity. Whether that was good or bad, she had no idea.

"Miss Fisher is awfully kind, Father. She thinks I should keep on with my prehistoric mountain man project."

"I think so myself. Miss Fisher has good taste."

Jamie hesitated, glanced at Mrs Peavis, obviously a signal, and said, "If only she could see one of my plays at the Old Mill!"

Thanks but no thanks, Roberta was saying to herself when Nicholas Demian answered his son.

"I think not. Edenbrook is no place for a young lady from Hollywood. Too slow. Too quiet. Boring. No, Jamie. I think not."

Would this man never stop prowling around her affairs, offering opinions like royal pronouncements?

She laughed as lightly and sardonically as she could.

"Do you think not Mr Demian? What a shame! I would be desolated to do anything you didn't approve of, but those poor villagers seem so anxious to talk over their romantic past with me. I simply couldn't disappoint them." He looked at her with what appeared to be a cross between a scowl and a laugh. She didn't let that bother her. "Just a little visit, you know. I really am a fair to middling writer. And then, I might be of some help to your son. I know so many people. Where it counts."

She really was surprised when he said in an odd, almost sympathetic voice, "I wish you wouldn't."

Mrs Peavis was fluttering all over the place and even Jamie Demian looked so pleased that Roberta felt that she could not go back on all her bragging now. She had, in fact, played right into their hands.

Chapter Seven

With everything she packed into her mother's worn Vuitton case, Roberta reminded herself, "I've got nobody to thank but myself."

The only consolation was that she had limited this boring adventure to three weeks. By that time she could get Nicholas Demian's village tenants started on their precious self-glorifying history. She seriously doubted it would help them against the Demian family in any court. Poor devils!

But most important to her, her expenses for the flight home would be paid by Sir Arthur out of the funds due her from Miss Halloway's estate, and her expenses at the village would be the responsibility of the noble villagers themselves.

"You're just to sign for everything," Mrs Peavis put in.

"Sounds so Hollywood."

It also baffled her that the villagers seemed to trust Sir Arthur so much. Surely no one knew better that he and Demian were good friends. Maybe they knew something about that relationship that Roberta didn't know. Was Sir Arthur actually on the side of the villagers and not his friend Demian? It certainly appeared so. Unless, as she also suspected, this was simply his way of getting a Trojan Horse moved into the enemy camp. Make that Trojan Mare, she thought wryly.

Roberta didn't like having to charge everything, however, she still had enough pounds sterling to keep her from the embarrassment of having to check with the villagers every time she wanted to buy an aspirin or a lipstick.

Just before she left Sir Arthur's office yesterday afternoon, she had given him her ultimatim on another matter which no one had even mentioned during the 'business' arrangements: Sir Arthur's earlier suggestion that she report any violence or sinister actions aimed at the Demian family.

She would do so only if the matter were serious, but the letter which offered Roberta the job was signed by five members of the village tenants, with whom Sir Arthur had an acquaintance. Over the telephone two of them had verified the letter's offer, the owner of the Edenbrook pub, a Toby Teague, volunteering to put her up for the duration. His lively voice on the telephone sounded as welcome to Roberta as a friendly, tail-wagging terrier.

Sir Arthur assured her that he had known Toby Teague since boyhood. "I was reared in Mincham, as I said. My family knew Veda, Nick's wife, quite well, by the way. A pretty little thing used to having her own way in everything; completely spoiled. But charming enough in small doses. Never had a thought for anyone else. I really believe she resented their boy. His arrival stole a little of the deference paid to her."

"I know," Roberta said, remembering her father's obsession with his own good, to the exclusion of all else.

Sir Arthur was pleased that she understood. "Nick stuck it out, but they were less and less together. He became preoccupied with his work. Those political cartoons and portraits. He spent more and more time trying to educate and amuse their boy. After Veda's death I'm sure he blamed himself for not having been there. It was an accident, you know, pure and simple. But it shattered young Jamie, of course, and the boy is Nick's whole life."

She shivered and changed the subject. "So Mr Teague is to be my landlord at Edenbrook."

"So to speak. Toby's pub has quite a reputation among overnight tours and day excursions out of London. I recommend the food and drink."

She was sorry for whatever tragedy had made Nick Demian what he was, but he needn't take it out on his poor tenants. She made that clear when the call came from the tenants in Edenbrook. By being strictly honest Roberta made herself popular with Edenbrook's citizenry over the telephone in the barrister's office. When asked about Mr Nicholas Demian, she said, "Please, I don't feel up to discussing the man. If this job depends on my friendship with your landlord, we may as well call it quits now."

Toby Teague had insisted, "Not a bit of it, Miss. Nick Demian don't think we've got a chance, just by telling our side. There's a long history here and there. We've made it liveable, like our near ancestors did. We'll show them legal chappies if you'll help us. Let one of our females talk to you. Here."

There was a little trouble with the phone at that moment. A soft, hesitant female voice came on seconds later to agree with the pub owner and his partner, a shopkeeper named Camberson.

"I — I'm Elly Camberson. We'll lose everything our ancestors have worked on all these years since 1901. It's the Demians. Mr Nicholas's great-grandfather was given the property back then. But you can help us tell our side. We're in such trouble . . ."

She seemed to be crying but somebody said something to her rather sharply and she broke off. Still, her words appeared to come from the heart. Roberta was beginning to feel a civic responsibility toward these unfortunate tenants.

There certainly was something odd in Nicholas Demian's anxiety to keep her out of Edenbrook. It might be a personal dislike, but the tenants' fear of him was an added factor.

Maybe Demian was just unsociable.

Still, those three weeks in Edenbrook might give her a TV plot at least. You never knew! The town against the villainous landlord? Old hat, but the scene might give it a little *lagniappe,* as shopkeepers in New Orleans used to say when they gave their customers an extra apple or tomato or sugar bun.

Tiny Tim against Scrooge.

Mrs Peavis, sounding triumphant for some reason, had told Roberta over the phone, "Sir Arthur and I will see to it that someone who knows the countryside of Edenbrook — such a woodsy little place — will drive you there. By the by, dear, that nice young Jamie Demian called to tell us how glad he was about your little literary jaunt. He said some of the people at Edenbrook are awfully nice and you musn't think they will interfere in his friendship with you."

"Can we count on his father for the same courtesy?" Roberta asked and was not surprised at Mrs Peavis's reply.

"Well — no. Not really. He doesn't want Jamie to hang about you and make a nuisance of himself, I suppose. I didn't mention Jamie to him."

"Lovely fellow," Roberta had said and cut the connection.

Afterwards, Roberta had repeated the word 'woodsy' to herself without enthusiasm. She had always been a city girl, but there was one consolation. Nowadays, three weeks passed rapidly.

She had just finished packing her make-up and 'extras' case when Mrs Sloan's daily maid knocked on Roberta's door.

"Taxi's waiting, Miss."

Roberta hefted her suitcase, a make-up and odds-and-ends case, and an old but still useful canvas shopping bag on which was emblazoned a San Francisco cable car. Actually, it was filled with all the junk that would make her writing task easier: a miniature word processor and a hand-held tape recorder plus tapes. They gave added weight to the tote bag but she regarded everything in the bag as necessary and only hoped she would find this three-week excursion worthy of what her stepmother had charmingly labelled 'her toys'.

"Coming."

She started down the stairs with as much dignity as she could, considering her luggage load.

The last she saw of Mrs Sloan was that lady in her doorway, arms folded, looking as if she wanted to be sure her tenant with the habit of exposing herself to the press, was really leaving.

Sir Arthur Laidlaw was in his office, though it was almost three in the afternoon and Roberta, comparing him with Hollywood producers, studio heads and other high and mighty personnel, was impressed. For once, Mrs Peavis was not present.

Sir Arthur smiled as she looked around for the adoring secretary.

"I really don't keep my loyal Mrs Peavis occupied seven days a week."

"No, of course not. I only —"

"Today is an important one in the Peavis household. Henry Peavis is, at this moment, enjoying what you Americans call a 'root canal'. He refused to appear at his dentist's office if his wife was not present to hold his hand. I might be married today if my wife had been so obliging."

She laughed. "I can't say I blame Mr Peavis. Anyway, I just wanted to thank her."

"I understand. I'll tell her so." He pressed a buzzer on his desk. "My young clerk will escort you down to the car. May I wish you the best of luck?"

They shook hands. She felt it only fair to warn him again. "I don't intend to act as a spy for you and Mr Demian. I think his tenants know that."

He nodded, unruffled as ever. "Nick understands. And I certainly do. This is just my way to keep the peace, if I can. You know. Give the poor devils some hope."

He might have given them hope by taking the tenants' case against his friend's, but she didn't mention that. The sooner she provided what little help she could give the villagers, the sooner she could get home and raise hell with the cheating Joel Sawyer.

The office clerk, a lanky youth with a prominent Adam's apple, hurried Roberta to the lift and almost pushed her in. He was certainly anxious to please either his employer or the man who would chauffeur Roberta to Edenbrook.

Out on the busy pavement the boy pointed to the grey American Lincoln that must belong to Sir Arthur. It looked like something a man of his station ought to have. The boy opened the rear door for her. She got in, thanking him, but he was already peering in through the open front window to give the chauffeur a cryptic report.

"One of 'em's up the street by the curb. This side of the theatre marquee."

"Thanks, Raleigh. I've been watching that ancient Land Rover a little further along. It won't be difficult to outdistance him. I know the fellow."

Roberta knew that voice and was still in shock when Nicholas Demian tipped his uniform cap back over his somewhat wind-blown black hair with his thumb, and looked around at her. He wasn't smiling, but his eyes seemed amused. Maybe this was the closest he came to smiling.

He always caught her with her mouth open in surprise.

"Shall we take off, Miss Fisher?"

She managed a careless, but not unpleasant, "Why not, Mr Demian?" It occurred to her that his nice son, Jamie, had probably persuaded him to drive her to Edenbrook.

But it seemed more than unwise. Plain stupid in fact. What about his tenants? Would they assume he had won her over to his side in their conflict?

He started off with a roar that she didn't associate with this smooth car and she wondered if he was sulking or angry, but decided he was really trying to avoid the ancient Land Rover back there near the theatre in the busy square. Silly and extreme as it seemed, undoubtedly the boy's conversation with him was on the level. He wanted to throw off his pursuer.

It didn't require an imagination to realise that

one of his discontented tenants must have parked the Rover.

"Are we to expect a shoot-out?" she asked lightly.

"Not quite. Sorry to seem so melodramatic. I simply wanted to have a few words with you with neither my tenants nor my peace-loving friend, Arthur, listening in. Do you mind?"

"Not at all. But won't it seem just a tad strange if you rumble up to your beloved Edenbrook with me when I've just told those nice tenants of yours I have no use for you?"

It seemed impossible to offend him. He raised his eyebrows but accepted her opinion with what she had to admit was a certain amount of charm.

"I'm really not such a bad fellow, when you come to know me. Would you mind looking back to see if our friend's rattletrap is on our trail?"

"No chance. My rescuer is out of sight. How exciting! I feel just like one of old Al Capone's victims being taken for a ride."

He was definitely in a better humour. "A pity. You might think better of me if we hadn't got off to such a bad start."

"Sorry about that. I should have guessed the moment I met you. Such a warm and gracious meeting it was, too!"

"First," he went on, ignoring what she thought of as her friendly sarcasm. "You will be seeing a great deal of the Demian tenants, and since many of them are friendly with my boy, I wanted to ask a favour of you."

She abandoned her humorous tone. "Of course. If it concerns young Jamie."

"I just want you to keep an eye on him for me. Sheila, my sister-in-law, can't always be around. She has a habit of speaking her mind and is always feuding with one or two of the villagers."

Roberta couldn't believe even Nick Demian thought a crippled boy with such warmth and friendliness was in danger from his father's tenants. This man must have a terrible paranoia over the people of Edenbrook, but she decided not to try and convince him otherwise. Maybe he actually did think the world was out to get him.

"I give you my word. I'll keep an eye on Jamie. But I don't think — well, never mind."

"Thank you. I wanted him to stay away until this business of the tenants had been worked out, but Jamie wasn't happy so far away, and now, if I'm not careful, he will walk into some kind of trap."

Trap? What on earth was he talking about? She wished he would stop talking in riddles. She leaned forward, holding on to the back of his seat.

"I'm going to Edenbrook for three weeks. That's all. And I wouldn't let them — or anyone — do anything to that boy during that time. But it isn't very long. If you feel the boy is unsafe, Mr Demian, I strongly advise you to keep him away from Edenbrook."

"Easier said than done."

There really was no hope that he could get

over this strange obsession of his. Trying to figure out how she could help young Jamie Demian in three weeks, she settled back in the car seat, looked at the street behind them, and couldn't make out anything sinister. There wasn't one vehicle still following that had been there at the beginning of this rather shivery ride.

They were finally beyond the spread of the city of London and on the motorway heading west. He glanced at his mirror and seemed to share her relief, but said, "In the circumstances, our friends at home should remain convinced that you and I are still at odds."

Her eyes were bright with amusement. "Aren't we?"

He looked around. Who would have believed it? No matter what his sensuous lips might do, his eyes were smiling. This affected her uncomfortably. She hadn't realised a man with his possibly dangerous psychoses could begin to attract her.

Watch it, old girl!

She pulled herself together mentally and was frank with him. "Mr Demian, I promise you, I was hired merely to write up a sympathetic history of the work your tenants and their immediate forbears have put into your land during this last century. That's all. If they hint at any violence, anything you really should know, I'll tell you at once. But I don't expect it."

"Thank you." His voice had softened a little. She liked what this new mood did to him. "I can't ask for more. I suppose Art Laidlaw made it clear that you and I were not to be seen as friends."

"I'll force myself to refrain."

He laughed at that. "Good. We understand each other." After a moment he went on. "McQuarry, our chemist — or druggist, I imagine you would call him — is trustworthy. If I should not be available and you need someone, you may count on Mac."

"McQuarry. I'll remember."

"The Cotswolds have their own charms, including a cottage owned by Art Laidlaw."

He went on. "Art's chauffeur will meet us at the little house and drive you to the river cottages of Edenbrook. Mrs Camberson, a tenant's wife, is to meet you there. We employ her daughter at Demian House. Jamie and Sheila, my sister, are fond of the girl. Especially since our French housekeeper made a temperamental departure several weeks ago. God knows what reason she took into her head. Just left abruptly after dinner one evening. Without a word to anyone, according to Sheila. A cool customer, she said."

Apparently Demian House wasn't the nicest place in which to work. Roberta could only say, "That's odd."

He shrugged. "I believe there were complaints that she was what they called in the village, 'a typical Frenchy'. Whatever that means. She seemed reasonably content here but she wrote often to her family in France, they say. So you never know."

"Thanks for the tip. I'll try not to act 'above my station'. That's the usual complaint against foreigners isn't it? And I'm certainly a foreigner."

She thought he was going to add something. He looked friendly enough. But he said nothing. She was almost sorry the villagers had given her such a negative picture of him. She would like to have known him better in this present mood.

The countryside towards the hills and valleys of the Cotswolds looked soft, almost sensuous to Roberta, who had been born in the west of the United States and been on movie locations that had taken her to some of the harsh desert country of the Mojave and Death Valley, along with the eastern shadow of Mt Whitney, the rugged, highest peak in the United States. Many a western movie and television series had been shot in that area which stood in so well for the lofty peaks and settings of India under the 'Raj'.

Roberta wanted to remark about the beauty of the scene and its total difference from what she was used to, but he had picked up speed and his expression as she glimpsed it in the rear-view mirror was serious again, very much the way he had looked the day she met him in Sir Arthur's office.

Better leave well enough alone.

There had been showers in this country area. Fields and trees, clumps of wooded little groves, were still damp, their autumn foliage scattered over the ground, no longer reds and brown but now soggy and dead.

She began to think about describing the recent history of Edenbrook and the work put into the land by the tenants of the last three or so generations. She had very little confidence in the idea or its hoped-for result, and thought her temporary employers were extremely naive. But all this wasn't her affair. She simply wanted to be paid for her three weeks and be on her way home.

She could hardly use the recorder here in the car. They were on a country lane now, barely wide enough for two cars and all bumpy with stones. No matter. She got out a stiff-backed shorthand book and jotted down some ideas for arousing immediate interest but taking care not to get clever or pathetic.

She became aware of Nicholas Demian's interest occasionally. He watched her in the mirror and once looked back. He said nothing but didn't look so forbidding. Maybe he was just curious.

Just before the neat, golden Cotswolds began to dissolve unexpectedly into fields broken by thick stands of trees here and there, and as Mrs Peavis said, more 'woodsy' than simple windbreaks, the horizon to the west was much darker in an area about two miles square, and Roberta wasn't surprised when her companion pointed it out.

"In something like half an hour you will arrive at the immortal Edenbrook. It looks its best at this hour, just after sunset."

"I know," she jeered, at what she assumed was his humour. "The Dracula hour. Darkness falls and things come out of the woodwork."

To her relief, he laughed, refusing to be needled. "On the contrary," he was all inno-cence, "the village street lights will be on along the brook, past all the quaint little cottages. Five minutes after you turn a corner to follow the brook, and pass our number one antique, the Old Mill, now defunct, you've arrived at the Piccadilly Circus of Edenbrook: a circle of build-ings around a square and a few straggling cot-tages in a line along the brook. And that's what it's all about."

She wanted to ask him point-blank, "Then why do you and the tenants fight over the end of the lease?" But she didn't. There was no explaining some priorities. Maybe Nick Demian had some deep, passionate regard for all his own ancestors to whom this land belonged. With a touch of irony she said instead, "Everything you describe makes it more fascinating, this Dracula land of yours."

He was still smiling when he began, "If I were you, Miss Fisher —" He broke off and laughed. "Well, never mind what I was going to say. We'll be parting company on the lane to your right. That first thatched cottage we come to. Art Laid-law's chauffeur, Weems, will take you on. A good fellow. Fond of his pint, but not while on duty."

"That's a relief."

"Oh, he's harmless. Been with the Laidlaws since General Laidlaw's time."

She was disappointed but wouldn't have told

him for the world that she would be sorry to lose his company, no matter how 'harmless' this Weems might be.

They rolled down a slight grade and pulled up on a narrow patch of unpaved ground still damp from the recent showers. The patch was beside a house which was separated a good quarter of a mile from its neighbour, a rambling little inn, almost concealed under blood-red autumn creeper. The inn was the beginning of the village, but in spite of a parked tour coach in the distance, only two people, a woman with a cloth-covered basket, and a boy running across the lane with a woolly dog, were visible.

Nicholas turned and looked back at Roberta. To her surprise he put out both hands, closing them around her fingers.

"I'm afraid this will be our last friendly meeting. You know what to expect when we meet in Edenbrook."

She made a pretence of indignation. "Do you consider our previous meetings *friendly?*"

He was amused but confessed, "At least, I enjoyed them."

This was news to her, but she liked it, none the less.

They heard a male voice calling "Mr Nick!" and Demian looked down at her fingers in the palms of his hands for a moment, then, to her astonishment, he raised her fingers to his lips. He released them with the unsmiling repetition, "Yes. I enjoyed those meetings."

She still felt the warmth of his lips on her skin and wondered if he had noted her own excitement at his touch. The small but sensual kiss reminded her of two occasions when such a moment had been cut from her scripts by the story editor on the grounds that they were 'Corny, dated, and unbelievable'. But such moments still happened.

A man in a chauffeur's uniform hurried up to the car. His figure was stoutish and his curly dark hair and uniform, being just a bit too tight, made his neck look thicker. He was polite, friendly as they were introduced, and seemed to be a long-time acquaintance of Nicholas Demian.

"Here I am, Mr Nick. Ready for the great adventure. Am I to expect a knife in the back from your delightful villagers? Or just a bat across the head, so to speak? We're old friends, Toby Teague and me, but if a bat across the head is in order —"

"Neither one, my friend," Nick said as Weems looked around at the quiet, deserted landscape before getting in behind the wheel. "This lady is a friend of my delightful villagers. Just as you say you are. Please treat her with respect."

"Wouldn't treat the young lady any other way." The chauffeur turned to Roberta. "You really going through with it, Miss? The best of luck. I'll just hop to it now. Nobody in sight, Mr Nick. You get out that side. Not that anybody here is going to see you. They're all up the street, busy with a glass or two of something."

"Take care of the lady," Nick called.

Weems promised easily. "You've my word."

Nick stopped between Sir Arthur's car and the house and waved a kind of half-salute to Roberta. She felt absurdly pleased and leaned far out the open window to wave back, adding her best smile as well. Her sympathies might be with the villagers in general, but Nick had caught more than her interest in this drive.

Or had that been his intention?

Never mind. It was as well to be honest with herself. Maybe he had his own side to the quarrel. As Weems drove up the lane and turned west toward the gathering darkness of the little wooded area, behind which the sun would soon be setting, Roberta said, "I hope Mr Demian can get back to the city. Or wherever he is going."

Weems was confident. "Oh, Mr Nick will manage. He's on his way to pick up young Jamie and bring him home to Edenbrook. I left his car behind the cottage. Mr Nick, he grew up fast after his father died. And then his wife, that nasty one."

She didn't want to know the 'nasty' particulars. Remembering the feckless and irresponsible men who had been Miss Halloway's lovers in the Sixties, one of whom had been Mr Demian senior, Roberta could see why it was necessary for his son to grow up fast. She had felt that way herself when her father's problem with mistresses and the use of his wife's money had led Roberta to go out on her own.

The car rumbled smoothly along in a westerly direction. They seemed to be moving directly into the wooded area. As she watched the scene ahead it went from sunset to dusk and quickly verged on darkness.

Roberta tried to absorb some of the Dickensian charm of the wooded scene which was obviously inhabited in spite of its fairy-tale quaintness. Within the trees she caught a glimpse of a thatched roof, though the trees, like an evergreen tunnel, enclosed the road now.

Seconds later she heard the faint bubbling of water over pebbles and then saw the little stone bridge, oddly out of place in this miniature forest. Weems pulled up this side of the stone abutment. Then he swung the car door open and bellowed.

"Oh, Mrs Camberson . . . Will you be showing your face now?"

His voice in this thick, closed-in wilderness, made Roberta shiver. "Could you tone it down just a little? I keep expecting an echo."

Surely, he could see that the place was deserted. From the way it looked, it could have been deserted for years.

Damn! Everything had gone wrong for her from the time she landed on Sybille Halloway's doorstep.

She didn't get much help from Weems. He frowned and sucked his thumbnail speculatively.

"The villagers get down from the bus here and take that path right there, just peeping around the end of the bridge. See?"

For two cents she would make him drive her back to London and start for the States with money she would chisel from Sir Arthur.

He went on in his amiable way. "She's just a mite late. Maybe she had a spot of spirits. She does that now and again." (Oh, lovely! Did Nick Demian know anyone who didn't like his or her spirits?). He went on, "You could just follow the brook but don't get too close. Those pebbles are slippery."

"That's nice. Luckily, I can swim."

He played along but she could see he didn't consider the matter very serious. "I have to get on to Mincham with the car, or I'd go with you. But don't worry about the brook. At the worst, you'd just get your toes wet. Never mind your luggage. I'll leave it at the village square with Toby Teague."

She started to get out. He obligingly gave her a hand. They both froze, hearing footsteps crackle on the stepping stones.

"Probably snakes," she remarked blithely to cover her nerves, but he didn't think this was funny either.

"Oh, no, Miss. Snakes don't make that crackling noise. It's someone come for you, so all's well."

How reassuring! Meanwhile, some of the rushes along the brook parted and Roberta thought she made out a figure.

Too late now to return to London and call everything off.

Chapter Eight

Weems, the chauffeur, straightened Roberta out.

"Well now, if it isn't the lady of the manor, and looking like an angel to us poor lost creatures." To Roberta he explained, "It's Miss Sheila Demian come to meet you, Miss. Mr Nick's sister."

Roberta had guessed at once that there was nothing inebriated about this trim woman with her free-swinging, bouncy stride and neat, athletic figure, wearing the blouse and timeless full skirt of someone who had no need to follow current styles, or even notice them.

She offered a ready hand to Roberta and seemed far from the wavery, unsure Mrs Camberson who had spoken to her on the telephone.

"Welcome to Edenbrook," Sheila Demian greeted her pleasantly. "You and I needn't be enemies, just because the men are behaving stupidly."

Roberta took her hand, more relieved than she wanted to express at the moment.

"It was very good of you to meet me, Miss Demian. The young woman on the telephone, a Mrs Camberson, seemed a little . . . unsure."

Sheila Demian exchanged a glance with Weems who nodded understandingly. She explained to Roberta, "I'm afraid it's a case of 'poor Elly'. Awful to think we speak of her that way, behind her back. She used to be a good friend of mine in our girlhood, but that was before her marriage. Then the villagers began to get closer to the end of the lease, and now we have a feud on our hands. Are you really going to make a plea for them?"

"Heavens, no! I'm no lawyer. I write. I'm supposed to present their side. The hard work they've put into the land, the length of time their ancestors worked. Not very legal. But who knows?"

Sheila Demian waved to the chauffeur. "Go on around to the square and leave Miss Fisher's things. I'll take her by the brookside walk. She must be starved by this time."

"Won't it look a little, inappropriate, if I were to be seen in your company, Miss Demian?"

"Call me Sheila, please. Everyone does." The woman watched Weems move off across the stone bridge and out of sight on what appeared to be a turn in the narrow road.

When the chauffeur was gone Miss Demian went on. "He's quite a gossip. He'll tell Toby Teague and Elly's husband everything he saw and heard here, and I don't want Orin Camberson to know his wife fell apart on my doorstep. She was on her way to meet you, obviously."

So one of the anti-Demian tenants had taken refuge in the enemy house. Roberta asked no questions but moved carefully along the little path behind Miss Demian.

Over her shoulder Sheila Demian assured Roberta, "It's only a two minute walk to Demian House. Lights are set up along the brook, beginning just beyond those trees."

Making her way through the undergrowth that was still damp from yesterday's rain, Roberta kept sinking an inch or two in rotting leaves or a twig whose sharp, broken end snapped at her instep. It was too late to wish she had abandoned high-heeled glamour and stuck to sports shoes and slacks. But in spite of this, the place fascinated her as a 'setting', something one sees on a screen. Not real at all.

Sheila Demain was right. It must have been only a minute before they came out of the little tunnel-like copse and found an enchanted brookside village meandering ahead of them. It might be the tiny, welcoming glow of the lamps along the brook, but the scene appeared to close around them like a warm hand. These lights gave a special Christmas feeling to the scene. The time-darkened thatched cottages with casement windows might otherwise have appeared as forbidding as the witch's house in *Grimm's Fairy Tales*.

Her foot slipped and Sheila Demian caught her arm momentarily. "It's the ground underfoot. Soft and springy. Muffles the sound. That two-and-a-half storey place on your left, next to the gardener's cottage, is Demian House."

After all the uncertainties of the afternoon Roberta could say frankly, "I love the brookside setting. And your house too."

"Actually it doesn't look like much, but out here it's Buckingham Palace. The land's worth a fortune, I expect. For development. That's old, toothless Samson Brinkby looking out of the parlour window of the Brinkby cottage. You've talked over the telephone to his son, the town gardener, and to Orin Camberson whose shop is on the village square. We Demians employ Brinkby the gardener by the year. He keeps the village looking pretty for the tourists."

It was odd to think of the village as a tourist destination. It seemed so secret and turned-in upon itself.

Sheila Demian explained. "The tourists love clicking away at their precious cameras every Tuesday and sometimes other days. The locals charge for the privilege, you can bet. Quaint. That's the going word with the tourists."

So all this 'quaintness' was deliberate. It disappointed Roberta somehow but she was careful to return the friendly wave of the grinning old man, Samson Brinkby, at the window of the gardener's cottage.

They had reached the doorstep of Demian House and Sheila Demian rattled the old brass knocker twice. She pointed it out to Roberta.

"Nick's and my great-grandfather had it installed. A ram's head. A tribute to the sheep men of the area around Mincham."

Roberta did not miss the reference to 'great-grandfather'. If the tenants were going to play up

113

their ancestry, the Demians would match them, rams for sheep.

"Sounds like the Hatfields and McCoys," she murmured, but from Sheila Demian's puzzled expression the story of the warring mountaineers in the States hadn't travelled this far.

Considering the atmosphere and the friendly, toothless old man next door, Roberta had expected an equally antiquated servant to welcome them at Demian House. Instead, a flashy, teen-aged blonde girl opened the door, looking relieved to see Sheila Demian.

"Oh, it's you, Miss Sheila, thanks be! I was afraid it might be my father."

Sheila was emphatic. "Heavens, no! And it's my hope he stays in Toby Teague's pub until we've got Elly — er — things straightened out. Do come in, Miss Fisher. This young lady is Merlina Camberson. Elly and Orin's daughter. She helps us out, and very useful she is, too."

Roberta offered her hand but Merlina was busy bobbing a curtsy like an upstairs maid in an old French farce. The girl's head nodded with her movements and spiky kinks of uncombed hair flew out. Roberta was about to draw her hand back, feeling foolish, when Sheila Demian looked at it in a startled way.

"Good heavens! I thought there was only one ring quite like that, with that setting and particular stone. An opal, of course, and very rare. You aren't superstitious, I see. Superstition is such bosh, I think."

"It isn't mine and frankly, I'd rather not have it," Roberta told her honestly, turning the ring to let her get a better look. "Miss Halloway insisted I take it. She really was superstitious and I must say, she was right, when I remember what happened to her. Anyway, the ring belongs to whoever gave it to her."

Sheila drew her own hand back. "I'm so sorry. It was rude of me. If it came from the Halloway woman, then she could have obtained it from anyone. Very likely male." She smiled. "I'm not much of a collector and to be honest, I'm just as happy without jewellery."

Suspecting it might belong to the Demians, Roberta started to force the ring off but Sheila stopped her as they entered the heavily panelled entrance hall. "No, no, please. We've had enough of that woman. Perhaps if you give it to some charity, the bad luck might fall away from it." She looked around the big room they had stepped into now.

Beyond the hall this large, oak-panelled room cut beneath a mezzanine landing where the stairs turned at an abrupt right angle up to the upper floors. Fortunately there was a bright lamp on the top landing side table and this, with the long French windows across the room opening on a wilderness garden, managed to illuminate what Roberta considered a movie set that should have been redesigned generations ago.

Young Merlina Camberson guessed who Sheila Demian was looking for when she glanced around the main floor and the girl said quickly, "Mother's better now. She's up in the sewing room. Your new cook is showing her some of the old clothes she found in the attic. Mother knows we need costumes for the Saturday night players at the Old Mill."

Sheila sighed but started up the stairs, motioning Roberta to come along. She explained. "Mrs Schramm is our new cook. Our French cook-housekeeper walked out on us a month ago, without a word to anyone. What a nuisance!"

Merlina followed the two women, talkative and clearly interested in Roberta, a newcomer.

"Schramm is awfully good, though. Her Viennese pastries with cream — not clotted, but good — and Wiener Schnitzel . . ."

"Yes, Merlina. We know." Sheila continued to Roberta, "But I did count upon Mrs DeVrees. She was immensely capable with sewing as well as the household."

Behind them Merlina giggled and then, catching Miss Demian's eye upon her, she covered her mouth but was not silenced.

"She was awfully taken with Mr Nick. I heard Father and Mr Brinkby say so."

Sheila rolled her eyes at Roberta and snapped, "Well, it was not reciprocated. I doubt if he knew she was alive."

Merlina began, "That's not what —" But this time, there was no mistaking Sheila's frown. The girl hushed up.

Had Nick Demian really been interested in the

French housekeeper? There seemed to be a difference of opinion on that.

They reached the upper floor with its timbered ceiling which, together with the golden light from two table lamps, was warm and welcoming. The oiled shades of the lamps glowed with scenes from the gentle village brook, an old mill on one shade and something similar on the lamp at the far end of the hall.

Roberta lingered behind the others, wondering if she was going to be an unwilling witness to the family squabble when Elly Camberson's husband came looking for his wife, drunk or sober. Would he also punish his daughter for her part in the conspiracy about Elly's drinking?

Quite possibly alcohol explained the voice of Mrs Camberson on the telephone that day when she spoke to Roberta in Sir Arthur's office.

What a place to come to! Nick Demian had been right when he tried to persuade her not to make this trip.

Sheila Demian and Merlina, with Roberta behind them, went into what appeared to be a sewing room full of Victorian female bric-a-brac, including an ancient treadle sewing machine and a chaise longue where a delicate, slender woman sat, drinking tea poured from a pot warmed by an old-fashioned tea cosy. She had the cup in both fragile hands but seemed sober enough. She raised her head; she had pale, frightened eyes, either blue or lilac. It was hard to tell.

"Ah, there you are, Elly," Miss Demain said

in a calm, unsurprised way. "Wouldn't you like something with your tea, dear?"

Mrs Camberson shook her head. "Not now, thank you. Oh, Sheila, I should be out at the bridge where the buses stop. That young woman I am to meet. I always get so nervous when it's something about Orin's business." She looked around the room, avoiding Roberta who had the sensation that the woman didn't know she was here. "Merlina, would you go out and see if the lady has arrived yet? Orin will be so angry if I don't come back with her. I was to show her the cottages along the brook, and all the work that our people put into them during the long years."

Roberta was about to speak but a small motion from Sheila Demian silenced her.

"Now, Elly, you've nothing to concern yourself about. Our guest, Miss Fisher, is right here. You brought her here yourself."

Elly Camberson stared directly at Roberta, blinked, and then very slowly gave her a smile that did not match the woman's speculative look. After a moment, Elly set her tea cup down carefully and held out one hand.

"I'm so glad I did find you. I forget so easily. I know it was terribly important; Orin told me. And Toby and the others. My! How pretty you are, Miss . . ."

"Fisher. Roberta Fisher. You musn't worry." Roberta went on hurriedly. "You were a great help to me." She caught Sheila Demian's nod. "Showed me through that little clump of trees to

118

the brookside cottages and then to Demian House."

"Oh. Of course." Elly Camberson was a little more certain, a fact that relieved the other women. "I remember now. It was growing dark and I stumbled over Sheila's doorstep and Sheila caught – no, it was my own Merlina who caught me. I don't recall meeting this young lady, but I must have. And here we are," she finished in triumph.

Merlina put in, "Isn't it nice, Mama? You are going to choose the wardrobe we'll all be wearing in our play on Saturday night. Mrs Schramm is up in the attic getting some things out of those old trunks this very minute."

"I'd like that," Mrs Camberson agreed. "I always like to see everyone dressed up. So different from the way life is every day."

Sheila reached for the teapot. "Won't you have a cup of tea, Miss Fisher? Just to give you a little sustenance before we get you past the cottages and over to your supper at Teague's place?"

Roberta wondered what kind of supper awaited her in Toby Teague's pub, but was determined not to make trouble at this stage of her own association with both sides in the Edenbrook feud.

Meanwhile, heavy footsteps in the hall attracted her attention and obviously excited young Merlina.

"It's Mrs Schramm. She said she'd found a very old trunk behind the others. She must have got it open."

The women weren't particularly curious. Sheila glanced at her wristwatch as Mrs Camberson drank the last of her tea and was about to set the cup down when a large woman of middle age came to the doorway, smiling with pride.

"These are very fine. Wide-hemmed trousers, worn long ago in South America. They would fit over the brace of young Herr — Master Jamie."

Sheila was especially pleased.

"Very good, Mrs Schramm. Jamie will be delighted. It's always better when there is a place for him in the shows. What else have you found?" She leaned forward, attracted as Merlina and Roberta were by the glistening bits of the gown Mrs Schramm held behind her substantial frame.

The hall lamplight had glimmered on the knee-length dinner dress and now all three women saw it in the full light of the sewing room. It was of clinging, off-white satin, sleeveless, with a trim of tiny seed pearls that put finishing touches to a severely elegant gown.

"Very nice indeed," Sheila remarked. "I don't remember it. Probably belonged to our grandmother."

"But it's too new for that," Merlina objected, clapping her hands. "It's gorgeous. Looks as if it's never been worn. It's mine, isn't it, Mama? I could wear it. A little letting out in the bosom, maybe."

Smiling, Sheila looked at Roberta. "Something tells me Merlina will steal the show."

"Mama, what do you — ?" Merlina began and broke off in a panic. "Mama!"

Roberta looked around. Elly Camberson stood up, wavered and took a step forward. To everyone's horror she began to collapse against Roberta who was stunned but managed to catch her, sinking to the floor with the fainting woman.

"Poor Mama. It's the drink." Merlina summed up the obvious explanation as Roberta knelt, propping up the frail woman against her shoulder.

Sheila poured more tea into Mrs Camberson's fallen cup while Mrs Schramm picked up the satin dinner dress, remarking, "*Ja.* Poor lady. It's a bad thing for some as haven't the head for it."

Roberta didn't think the alcohol had reacted on Mrs Camberson belatedly, stripping her face to an alarming pallor and her breath to that terrible gasping for air. But she knew better than to contradict these women who had doubtless known Elly Camberson all their lives.

Chapter Nine

Kneeling, Roberta held the woman's head and shoulders against her arm and looked up, more concerned than anyone else seemed to be.

"She's coming around. Mrs Demian, could you try the tea again?"

Sheila held it to Elly Camberson's lips while Merlina, seeing her mother begin to move and reject the cool tea, asked in a loud stage whisper, "Is she still smashed? I thought she would be okay by now."

The fainting woman opened her eyes, the eyelids fluttering. Her right hand made incomprehensible gestures to the cook.

"Not that . . . Colour bad. Makes Merlina look . . . sallow."

"Oh, Mama!"

"Of course, it's bad," Sheila agreed briskly and added to Mrs Schramm, "just put it back where you found it. We'll use something else later. Give me that cup, Elly, and breathe deep. That's better."

The cup rattled in its saucer as Elly Camberson replaced it with shaking fingers. She stirred against Roberta's arm and tried to get to her feet. When Roberta had helped her back into her chair the woman looked groggy but seconds later she gently protested at the excitement she had caused.

"I was just too warm. That's the thing of it. Came over all faint-like. But I'm quite myself. I can walk."

Sheila washed her hands of this curious business.

"Well, thank God for that! Now, dear, if you are done with your vapours or whatever, I'm afraid we must get Miss Fisher to Teague's pub, else we'll have that husband of yours marching on us with the entire village population. He should have come to meet Miss Fisher in the first place. She is your problem. Not mine."

She gave Roberta a significant little message with upraised eyebrows and Roberta understood that unlike her brother, Nicholas Demian, Sheila did not take this 'feud' with their tenants seriously.

The cook threw both the satin dress and male slacks over one arm. "I'll just be putting them away for the time being, Mrs Demian. I'm sorry for all this, to be sure."

She hurried from the room, shedding old-fashioned bone hairpins in her haste.

Roberta noticed that the mention of Orin Camberson had aroused Mrs Camberson, putting her in something very like a panic. Whatever troubled her, she certainly was in a bad way. She shrank from Roberta and held out a hand to her daughter. Her voice was timid and hesitant as Roberta remembered it from the phone call but she seemed to be doing her best to fortify herself, despite her sick pallor and the thin fingers that still trembled a little.

"Merlina, finish your work for Sheila and then come along home. Papa will expect you."

Merlina bobbed a half-curtsy to Sheila Demian and hurried away. To Roberta's surprise Mrs Camberson straightened up, raised her head, and started to follow her daughter. As she left the room she turned back briefly to Sheila Demian and then to Roberta.

"I'll just make myself more presentable in the little bathroom downstairs. Then, Miss Fisher, I will be happy to show you our brookside and take you on to the pub. It faces on the square, you know."

The minute she was gone Sheila and Roberta looked at each other. Sheila remarked, "I'd give a good deal to know what that fainting was all about."

"Was it genuine?"

"Oh, yes. She isn't well. But what was that silly business about the dress? She never even knew our grandmother."

Roberta was still puzzled. "Are you sure the dress is that old? The material seemed so fresh and new to me."

Sheila shrugged indifferently. "Even so, what has it to do with Elly? Well, come along. I suppose there are some things we'll never know. Meanwhile, comes more unpleasantness. You will have to meet Elly's husband. A dried-up prune of a man if ever I saw one."

"I hope all my so-called employers aren't going to be dried-up prunes," Roberta said lightly as she and Sheila Demian went down the stairs together.

Sheila shook her head. "Unlikely. Though there has been a growing malaise in the village for many years. Even I've felt it. First, there was Father who died. He was quite a rogue with the ladies, as you must have guessed in writing Miss Halloway's memoirs. Not at all like Nick, as anyone may see who knew them both at all. After that, things have gone steadily down in our relations with the tenants. They didn't get any better when Nick's wife, Veda, was killed, and our Jamie was injured. An accident involving the mare who belonged to one of the villagers, the chemist. A friend of Jamie's."

The chemist.

And he was still a friend of Jamie's, the boy whom his horse crippled, perhaps for life?

Why had Nick Demian told her to count upon that particular villager? It didn't make sense.

Roberta made a mental note of this, intending to question the tenants about the chemist and Jamie's injury. But she would take care not to mention Nick Demian's view that the man could be trusted, presumably not by the villagers but by the Demians.

By the time she and Sheila Demian reached the front door Elly Camberson was there waiting and looking almost normal. When she had concealed her pallor with a little make-up and conquered whatever fears afflicted her, she proved to be a lovely woman, in spite of her delicacy.

"Such a stupid fall I had, Sheila! I don't know how I came to be so clumsy."

"Not at all, dear. Drop in any time." Sheila laughed at her own joke and patted the woman's arm with one sturdy hand. "That is, my door is always open to the villagers in spite of my impossible brother. Tell your husband so."

"Oh, I daren't." Elly Camberson hugged Sheila, then broke away. "But Miss Fisher and I must hurry. My husband will be so cross. You will send Merlina home as soon as you've had dinner? You know how Orin dislikes our girl working here."

"Certainly. Certainly. Now, run along. I'll walk Merlina home myself."

Elly Camberson hesitated. "Well, perhaps — I don't know."

Sheila Demian muttered to Roberta, "My God! I'd shoot a man before I let him bully me that way. Run along now."

Roberta was sorry for Elly Camberson but her instincts agreed with Sheila Demian. However, she did as she was told, joined Mrs Camberson, and they walked along beside the brook, carefully stepping from stone to stone, avoiding the water which was illuminated by the lamplight overhead.

"What a setting for a Victorian murder!" Roberta remarked and then, seeing her companion shudder, she explained, "On TV, of course."

Elly Camberson forced a laugh. It was hardly more than a grimace dredged up from somewhere in her frail body.

To Roberta it had begun to appear that half the villagers were ready for the loony bin! She changed the subject, wondering if it would be necessary to protect a battered wife from her husband as well as the villagers from their 'cruel and inhuman' landlord.

Small wonder that Nick Demian had tried to prevent her from getting mixed up in this vicious affair.

As if vitally interested in the unknown night scene around her, she asked, "Does this little brook ever overflow these stones? There doesn't seem to be a proper bank."

Obviously, this was a subject more pleasing to Elly Camberson. "Only around the Old Mill further along on the opposite bank, just below the square. We tried to grow courgettes and other vegetables in that patch. Sometimes it works. Mostly not. It can get boggy and waterlogged there."

Walking along the edge of the brook, Roberta noticed how extraordinarily dark it was behind the hundred-year-old cottages they passed. This must be due to the extension of the woods which crowded the space devoted to the tiny village itself. The village certainly was closed in. It gave her claustrophobia. What would such a background do to people who had allowed themselves to be shut away from the world for centuries? Or, for the purposes of her 'report', one century, in any case.

Roberta said, "I suppose the young people leave as soon as they can."

Elly Camberson seemed surprised by this obvious conclusion. "Some do. Some come back, hoping it will be better later on."

Why later on? But Roberta did not repeat the thought aloud. Were the tenants here that sure they would have it all very shortly?

Elly said, "The brook curves around a corner here. It's rather pretty by daylight. Past the chemist's cottage belonging to McQuarry. From here the brook rambles to the north and then west into the Mincham Weir."

Roberta could see what she took to be Edenbrook's public square above their side of the shallow bank. It was slightly shadowed by a big, grey, wooden building across the brook. The grey building's waterwheel announced it had once been a flour mill.

Mrs Camberson saw the direction of her interest. "That's the earliest building still standing in Edenbrook. Just a big, empty shell now. Even the wheel doesn't go round, unless you give it a good push. Back of the mill is the patch I told you about which catches the excess run-off water from the brook. There's a tiny rivulet between the trees that feeds that patch. But it's all useless. Either too much water in some seasons, or not enough. And now, everything is so uncertain they just get busy on other projects and there's an end of the matter."

"Too bad. I love fresh vegetables. They are pretty scarce in the areas I'm used to."

Her companion ignored that. "The ground floor of the mill is used for showing films."

Roberta laughed at this show of civic pride but Mrs Camberson was already transferring her interest to the village square on a gentle rise above the brook where they stood. She seemed to grow in strength when turning her thoughts from her husband to civic interest.

"There. That's the heart of Edenbrook."

The tiny golden lights along the brook illuminated just the path up into the centre of the square, and Roberta stopped suddenly, feeling more chilled than the cool, early autumn night warranted.

"Did you see that? Across the little footbridge from the Old Mill? Now, see the movements and lights among those rushes?"

Elly stifled a nervous giggle. "They're coming from the cinema in the mill; most of the village. They were showing an old American film early this evening."

Over her own uneasiness Roberta reminded her, "It's the villagers like that who will be the chief sources for my book. Their memories of the work their ancestors did."

"How very true! You can see their faces now. Look."

Was it possible that these people still used

lanterns on a walk of a hundred yards or so? But it *was* dark out here.

Suddenly, Elly Camberson made out a thin, small male figure in the crowd and waved to him. She seemed frightened again but obviously was making an effort, proudly showing off her conquest, the 'late' Roberta Fisher.

She said quickly, "That's Orin. He is the projectionist, and very good too. He used to have the matinees at the Revivals Cinema in Mincham. That's why I was sent to meet you. He was busy here."

To Roberta's embarrassment most of the moviegoers, instead of separating and making their own decisions about meeting her, buzzed as if debating whether to take Elly Camberson up on her invitation when she called again, "I have Miss Fisher. Come and meet her."

Then, having come to an agreement after waiting to see that Orin Camberson was going to meet his wife and the newcomer, they came to an unspoken agreement and crossed the bank toward Elly and Roberta.

By this time they seemed curious to meet her, perhaps anxious to be liked, and she was touched.

Under the scattered brookside lights, one or two beside wooden benches, Roberta made out the country faces she had hoped to find: some rough-hewn, male and female, a few, also of both sexes, with pink and white complexions that looked as fragile as china.

Some appeared shy with her even after the handshakes they offered hesitantly, and she realised she had been wrong. They were not anxious to be liked. *She* was the person on trial here.

Roberta tried to sort out the various families and their parts in the life of the village. At the start it seemed almost as simple and easy as a card game in which one family represents each suit on the board, but this very soon proved to be inadequate.

Aside from the thin, small man Elly had called to, Roberta couldn't tell one from another of the suddenly chattering, nervous villagers under an overcast night sky, with only shaded lanterns to illuminate the scene. She smiled at everyone, agreed to everything they said, whether she understood their slight accents or not. She ended by being escorted up from the brook path and into the more modern centre that they called the Edenbrook square.

This little area reminded her of other villages she had seen in the Home Counties, with touches of ancient Rye and even the beach cottages of Hastings. She guessed that the area had been built long before the brookside cottages, though the square had been modernised and made more utilitarian.

The pub, apparently the only one, was easy to spot even if the little polished brass sign hadn't spelled out the three letters or the inn sign hadn't been swinging darkly overhead. She suspected this self-advertisement was more for the benefit of the 'Tuesday tourists'.

The lean-faced Orin Camberson, with thin, greying hair and pale, narrow eyes looked Roberta over, not appearing to like what he saw. She remembered the beautiful Merlina at Demian House and wondered how the girl fared with a father like Orin Camberson.

Eager to indicate she really was on their side, Roberta told Camberson brightly, "I saw your daughter when Mrs Camberson met me. Both were charming."

"It wasn't my choice that Merlina should be slaving away in that house," was the only reply Roberta got to her bid for friendship.

Elly Camberson spoke up anxiously. "Mrs Schramm will be bringing her along shortly."

"I hope so. This is our girl's payday. We'll expect an accounting," Camberson reminded her. He took his wife's arm tightly above the elbow. "Come along, Elly. Leave the young woman to Toby Teague. He'll see to her comfort."

"Yes, Orin." The woman looked back at Roberta, then avoided her eyes and went along meekly, still with one arm held tightly to her husband's grey sweater. When they were going down the path Roberta and Elly Camberson had just taken on their way to the square, Roberta stopped long enough to thank the people of the village for greeting her. But some of the villagers had their backs to the pub and were sauntering off to their respective cottages in and around Edenbrook square.

The pub's heavy door opened upon the scene and the electric lights from within cast a cheerful glow on the paving stones in the square. Roberta was relieved when a big man came lumbering out to the street. He had tousled hair and a wonderful, toothy smile. He looked to be about fifty or more, but she had no doubt he could handle any drunks who gave him trouble in his pub.

The remainder of the crowd began to shuffle around. Spirits seemed lighter and several people, all male, called to the huge, friendly looking man in the doorway.

"Hi, Toby. We've brought your young lady, like she was promised."

Another of Toby's customers yelled, "Hope you've swept up the dust and that, under the rugs."

"What say, Toby? She's prettier than you thought; wouldn't you say?"

Embarrassed, Roberta offered her hand, apologetically "I hope I'm not putting you out. I'll try and make my short visit as profitable to you as possible."

He protested, "No trouble, Miss. Sir Arthur Laidlaw's driver, he left your cases here with me. I'm Toby Teagarten. Toby Teague, for short."

He grinned. "My Pa and Sir Arthur Laidlaw, he was a young lad in those days. He used to hire my Pa to drive him to the bookshops and places in Mincham town. But come along in, before these good folk talk your ears off. You there, Barney, off you go home. Pub's closed for the night so this lady can unpack and get some rest. She's going to be pretty busy working up the book on our grievances against the Demians."

In spite of his words, the publican certainly didn't seem as hostile as many in the village.

"Night to you, Toby," most of the people shouted, including some of the women. She was beginning to understand his popularity. He certainly made her welcome.

He ushered her in through a short, narrow passageway to the warm light beyond, hardly giving her time to address the villagers over her shoulder: "Thank you, all of you. I hope to see you tomorrow."

Toby Teague assured her, "We won't ask anything of you tonight, Miss. You being tired out and all. But you'll be wanting a nice dish of supper. How'd you fancy our fresh lamb stew?"

After all her ups and downs and slightly sinister experiences today, she was more than grateful for his thoughtfulness.

The pub's entrance passage opened into two large rooms, a public lounge on the left made more comfortable by a fireplace in which a modest fire burned, suitable to early autumn. On the right side was an unpainted, panelled bar room. Scattered around the room she saw a hand-carved table and six chairs, plus two stiff, uncushioned settles under the shuttered front windows. The cheerful tulip-shaded lamps in the lounge and bar undoubtedly attracted the villagers.

Toby Teague made a sweeping wave toward the bar. "We get a deal of supper trade there. At the table and chairs. Nobody wants the settles. Too stiff, uncushioned and all." He grinned his big, toothy grin. "So we put a lad on the settle when he's had a dram too much. It's long since dinner. We have it early in these parts. But a microwave'll do the job, don't you fear. Serves me when there's a bit of a crowd. And like tonight. I can have supper heated for you in a shake."

She thanked him but he dismissed such petty considerations. He led her up the stairs beside the bar and into a narrow, low-ceilinged corridor where her room awaited her at the front of the building, very close above the street. It was modestly furnished with what appeared to be a comfortable double bed and mattress, along with a night stand, a round table covered with a crocheted cloth, one chair and a big, armoire-type of wardrobe.

The shutters had not been closed and the window was partly opened, with a view of the town square. It was interesting to get a good idea of the activity in the heart of this miniature town.

There wasn't much activity now though, it being nearly nine o'clock. Like hard-working country folk, they probably rose at the crack of dawn to begin their day's work. A little knot of people, probably some who had left her here at the pub, was gathered across the square and kept glancing towards the pub. Undoubtedly comparing notes on her.

Roberta heard voices now below the window but they faded as Teague turned on the room's ceiling light and the more cosy pink lamplight, and told her about the 'facilities' down the hall.

"Thank you." She was careful not to smile.

After pointing out the water in the white pitcher on the stand he went away as if afraid he might have to show her the 'facilities' in person. She heard his heavy-soled shoes clomping down the staircase and finally felt that she could relax.

After removing her wristwatch and the opal ring and setting them on the little round table, she began to unpack. She was glad she didn't have to be on display tonight and was just laying a nightgown, robe and slippers on the bed for use 'down the hall' when she became aware of voices again under the open window.

"Not bad to look at. If only —"

"What was you expecting? From that Hollywood."

Roberta dropped her slippers and listened more carefully.

"That's the trouble. She's nothing like the others."

"She seemed right, somehow. What with the London papers and all."

Whatever the other male voice replied was inaudible. She looked out. Two men were walking down the little slope, past the chemist's shop and house below, where the brook began to turn north between the village square and the Old Mill.

She sat down on the bed and closed her eyes, trying to figure out just what she had got into here. It was only when she felt the prick of her slipper heels against her forehead that she dropped the slippers beside her watch and the opal ring.

Remembering Sheila Demian's interest in the opal, she picked it up and examined it. The ring's owner must be the man who reluctantly gave it to Miss Halloway. Had that man been the father of Sheila and Nick Demian? Then the ultimate owner was young Jamie Demian, the original owner's grandson. She wondered if Jamie's father would forbid him to keep it. But Nick Demian looked much too sure of himself to be superstitious.

She settled down to do some unprofitable thinking about her situation.

Chapter Ten

The strange bed was comfortable and helped to bring Roberta Fisher some dreams that included her complicated feelings about Nick Demian. She found him attractive in spite of her early experiences with him. Probably nothing more than a sexual allure. It would vanish the next time he showed his true colours. Whatever they were. She didn't like this attraction she felt toward him, but it was easier to analyse than to conquer.

At least, it had nothing to do with poor Miss Halloway's accident which had lingered in her previous and unpleasant dreams.

She got up a little after a hazy autumn sun had risen and the village seemed fully awake. She pattered down the creaking hall to the 'facilities' which were divided, European style, into two compartments: a bathroom (but no shower) and a tiny cabinet with a flush toilet and a box overhead that kept dripping lightly between pulls on the chain.

Floorboards squeaked painfully in the hall. The footsteps retreated and she escaped to her room with her hands still wet, because she couldn't find the towel in either the toilet or bathroom. Luckily, she was dressed by the time her landlord called through her bedroom door.

"Breakfast on the hob, Miss. In taproom."

"Thank you."

It turned out to be a tourists' breakfast: eggs, mushrooms, sausages, squeezed orange juice, toast barely warm with the edges carefully shaved off, but tasty all the same, and of course a pot of strong tea.

"Not like that Frenchie female ordered, eh, Miss?"

What Frenchie? Oh, well, it was too early for mysteries. "It's perfect," she managed, with her mouth full of toast.

Toby Teague had been standing there in his big butcher's style apron, waiting for just this compliment and hearing it, he rubbed his huge right hand on the apron before offering the hand to her.

"Well now, it usually goes down with my tour folk, but they don't always say so. I'll leave you to enjoy it and wish you a fine day ahead. If you're looking to find what the villagers have been up to these past years and long ago, there'll be records of payments and carpentry, new buildings, sheds, patching up the bridges, work on the weir — Mincham never does its bit. It's all our labour. The lounge is being cleaned now but in no time it'll be ready."

"I'm to make all this interesting and readable. I'll keep my fingers crossed." She thanked him and they shook hands very formally. Then he sloped off to his kitchen behind the taproom. For once, Roberta's habit of rapid eating served her well. The taproom soon began to fill up with various townsmen and brookside cottagers who looked vaguely familiar from the meeting outside the pub last night.

There were no women and the men seemed even more curious about her by daylight. Some spoke to her, with a hesitation which surprised her by either their shyness or a not-too-friendly curiosity. They apologised stiffly when forced to intrude but no one shared her table, though it was the only one in the room.

She caught them looking furtively at her from the bar and then at each other. Was it necessary to be so sneaking in their exchange of glances? How could her little effort to help them, carefully censored and edited by them, cause this alienation? Or was it something else, her presence itself? If so, why make such an effort to invite her. Not for the first time she felt herself to be on trial, and far from welcome. She hurriedly finished her breakfast and was about to leave the taproom when she came face to face with one person who definitely did not like her. She didn't need any deep study to discover that.

She looked into Orin Camberson's frigid, almost colourless eyes, which stared back at her without blinking, and was chilled. However, she gave friendship a try.

"I do hope Mrs Camberson and your daughter are well. They were a great help to me last night."

"They are well, certainly."

His wife wasn't with him. Poor woman. Probably home eating leftovers in her kitchen.

One of the men drinking at the bar looked around and called, "Orin?"

She thought at first that he was asking Orin Camberson to join him and the others at the bar but the way almost everyone in the room turned to look at Camberson made her wonder.

Camberson ran a hand over his grey hair which was so thin she could clearly see the shape of his skull. It was not a pleasant sight. Roberta felt sure that when he did speak to her it was an effort against his belligerent nature.

"You started to ask me, Miss?"

"Just if there are records about the tenants' contributions to the village elsewhere. I thought I ought to read whatever else I can about Edenbrook, as well as the files in the parlour. I mean the lounge."

One of the men at the bar called out with startling promptness, "Nothing to hide here, Miss. Just good, hardworking village folk. That's what we've got to make them City lawyers see. The work we've put into the place."

"Ay," several agreed.

They all looked with one accord to see if Orin Camberson replied to Roberta's question.

"As to that," he said after he had apparently thought it over, "McQuarry, the chemist, keeps records. What with medicines and poisons for field pests and that. Of course, he's a newcomer. Only took over the shop some ten years gone by."

One of the men put in helpfully, "Tight-lipped, for all that he's Irish as any Paddy."

"Thanks. That should be a place to start, anyway."

As she left the room one of the drinkers muttered, "Awful tight-lipped for a Paddy, that McQ."

Another added what Roberta found to be the most curious thing she had heard from them.

"But suitable. Him with his damned poisons and his dealing out the powders like he thought we was all fiends for the dope and that. Well, we aint."

Roberta slowed her steps. Another of the villagers said, "She'll get nothing from him."

"Ay. That's so."

"A pity, if she wants to get famous," someone else put in.

This seemed to strike some of them as humorous. "Looks like there's no goin' up to London and on the films to play ourselves," mourned another.

Roberta went into the lounge across the hall but it was being vacuumed by a small, dark-haired girl in her teens who looked up as she came to the doorway. The girl glanced behind Roberta before giving her a mischievous wink.

"I was at the movies in Mincham last night with Gordon Brinkby, the gardener's boy. Don't tell old Toby, will you?"

Roberta laughed. This seemed to be the most human encounter she had come across since she arrived in Edenbrook. She waved at the girl and backed out.

Toby Teague was suddenly so close he made her jump. He muttered in her ear, "That's little Pamela Perth. Lives in one of the brookside cottages with her grandmother. We don't have the best help hereabouts, Miss, but she works cheap."

Roberta shrugged and went out into the square reflecting that this assignment was going to be harder than she expected. In her experience country people who lived cut off from the nearest metropolis were usually secretive, probably in self-defence, so how could she put together their side of the quarrel with the Demians?

Was there some other reason for her presence here? She couldn't imagine what it would be. Nick Demian must know. Perhaps it was one of the reasons he hadn't wanted her to come to Edenbrook.

She studied the square. Villagers crossing or coming up over a humped wooden bridge from the direction of the mill across the brook looked at her and then quickly away. She decided they were deliberately staying away from her.

This was a point to discuss with her landlord. Toby Teague would have to explain how she must write the tenants' side of the dispute when most of them avoided her.

She saw the chemist's house, two stories high, probably with his living quarters under the thatched roof. The ground floor was his shop, with dark casement windows and a weather-worn sign indicating his profession. She decided to take the advice of those not-so-friendly fellows in the taproom. McQuarry, the chemist, might know something about the tenants and their many worthwhile contributions to the village during a few scores of years.

She tried to smooth her wind-blown hair and hoped her sweater and close-fitting cream slacks wouldn't strike the village people as 'unsuitable'.

For a minute she thought the chemist's shop was locked, but a little pressure opened the door. Bars and squares of light illuminated the otherwise gloomy grey interior and she made out various British product names with a sprinkling of continental products. Those on view were all over-the-counter medicines.

She was amused to find no magazines, toilet articles or makeup such as she would find in the drug stores in the States. This place was strictly limited for business. She was still fingering the medical salves and some bottles of what appeared to be horse liniment and/or castor oil, when a voice out of the indistinct shadows made her drop a small round tin of salve.

Nervously she cleared her throat and called, "It's me. A customer, Mr McQuarry."

A flash of light appeared under a door behind the far end of the counter. Probably the chemist had been in the rear of his shop or just come in from the outside.

She called again. "I'm new here, Mr McQuarry. May I speak to you?"

The inner door opened and Nicholas Demian came in from somewhere in the back of the shop. She looked around hurriedly. If his presence here was secret from the villagers, he was safe. She had been alone in the shop.

His reaction at the sight of her was all she could wish for. He strode over the narrow strip of linoleum and reached across the counter to take her hand. She hadn't forgotten his strong fingers and winced, but smiled so he wouldn't get the idea that his touch wasn't welcome. Those days were over, she hoped.

"Now, this brightens the day," he told her looking as warm and welcoming as she had seen him. "How was your first night? No ghostly visitations in the old pub?"

She pretended to shiver. "Should there have been?"

"Certainly. Teague's place has been up there opposite the square — which used to be the Old Market Place — since the sixteenth century." He came around the counter and looked her over, apparently pleased by what he saw, though he criticised her. "You look so infernally young. I can see them now, asking me in Mincham if I have robbed the cradle, so to speak."

"In that case, I'll change at once into something more suitable to my august middle age."

He raised both hands in surrender, palms up. "Spare me. Look just the way you are this minute.

The devil with what people say. I'll tell them all that you are Jamie's sweetheart."

That made her laugh. So they were going to Mincham together. She had no objections in the least.

He led her around the end of the counter, stopping momentarily to lock and bolt the brookside door from the inside. Obviously, he hadn't wanted to be seen by villagers. It was much lighter in the back room where she noted a refrigerator with a heavy lock and an intricate bar securely fastening it to the wall behind.

On one of two kitchen tables were piled what must have been at least a dozen wooden cigar boxes and several cardboard sweet and chocolate boxes held together by rubber bands.

The other table held pieces of silverware and steelware covered by acrylic cases. They were probably adapted to surgical instruments. Aside from his own profession McQuarry must also dabble in minor surgery when time was pressing and injuries required treatment in seconds. She had half expected to see the chemist back in this chemical kitchen and Nick Demian guessed her curiosity.

She glanced at the cigar and sweet boxes but said nothing. They were not her business and she was trying to keep him in his pleasant, friendly mood.

"Drugs and the rest are fairly secure."

She was more interested in what Nick Demian was doing here, and with entry to the shop. She couldn't help saying, "I hope others haven't got access to this place."

He frowned but didn't seem as angry as a man of his temperament might be.

"None that I am aware of at present." He added sharply, "And I am aware of most things that go on here. I've come to know old Mac since the accident to my wife and our boy."

She said awkwardly, "Your sister mentioned it. It was a dreadful tragedy."

"Yes. All of that."

There was an awkward little silence. He changed the subject. "McQuarry is off to Mincham with my boy. At Demian House Jamie left a note which brought me here. I came by the fields, as Jamie often does. And out there on the counter I found another note saying Jamie had persuaded Mac to drive him to Mincham."

"Then you do trust the chemist."

"Yes. I've had some years to satisfy myself on that point. All the same, I take very little at face value these days. That's why we are going into Mincham as well. To bring back Jamie. You see, there are others who may be in Mincham. I've got to persuade Jamie to return to Switzerland, a place I am sure of."

He opened the back door onto rolling, un-ploughed fields where a small flock of sheep wandered around in autumn debris that carpeted the ground.

Belatedly, he said, "It isn't far to Mincham. Twenty minutes or so. I hope you will make the trip with me. I need company; I'm not in my happiest mood."

She wanted to accept but felt bound to ask, "What if someone sees us?"

"If one of my noble tenants sees us together, we will put on a performance of my bad manners and your righteous anger."

Roberta laughed. "I'll work myself up. To tell the truth, my own work hasn't begun yet. They are busy cleaning the lounge. Mr Teague says most of the tenants' history is collected there, and a little of it with Mr McQuarry." The pleasant autumn scene with the sheep spread out before her was entrancing. She added, "No wonder they call this place 'Eden'."

"*We* call it 'Eden'," he reminded her. "The tenants have nothing to do with it."

She did not disagree but she was growing more and more aware that the divisions between Demian and the people of Edenbrook were deepening, not being repaired. Just how serious were they? This double hatred was close to a blood feud.

She hoped not. There were things about Edenbrook that fascinated her just as there were qualities about Nick Demian that made her anxious to hold his friendship, if that was possible.

Beyond a clump of trees still shedding maroon leaves, by which she assumed they might be a form of maple like those back in the United States, she saw a little black English car. Nick Demian looked around but nothing human was in sight and he opened the passenger door for her.

"Not quite a Rolls or a Bentley," he apologised, "and it kicks up at the most awkward moments, but suitable for our purposes of — shall we call it 'disguise'?"

She got in, feeling warmed by his unexpected smile. She promised jauntily, "I'll try to live down the shame if you will."

That made him laugh as he started the car whose engine was true to Nick's prediction and took a little coaxing to start. At last they heard its welcome purr and started across the bumpy road, hardly wide enough for two.

He avoided the flock of sheep which threatened to panic and scatter, and the woolly sheepdog which watched the car's progress with baleful eyes, until the car bumped out onto a country lane fairly well bordered by more trees, thinning but not yet denuded by the autumn showers.

In a few minutes Nick turned into a more prominent westerly road which he called Mincham Lane. This was bordered on the southside by the steep bank of a stream. Roberta was surprised and somewhat repulsed to note that the bottom was covered by the accumulation of the year's leaves, branches and debris of every sort, including a few bed-springs, dilapidated rocking chair and the back seat of a motor car.

"Your local junk pile?" she asked.

He didn't like what he saw any more than she did. "All this area beside the lane belongs to

Mincham and as you can see, nothing is done about it. God knows I've tried — those meddlesome Demians, you know. But since my trouble with my tenants, they've gone over to the enemy as well."

"But that's ridiculous. Their own property may be involved."

"Demian property," he corrected her harshly.

What on earth made him so bitter?

He changed the subject rather obviously, indicating on the horizon what appeared to be miniature towers — church, high-rise moderns, and occasional treetops that he said were the sentinels of Edenbrook's nearest city, or the illusion of one.

She looked at him. "I'm a firm believer in illusions myself — aren't you?"

He was silent. Then he looked down at her hand. She thought he would cover it with his own, but he didn't. Too bad. He did puzzle her with the remark, "Perhaps. But as I grow older I find the real thing much more satisfactory."

Whatever that meant.

She was relieved when they drove up toward a stone bridge leading into the bustling little town, although it was clear this area required all his attention. Cars and lorries came from several directions, trying to pass each other and manoeuvre their way onto the bridge at the same time from three directions.

Obviously, the town was the hub of activity in this secluded area of England, so little known it seemed to be cut off, not only from London but even from present-day Britain itself.

She asked him curiously, "Don't you live in London? I mean, for your work and all."

"I commute. That's very American of me."

She laughed but the way he had said it struck her as more sarcastic than merely a confession of preference.

"Then why — ?" She couldn't go on. She would certainly provoke an argument.

But he was aware of what she had been about to say. "Then why do I care so much about Edenbrook?"

"Well — yes."

"It isn't Edenbrook, you know. It is the methods being taken by my enemies to remove me and mine."

This sounded very like a paranoid fear of his tenants and God knew who else besides. His 'enemies?' She didn't pursue the matter but felt that she couldn't give up her work for the tenants of Edenbrook quite so soon.

He broke into her painful thoughts. "I'm sorry I forgot it was market day. That explains all this mob bringing their produce into town. But to change the subject, have you any objection to churchyards? Cemeteries, that is?"

"Of course not. Is that where we are going?"

"I hope to meet old Mac and Jamie there. At the grave of Jamie's mother."

All she could say was "Oh." Would Jamie welcome a comparative stranger to somewhere as

151

private as his mother's grave?

She was more nervous than she had any right to be, and noticed little of Mincham aside from wondering how this country town, with its circular park surrounded by imitation Regency shops and parking places for touring coaches, had spawned the unexpectedly busy citizens everywhere.

This ought to be a safe subject.

"There seems to be more activity here at this market town than outside my landlady's bed and breakfast in London."

"It's an interesting little place in its way," he agreed. He was looking ahead, toward a churchyard which seemed to be at the rear of a small country church covered by dying ivy vines.

She began to worry over Nick Demian's expression. Then she, too, heard the ominous 'clank-clank' of what she supposed was the car engine.

"Is something wrong?"

The car answered her question by coming to a tired, coughing halt beside the cemetery fence.

Nick looked over at the vicarage beyond the heavily occupied little church cemetery.

"I'll borrow the curate's telephone and call the garage. Old Mac may find himself with two extra passengers going home today."

They were beside a little wooden gate that needed painting. All the green colour had apparently peeled off some time ago, thanks to the weathering. Nick opened his car door.

"I'll only be a minute. Do you mind?"

"No. Of course not."

He was true to his word. While she remained in the car, physically comfortable but a little nervous, he opened the gate, crossed the cemetery and disappeared along a narrow brick walkway to the front of the vicarage. Meanwhile, she studied the cemetery, wondering which grave was that of his dead wife.

She was just beginning to feel sorry for those lonely dead when Nick came back across the churchyard to the car.

"The housekeeper will take care of everything. She knows Jamie very well. He comes here every month when he is home. Would you like to see the family plot?"

"Yes. May I?"

He opened the door for her and then went around to the back of the car. Seconds later he had retrieved something from the boot and then came alongside her to take her arm. His free hand was closed around the crowded stems of several dozen violets. She hadn't seen genuine wood violets in years but she knew the Parma violets in their centre, whose enchanting scent overpowered the beauty of the wood violets and she remarked on the fact.

He looked down at the flowers. "They have always been Jamie's choice for his mother. Actually, Veda preferred those small orchids that grow wild in the Hawaiian islands, but I prefer Jamie's choice."

She didn't discuss the matter. She had expected him to look depressed and sad, but it seemed to her that his features hardened. He was certainly a puzzling man.

The churchyard was crowded with tombstones dating back through the last two centuries. Many slabs had fallen over the sunken graves. Some were propped up by small rocks from local watering places, possibly even the Edenbrook stream which wandered into the sinister little weir that she and Nick Demian had passed about a couple of miles east of the town's stone bridge.

Roberta had no difficulty finding the Demian section of the churchyard near the little brick-lined cloister and sheltered by a tree now shedding its golden autumn leaves. On the well-kept grave, dated ten years back, was carved 'VEDA YARROW DEMIAN, REMEMBERED BY ALL WHO LOVED HER'.

It struck Roberta as an odd inscription but she didn't know why. Without seeming to, she watched her companion.

He touched the stone cup used to hold flowers in front of the tombstone and smiled. "Full of water. Rainwater from two days ago, I suppose." As he arranged the little violets he looked around, frowning. "They haven't arrived yet. Must be Jamie's doing. When he's been abroad for any time he misses all the little details of the towns near home."

The street was empty for some distance until Roberta could see the edges of the Regency Circle with a number of stalls set up, each of them parked around the grassy circle. By this hour the market had already come to life, but no cars were headed towards the silent churchyard.

Nick said, "I'm sorry about the wait. I imagine Jamie wasn't the only one delaying things. Mac had to stop by one of the chemist's here in Mincham. Besides filling prescriptions he delivers a great many prescriptions for the villagers at Edenbrook. He is invaluable to the community, though I doubt if they appreciate it. He's not the type who gushes over people."

"I only wish we had some like him where I live."

He smiled. It was a winning and unusual smile. Not commonplace, she thought.

He took her arm again. He didn't look back at the grave but said warmly, "You really do like Jamie, don't you?"

"Very much. I hardly know him, but I think he's done wonders and he doesn't seem to resent his injury."

"Very true. God knows he's had his problems, but he's handled them superbly, in my view."

"And in mine. It was an accident, wasn't it? He wasn't born with that terrible injury?"

"Oh, no. Horrible business all around, but he has survived it magnificently. No grudges. Matter of fact, Jamie's friend, McQuarry, was involved indirectly. Some time after McQuarry took over the chemist's shop about eleven years ago."

"Surely, it wasn't this McQuarry's fault? Jamie

wouldn't be so fond of him. Would he?"

He agreed. "It was actually a horse that was responsible. Old Mac's beloved bay mare, Sultana. She was a beautiful creature. Gentle. Children loved her. There was no harm in her. I sometimes think she was the only thing McQuarry loved in this world."

"Then it really was an accident. And the mare did this to Jamie? How ghastly!"

"Yes. Especially because Sultana was a friend to all the village. And certainly to Jamie. The mare got hold of some poisonous grass or plant. God knows what or where. But she went mad."

"Loco? There is something called locoweed." Roberta caught her breath. "We have it in the western States."

"Whatever it was, the morning Sultana was poisoned, she got out of the field at the back of Mac's shop and rampaged along Mincham Lane where we drove today. She met Veda, my wife, who was jogging. Jamie had run after Veda. He was not quite five. For some reason Veda had refused to let Jamie come along with her that day. When she refused, he tagged along behind her." He frowned into the mottled sky, still blue, but with signs of approaching rain clouds.

"I often took Jamie up to London with me. I was thinking of buying a flat in the City where Veda might find more interests, as she had had early in our marriage. But about this time I realised it wasn't lack of interests, but me who bored her. We were just drifting along. Poor

Veda. At seventeen she thought she was marrying one of her idle rich dream men. But after six years she found her dream hero wasn't me. Not quite like the poor girl's boasts, as I was discovering. Then — there was the accident."

"The morning the mare was poisoned she attacked your wife and Jamie?"

He hesitated. "When Veda saw Sultana in the road galloping towards her my wife screamed, turned and ran. Jamie got between his mother and Sultana. He knew the mare so well he was undoubtedly not afraid of her."

"Good God!" Roberta's horrified voice was barely more than a whisper.

He cleared his throat. "Well, Jamie was kicked down into that trench near Mincham Weir and the mare took after my wife. She was still running away. Then she slipped and fell. Right under Sultana's flailing hooves."

Roberta was sickened but she had dealt with horses on various movie locations and moistened her dry lips. "What happened to Sultana afterwards?"

Trying to strain out all emotion, he said finally, "There was no hope for Sultana, of course, even if she recovered. She had to be destroyed."

"By — ?"

"Oh, yes. By McQuarry."

She blinked, feeling shock and compassion at these tragedies to Jamie and his mother, though the woman hadn't behaved in a very heroic fashion. But Roberta found herself also deeply sorry for McQuarry and Sultana.

Demian said suddenly, "They're coming now. That's Mac's car."

She felt Nick's arm around her shoulders and she warmed to his touch, wondering if the demonstrative gesture had been subconscious or deliberate.

He warned her, "Don't mention Veda's death to Jamie. There are moments when he still believes it was his fault because he disobeyed his mother and ran after her. She had told him to stay home, of course. Twenty-three operations haven't convinced him that he has paid too great a price for his imaginary guilt. There seems to be no convincing him otherwise."

"But that's terrible."

"Yes. Terrible." In a voice almost expressionless he explained. Only his dark eyes were bright.

"That's one more reason why Mac and I still want to know how Sultana found that poisonous stuff. Whatever it was."

Chapter Eleven

Roberta was still haunted by Nick Demian's story when the black saloon pulled up behind Nick's car and she saw Jamie Demian leaning out of the open window, waving to his father and to Roberta.

He yelled to them as Nick stepped into the street to explain about the broken-down vehicle. Nick took his son's hand, squeezed it, and turned to McQuarry, the driver of the saloon who listened, but with his hooded gaze fixed on Roberta.

His austere face was lean and forbidding, the high-bridged nose and thin lips no friendlier than the heavy-lidded eyes.

He certainly showed her no recognition or even politeness, but she hadn't expected any, and when Nick introduced McQuarry to her, she said "How do you do" and let it go at that.

He said nothing whatever to her but she respected his apparent dislike (or distrust) of humanity, and remained cool but not discourteous.

Jamie climbed out of the car, with a bouquet of slightly crushed violets. He limped through the gate his father held open for him and then moved quite efficiently among the graves to that of his mother. He remained there a couple of minutes after squeezing the flowers into the vase beside his father's, then limped back and climbed into the rear seat of the car. This required careful manoeuvring to get his braced leg in but he made it and leaned over to talk to Roberta as his father helped her into the back seat of the saloon, beside him.

Roberta noted that he did not help his son. She suspected Jamie preferred it that way.

"What a crowd in town today! Not like Zurich. I saw the market stalls here. We bought some vegetables to bring home to Mrs Schramm, if we can get through that crowd of lorries and cars at the bridge."

"One good thing," McQuarry remarked without addressing anyone in particular. "We'll be off to Mincham Lane against the traffic."

"I usually sit in the front," Jamie piped up, as the pharmacist slid into the boy's usual seat next to the driver. "But I wanted to sit by Roberta so we could talk about screenplays."

Jamie gave McQuarry a grimace but agreed.

A stout, authoritative woman in an enveloping apron came out of the cemetery gate and called to them, "Garage is here. I'll see to it, Mr Nick."

He called out his thanks and started the car, driving it smoothly away from the churchyard.

Nick pointed out several buildings to Roberta, including a theatre and a wool factory that had been adapted to the making of television commercials about the re-emergence of wool products.

The area grew busier. Even the little side street

along the churchyard had picked up traffic. A lorry-load of produce seemed to be trying to crowd its way past a midnight blue Italian car, although both would have to wait for the main street traffic which had priority at the bridge.

Nick had stopped talking and leaned forward in concentration, carefully making his way toward the outer of two traffic lanes on the bridge. The other one was incoming at this hour. At that minute an oncoming car in the middle lane ploughed into the passenger side of McQuarry's saloon.

Nick was thrown against McQuarry's seat. Though heavily shaken, he twisted to Roberta who had been flung against the back of the driver's seat but she and Jamie were luckily unhurt. Nick then turned his attention to McQuarry.

Everything had stopped. Some woman's scream had made Roberta shiver. An elderly woman was in the car that had hit the front passenger side of McQuarry's vehicle and Roberta could hear her protesting as the lorry driver helped her from her car.

"I don't know how it happened. My car just lurched forward. No. No. I'm perfectly well. Just jarred a bit. But that poor man!"

The 'poor man' was McQuarry who had been in the passenger seat that had received the impact of the crash. He groaned and his lean frame was curved inward in a painful-looking twist with his right arm locked against his chest.

"My shoulder," he muttered as Nick and Jamie leaned over him. "Nothing. No fuss. Just the shoulder thrown out."

Some of the onlookers, mostly men in stalled vehicles, were milling around, examining the damage done to both cars. The old lady's — a heavy machine probably fifteen or more years old — had stood up well; only a little battered and scratched. It had clearly saved the woman by its tough strength.

McQuarry's car too was strong and except for the door which was badly crushed it received the dubious praise from the crowd: "Could have been worse."

The glass was shattered in the door but when Roberta and Nick gently brushed off the injured man, they were relieved that none of the crushed glass had cut him.

Roberta was surprised at how quickly Nick Demian alerted a policeman and ambulance men, the latter carrying McQuarry off to the local hospital.

The cause of all this commotion, the elderly Mrs Constance Seddley, was unnerved and had to be helped into her own car, but otherwise, she was very much herself.

"My address and insurance details — I've written them here. I still don't know how my car pushed into the gentleman's one like that. Naturally, the damages are my responsibility and whatever expenses the gentleman incurs."

Nick told the lady, "I would like to see you

soon, if I may." The lady's faded blue eyes looked apprehensive and he assured her, "Not about financial matters. Something else. Something you may have noticed."

Troubled again, she looked around as if for help. "Noticed? Well, the car leaped — I really don't know what else to say."

"But you won't mind my calling, for a brief time? You might have someone else present. So you will feel secure."

She smiled. "Oh, no. I've lived in Mincham since time out of mind. Very nearly. I know you by sight and reputation, Mr Demian."

They shook hands and she was helped into the car by the policeman, who also had questions for the poor lady.

A few minutes later a rented car came along from the garage where they were repairing Nick's own vehicle. Nick said, as he gave Roberta a hand into the passenger seat, "We are going to the hospital to see how old Mac is doing. You don't mind, do you?"

"No. Of course not. I certainly hope it was no more than a wrenched shoulder. It must be very painful."

Jamie explained, "That's where I stayed when I was young and the accident happened. I know all the nursing sisters. They're very nice. I want them to be specially nice to poor Mac."

Nick assured him, "They will be. We can count on that."

Jamie had decided to sit in the back seat again.

Nick helped him in though Jamie insisted that he needed none, so Nick turned his attentions to Roberta, his hand lingering on hers through the open passenger door which was grasping the handle, ready to shut it.

Then he got in and started off. Both Jamie and Roberta were shaken, mostly from nerves, and Nick made his way a little easier this time, as traffic reverted to its normal pattern. He followed what appeared to be a main road, driving north past a bookshop, a bakery with a 'Genuine French' sign in the window above one that promised 'Cornish pasties' and which Jamie pointed out as his favourite shop. A supermarket of modest but inviting proportions followed. A few streets beyond was bed and breakfast accommodation beside the four-storey hospital.

The hospital was forbidding, even to the long, barred windows, but when Nick and his son ushered Roberta through the freshly painted main corridor she changed her mind, impressed by tall Sister Longacre's welcoming smile, and by several ambulatory patients being assisted by other nurses.

Jamie led his father and Roberta into a waiting room where worn couches, chairs and a table stacked with papers and magazines created a cheerful atmosphere in spite of the overcast skies that looked as if they could push in the windows.

Probably because the day was still early, only one person, McQuarry, with his arm in a sling, was in the room. Jamie made his way to the pharmacist, limping but happy.

"You're looking better. We were worried, weren't we, Father? Roberta?"

"We were that, old friend," Nick said and took McQuarry's free hand. "How are they treating you? Say two words and Jamie will march out and raise the roof, as he says."

The vaguest of smiles appeared around McQuarry's mouth. "He is a good lad, that. But I have my friends here, too, you know. I'm just waiting for the result of the X-ray on my shoulder."

Demian nodded in acknowledgement, then said, "You know why Miss Fisher is in Edenbrook? Art asked her to do what she could for my tenants. I have been placing various obstacles in her way, but we understand each other." He looked over at Roberta and she nodded.

"Indeed. No matter how long Mr Demian and Sir Arthur have been friends, I am inclined to think Sir Arthur Laidlaw is a bit naive about his beloved put-upon villagers."

McQuarry surprised her by looking at her thoughtfully and saying, "There are villagers who mean well. Take care, Miss. Discover which of them fall into which category."

Nick laughed but said ruefully, looking at Roberta, "I seem to have an enemy in camp, close to home."

"Not an enemy," she reminded him, "But I'm cautious."

She had said it because it leaped to her mind,

but she was rewarded by the serious old pharmacist's nod of agreement.

Worried by this contradiction of his beloved father, Jamie began, "Oh, I say, I don't think Roberta meant —" But his friend McQuarry cut him off in his quiet way.

"Mr Nick, you young Jamie and Miss — the young lady — were not hurt today because they were on the opposite side of the car."

"That's right," Jamie began, only to be cut off again.

"Very true," Nick agreed, watching the injured man, who remained thoughtful.

Jamie put in quickly, "But it was a good thing for me. I'd never have got this rotten brace out of that twisted door, with the glass and all. I'd have been stuck there and —" He stopped. He looked paler than Roberta had seen him in the past, and she had a deep fear that he guessed the men were talking of something very serious to him.

McQuarry went on, "I think we may dismiss it publicly as an accident, as indeed, it probably was. But we may be thankful that Jamie was in the back seat today and on the opposite side of the car. Yes, Miss. An accident. You do understand?"

He must think she was worse than stupid, and deaf as well. But it was in the interests of Jamie Demian, so she did not let herself show any sign of resentment.

"I do understand. If my word is worth anything, I give it to you and I might say — especially — to Jamie."

"Well." McQuarry sat back, winced and eased himself further into his chair. "Sister Longacre will be back shortly to take me up to a private room while they sort me out."

Jamie was still pale, but he picked at Roberta's sleeve as a hint and said, "We'd best be on our way now then."

"Not quite so fast. One more moment. Mr Nick!" McQuarry called.

Roberta and Jamie had already turned away but Demian waited, speaking to McQuarry. "Of course. I am going to talk to the woman who ran us down. I'll drop by later in the day to let you know just how the matter lies."

"Thank you. That takes care of one matter. And one more which I'd forgotten, not expecting to be detained in this abominable place for God knows how long. Miss Fisher — is it?" He was in obvious discomfort but he seemed determined on an extra word or two with Roberta.

"There are a few bills of sale, bills of work, notes, not many, but they might be of aid to the villagers. You will find them of some trifling use for the defence of their aims." He saw her surprise and went on, "Mr Nick trusts you. All well and good, Miss, but you must forgive me if I refer only to the daily public records I have kept for the last dozen years. Brinkby, the gardener, works for me now and again. Deliveries and whatnot. He knows where I've kept the ledgers.

Nothing private, as I say."

Roberta barely glanced Nick's way but saw his nod. She said, "If necessary, Mr McQuarry. If there really is evidence of the villagers' payments on work, it would add to their plea. Obviously."

Why not ask Nick Demian to turn it over to them? No. Perhaps that would spoil Nick's supposed hatred of his villagers. These men must have their games. In some ways, they were as childish as the villagers.

Sister Longacre and a young nurse came back into the room to take McQuarry upstairs. She warned him, "No excitement now, or it's more pills for you." She looked around. "It's only fair. Mr McQuarry is our pill man in all emergencies."

Everyone laughed except McQuarry.

Nick assured him, "I'll give you the report on the woman after my visit late today if they let me see her."

"Just so. I expect we both have thoughts on the matter."

Sister Longacre gave a great sigh at the wasted time of her patient and Nick spoke quickly. "We are wearing out our welcome Mac, see you soon. We'll be off now."

McQuarry had no objection. Everyone said goodbye, Jamie touching Mac's good hand in an unspoken moment of affection, and the visitors left McQuarry to be wheeled out of the room by the young nurse.

In Sister Longacre's office with its one small window too high for anyone to see in or out, the

168

senior nurse presented Nick with a number of legal-looking papers and indicated where his signature must go.

To Roberta Jamie explained proudly, but in a low voice, "Father pays for many things our people need, in a private capacity. Whatever the government doesn't pay for via the National Health Service. Aunt Sheila says it was done in the family, even before the NHS."

Roberta was surprised but pleased and a little resentful that none of the villagers, or even Sir Arthur Laidlaw, had told her of this. She wondered what other kindness and benefactions had been kept from her.

Sister Longacre surprised her again when she told Nick, "You may be sure we will see to our good friend, and yours, Mr Demian. Won't be anyone near him without one of us, while he's here."

"Thank you. I'll count on you."

"Indeed, you may."

The nurse shook hands with him, then with Roberta and made a nice little ceremony of her handshake with Jamie, telling him, "You handled that accident very capably, Master Jamie."

When they left the hospital Jamie was elated by his treatment. Clearly, he had spent time here in his boyhood and was, in more than one way, the nurses' 'fair-haired boy'.

Was there anything odd or mysterious about the chemist's injury?

When the little car was bumping its way along

Mincham Lane toward the village square of Edenbrook Jamie remarked more to himself than to his present company, "Poor Mac. It was my fault he got hurt."

Nick was frowning into the watery morning sunlight and asked casually, "How do you make that out?"

"Well, I was in the back — suppose I had been in the front passenger seat as usual? With this cast, I'd have been jammed in so hard I might have been completely squashed with this idiotic steel brace."

Roberta was chilled but she left it to Nick to express what both of them were feeling over Jamie's remark. He didn't speak for a minute. Roberta saw that his jaw muscles were set.

Then he said calmly, "It's just as well you weren't hit. You'd have been a remarkable sight with your leg and shoulder both battered up."

Jamie giggled. "I would, wouldn't I?"

Nick looked over the boy's head at Roberta. She closed her eyes momentarily but said nothing.

When she opened her eyes again they were passing the deep gully on the south side of the road and the weir with its tangled debris beyond. She wondered if Jamie thought about that other accident long ago, and about the place somewhere in the road ahead where his mother had died.

From the tight look on his father's face, she was sure Nick thought of it.

Chapter Twelve

They would soon be passing Edenbrook square and Roberta suggested, "Considering that I'm supposed to be working for your tenants and against you, I shouldn't be seen travelling around with you. Shall I get out now?"

He surprised and pleased her by his quick objection. "I wish you wouldn't. Jamie and I will miss you; won't we, old lad?"

Jamie, who had squirmed about painfully while she spoke, insisted, "You just can't, Miss. You were going to show me how the telly or the films put stories together. Besides, it'll be time for lunch soon and old Schrammy makes great omelettes."

His father's stern features relaxed and he grinned but reminded Jamie, "You're not being very respectful of our good Mrs Schramm, Jamie."

"Well, she's ever so nice. She talks more than that Frenchy housekeeper. She kept asking things about the village people."

His father dismissed this without interest.

"You'll have to learn to distinguish between conversation and plain gossip. Your Aunt Sheila said she was quite competent. That's all we need to know."

To Roberta's surprise Jamie persisted.

"But Aunt Sheila didn't like her much either. I heard her and Mrs Camberson the day you and I went off to that silly academy in Switzerland. Aunt Sheila said Mrs DeVrees wrote letters all the time. And Mrs Camberson said, 'Maybe to a lover'."

"Jamie, for God's sake!" Nick Demian looked over at Roberta. "He doesn't behave like this normally. I don't know why he is acting like a damned village gossip today."

Jamie did not seem abashed as Roberta had expected and she was embarrassed, not to say astonished, by his reply to his father's scolding.

"Oh, it doesn't matter about Miss Fisher. I like her. And you do too. I can tell."

Nick stared at him, speechless, and then at Roberta who recovered quickly enough to burst out laughing. Luckily, he laughed too. It was a good way to relax an awkward moment.

She said breezily, "On that note, gentlemen, I think I had better get out while the going's good."

Both Demians looked at each other and then at her. She was touched when Jamie asked plaintively, "When will we see you again?"

Nick said, "Add my name to that. What about making up a quarrel of some kind? We stalk to Teague's pub to see you home or something of the sort, and begin to quarrel. About anything. Our little difficulties in London, for example. We can always keep on quarrelling as we walk, clear to our doorway. One of the gardener's family, old Samson Brinkby, or the boy, Gordon, will be sure to report it in the right quarters. Wherever that may be."

Jamie was delighted to be in on this game. "Make it near dinner and we can pretend I invited you even though Father said no."

"That's the lad. Make me the villain. My son is a born writer."

"Of fiction?" she asked, trying not to be arch about it.

"Strictly non-fiction."

Even if she had wanted to, she could not have resisted the smile that illuminated his dark eyes.

"Done." She studied the scene around them. So far as she could tell, nobody from the village was in sight, but cars kept passing them, going to and from Mincham. Any one of these might carry some 'tenants' from Edenbrook.

"Shall I seem to boot you out of the car?" Nick wanted to know as he slowed until the motor was idling.

Jamie clapped his hands. "And Miss Fisher shakes her fist at us."

In excellent spirits, they all played their parts until she had haughtily crossed the flat stone bridge over the brook from Mincham Lane to the square. Afterward, she watched the little car chug away toward Edenbrook, past the rear walls of Camberson's souvenirs and tobacconist shop that provided part of the northerly border of the little square.

Preparing herself for her performance as an insulted partisan of the Demian tenants, Roberta made her way towards the pub with her habitually long strides. Approaching the square, she turned her ankle on a pebble and used this to good advantage, seeing a powerful, red-haired man, probably in his early forties, turn the corner beside Camberson's store and march along towards her, swinging a large and lethal pair of gardening shears over one shoulder.

She rubbed her ankle, grimacing, and pretended to see him just as he was about to pass her. His red hair was unkempt in the morning breeze and he smoothed it down with his free hand. He obviously made an effort to be polite to her, though she felt that his grin was a trifle overdone, almost too wide, anxious to please. Or maybe it was her own guilt, the attempt she knew she was making to befriend both sides of the local feud.

She called out "Hello. Are you from the village?"

He seemed relieved at her friendly greeting. "That I am, Miss. Born Bovril Brinkby, Miss. I tend the local gardens and whatnot."

Hoping to break the ice, she asked with amusement, "Bovril?" She was relieved that he didn't seem to be annoyed.

"Well now, Miss, you have me there. My Mam was that fond of those old lights in Piccadilly Circus and Bovril — well, she drank that a lot. But I was pinned up to the name of Bovril. I soon put that in the rubbish and become 'Will' Brinkby. Don't much fancy it, but it's better than — But here now . . . you've gone and given your ankle a twist. Take my arm. I'll get you back to Toby's pub and have old McQuarry look you over."

She accepted his offer with thanks and he looked pleased. With his help she limped to the little village square which was perched above the brook and looking across at its rival for attention, the Old Mill.

Her condition was noted with curiosity by several villagers: one man entering Camberson's tobacconist shop, two women on their way to a tiny haberdashery shop next to Camberson's, and one boy with a skinned knee, heading down to McQuarry's closed and shuttered chemist's shop below the square, on the west side of the brook.

Brinkby seemed very satisfied with himself. "Expect you wouldn't be remembering me. I chatted you up, along of Orin Camberson, over that fine Sir Arthur Laidlaw's call, other day. No doubt, you wouldn't recall, you being so busy-like."

She remembered the phone call and especially the difference in the two men. She had much preferred the gardener, Brinkby, and having met the nasty, dry little Camberson, saw no reason to change her mind. She told him so, gently polishing off her opinion of Camberson whose wife was so browbeaten.

Brinkby shrugged off Camberson's ill nature

and she noted that Nick Demian's tenants took care not to run each other down. Probably, they had all agreed to band together against 'the common enemy'. She didn't know why this should annoy her. The villagers no doubt had good reason to hate — or at least fear — the Demians; the way Nick paid so many bills for 'his' people certainly smacked of paternalism.

But Nick Demian must know that. He was an intelligent man. Why was his feud against the villagers so prolonged and bitter? She felt that some of the pieces of the real story were missing.

Roberta came back to the present when her companion stopped speaking and she realised he expected an answer to something he had said. He was looking at her expectantly, his pleasant, broad face bright with anticipation.

He repeated, "See? It's true, Miss. Your ankle's good as new. Pain all gone?"

While she frowned at her own absent-mindedness, he called to her landlord, the pub owner, to prove him right.

Toby Teague had dragged a big, wooden captain's chair out of the bar and propped it up against the pub wall where he sat, leaning back in comfort. He had been polluting the square with pipe smoke but took the pipe out of his mouth to wave at Roberta and Brinkby.

"Like you say, Will. That pretty foot looks good enough to me."

She reddened and was relieved when he changed the subject rapidly. "Getting your facts from our prince of gardeners, Miss? Will here, on off-days, he works for old Mac at the chemist's shop down yonder, and Will can give you old Mac's ledgers as he calls them. He promised them to us, you know. Personal remarks mighty helpful about the work of the villagers on Edenbrook. It's most of his records about medicine and treatment and that. General stuff, not confidential. Goes back to part of 1986. Not all. But most."

Will Brinkby gave her a big grin, puffed a bit at his own new importance. "That'll be my job, I'm thinking, Miss. He pointed 'em out to me last night, 'fore I left for the cottage."

Toby Teague waved his pipe.

"Hold you now. He don't include 1985, nor the first of '86, like I say. I just heard he's in hospital in Mincham. Nothing serious. Just a bit of a shoulder bone not where it ought to be, but won't you be wanting the early years too?"

So they knew about McQuarry's accident already. And they were certainly hinting about other material, which she saw now, was not to be given to them. Undoubtedly, the 1985 and early '86 years were the ones he had forbidden her to take.

Before she could ask more about their version of McQuarry's accident, discovering what they knew, and how they knew it, Toby added, "So long as we give you only what he has laid out on the kitchen table . . . That's it, am I right, Will? In his lab, as he calls it, there's use you can make of them for the village."

"That's as how I heard it. He don't like any touching of his bottles and work things. Pills. Tablets. That sort."

"Or poisons?" Roberta asked, to see how strongly feelings were running between these men and the Demians, or whether they saw McQuarry as actually being on their side.

The two men laughed at her obvious joke. Toby Teague waved away the absurd idea of poison with his pipe.

"Nothing like. Anyway, Will just works at ridding the place of oddments after there's an accident. Things like that. Yesterday, it was Samson. He's Will's father."

Will put in, "Dropped my clippers on his leg, he did. Not too bright in the upper-works nowadays, is my father. Means no harm though. Poor old bastard."

A little jarred by this remark, Roberta still wanted to get to the root of the record dates she might use. She wished these fellows weren't such gossips.

"I've seen your father around. He seems most cordial."

"And then there's last week, wouldn't you say?" Toby went on, ignoring her comment. "Some tourist buys one of them sharp knives for opening mail. Spanish, sword-like. Stuck herself, she did."

Will added, "Being off the tour bus — well, you'll never hear the likes of that creature's snivelling. McQuarry wrapped her up. Her hand, it looked like one of them mummies when she got into the bus. Showed it to one and all. It was hardly but a scratch."

Toby shook his head. "That'll be about Mr Nick. The tourist lady liked his looks. Orin Camberson and some other locals was in the bar. The lady said she'd made as if she'd fall, out there in the square. Seemed like she'd had a bet with this other female that she'd get old Nick's eye. So she was about to fall and Mr Nick picked her up like anybody would."

"But not caring, one way or other." Will nodded wisely. "You know him. Hating the females like he does."

"Well, now —" Toby glanced at Roberta, saw that she had been caught by this and grinned, waving his free hand to banish Will's remark. "You made it worse. Anyhow, Camberson and the others said the lady was showing her friends the letter opener she bought from Orin, while she talked about Nick. Quite gone for him, she was. She made as if to show how she'd fallen and he picked her up. She pointed the letter opener right at my old carpet in the bar room. The opener twisted in her hand and give her a little scratch, like you said."

Roberta was not too thrilled by this subject and was relieved when she and the two men were distracted by giggles behind them as several of the young people crossed the square and headed for the brookside where, still chattering, they settled in a circle around Jamie Demian and a lanky boy about his age.

Will Brinkby called out impatiently to the lanky boy in the circle, "Gordon, take care now. No rough play." He turned to Roberta. "My boy Gordon. Such as he is. Him and the lad Jamie, they hand-wrestle a bit now and again."

It was surprising to Roberta that Jamie could hand-wrestle or any other kind of wrestling, with Will Brinkby's boy who, though rather skinny, looked as if he had some of his father's strength fast developing in his shoulders and arms. But Jamie too was well developed about the shoulders and the little group of boys and girls, including a stout, red-haired girl they called 'Billie', furnished both participants and audience in the 'Great Hand-Wrestling Contest'.

Roberta called "Good luck," and added carefully, "both of you."

Jamie waved back but she got no reaction from Gordon Brinkby except a flat stare, first at her and then at his father. Then the boy and one of the audience began to discuss the technicalities of the contest.

Will Brinkby had already lost interest in it and turned to another subject.

"Miss, do you go now to old Mac's shop for the ledgers? I can carry them to the pub for you, if you're willing to take what you need from them that covers just part of 1985 through 1996, far as he's gone."

She gave way to her deep curiosity and asked,

"I wonder why his records of 1985 and the first months of 1986 aren't included."

Brinkby was quick to say, "Funny fellow, Mr McQuarry. Secret-like, but I wouldn't know. Not my concern."

However secret they might be, Nick Demian was familiar with them. The dates of the forbidden records covered the time of Veda Demian's death, Jamie's injury, and the death of Sultana. Maybe it was the latter, a sentimental reason. McQuarry might not want to expose his own deep feelings over the death of his beloved mare.

Brinkby added after a quick look, not meeting Toby's eye, "If Mr McQuarry says you can take out the ledgers, we might make a mistake, an accident-like. No harm done, but you'd have the whole notes about everybody's work on the cottages and grounds. 'Course, I'll not be doing that unless you're with me. Make it all proper."

I think not!

But she didn't say this aloud. The village was too curious. She would discuss the matter with Nick when he returned from Mincham.

Both Toby and Brinkby appeared much too interested in seeing the early (and forbidden?) records. But they wanted Roberta to take the blame. She was having no part of that, just to get some doubtful evidence of the villagers' 'good works'. Whatever McQuarry's emotions and thoughts on that village tragedy, she didn't want to read them without his permission.

But he should be told about the interest of

Toby Teague and Will Brinkby in Mac's private records before she gave Brinkby an excuse to fumble around among McQuarry's ledgers.

Meanwhile, Will Brinkby kicked pebbles away from under his muddy boots, frowning down the slope toward the chemist's shop.

Toby saw him and looked at Roberta.

"Will's the impatient one. You know what I'd do, Miss Roberta?"

"Mind my own business?"

He smiled. "No. I'd use the telephone, is what I'd do. They told me McQuarry's over to the hospital in Mincham."

"Yes. I heard that too." She didn't think it prudent to say she had visited him there. It might lead to awkward questions and reveal her earlier association with Nick.

"That's all the better. You just call and check with him. Double-check, you might say. Find out if there's things we're — you're not to touch. Private, you know." He tilted his head. "Phone's right inside." As she thanked him and turned away, he reminded her, "We'll charge the call to the tenants' committee. All's fair in love and war, eh?"

"Right you are."

She slapped his shoulder lightly and opened the pub door without waiting for him to do it for her. It was just as well; he didn't. Holding the door open she looked around and saw that Toby Teague had turned back to watch her.

A little uncomfortable about his attention, she

called brightly, "You see? I'm going to take your advice." It was awkward, though. She wouldn't be able to say what she would like to have said over the line to McQuarry. He studied her for an embarrassing few seconds, as if reading her mind. Then he made a playful little gesture with fist raised. "Stand by your guns, Miss. And a mighty pretty figure you make doing it. Oh, Miss, just a mite of a word."

Puzzled, she stopped. "Yes?"

"Old Mac, he's a good one and means the best. But he has some little thing he knows, or thinks he knows, about Mr Nick."

"Oh?" Was he afraid she would go over to the Demian side in their dispute?

"Ay. Just you talk with Mac alone. Keep to Mac. Not Mr Nick. Understood?"

If this was Toby Teague's way of acting against Nick Demian, she would make her own judgement on that.

She nodded and went on along the passage, past the staircase, toward the taproom on the right and the lounge on the left.

The telephone was perched on a little shelf jutting out from the wall just at the open doorway into the taproom. Not only was it very much in the way, and anything but private, it was probably bumped by everyone going into the bar. Ahead of Roberta, several people in the lounge were rummaging through an old trunk which was positioned between Sheila Demian, Elly Camberson and the pert little brunette teenager,

Pamela Perth, who had been operating the vacuum cleaner that morning.

Now, the girl was folding and unfolding garments, lunch cloths, old hosiery, an aged mink stole, and bedroom slippers, all of which she replaced in the trunk's faded interior.

Roberta would like to have looked through the village account books that Toby Teague had promised her would help the tenants' cause, but there was no use in interrupting the three women. They were all chattering away. Even the lachrymose Camberson wife seemed in good spirits.

It occurred to Roberta now as she turned to the telephone that she must be losing her mind. She had no idea what the number of the hospital might be and there was no book handy. In self-disgust she cleared her throat to attract the women's attention. The sound she made was only half audible, thanks to young Pamela's excited exclamation.

"Here's the pattern that Mrs DeVrees used when the children did the Cinderella fairy tale. All spangles she was, as the fairy godmother. Just for the men, and that's a bet!"

"And didn't she know it!" Sheila remarked.

Pam shrugged and suddenly, seeing Roberta, dropped the envelope with the yellowing paper pattern. "Oh! It's Miss Fisher. I didn't know you were there."

Roberta was about to apologise when Sheila Demian looked around. In her practical way she raised her eyebrows but said pleasantly enough,

"Don't mind us, Miss Fisher. We're rescuing costumes to dress the cast on Saturday night. Were you looking for someone?"

"Some thing, actually. A telephone book for Mincham."

Sheila scrambled to her feet, rubbing her left hip and shaking her head. "Not as young as I once was. All this crawling about on the floor. What number were you looking for?"

Roberta explained about the hospital and was aware of the interest she had aroused in Mrs Camberson and young Pamela.

Sheila said in her calm way, "No trouble. I know the number by heart. Jamie has been there several times. Let me get it for you."

Before Roberta could even thank her she was on her way to the telephone. This put Roberta in a difficult position. She hadn't wanted anyone in Edenbrook to hear her conversation.

She need not have worried. Sheila got her number, spoke to Sister Longacre at the hospital whom she obviously knew well, and then explained over her shoulder to Roberta.

"He's gone."

"Gone?" Maybe he was coming home. Roberta was relieved. She would let McQuarry show her his records which he apparently kept faithfully. Meanwhile, there were always the village accounts here at the pub. They would give her some facts to help the cause of the villagers.

If there actually was a cause.

She said, "Fine. It doesn't matter. Mr

McQuarry may be back any minute. Though how he can do so when he looked pretty weak a few hours ago, I can't imagine."

"Oh, Mac's a tough one," Sheila said as she replaced the phone. "He's busy in Mincham already. According to Sister Longacre he's going to see some old lady who ran into him. Probably a lawsuit. I wonder how much he will get for the bumping he took."

Roberta thanked her, not sure what to do next, since the logical answer was to dig through the records in the lounge relating to improvements to the Demian property made by his tenants during the past decades. This, at present, would prove difficult, since she did not want Sheila Demian's businesslike and unsympathetic observation during the time she worked on evidence for the Demian tenants.

She was about to excuse herself when the gardener, Will Brinkby, pushed open the pub's front door and called down the short passage.

"There'll be fighting ahead. I warned that lad of mine."

Roberta thought of Jamie and didn't like the sound of this. She looked around, then decided that her own concern was greater than Sheila Demian's, and furthermore, that the village files could wait. She would return later and get to the job she had been contracted to do.

Only half joking, she told herself, "Blame it on the luck of the opal upstairs."

Running now, just as raindrops began to sprinkle the square and the brookside, she followed Will Brinkby down the slope to where the young people had established their hand-wrestling contest.

The youthful voices were audible as the cheers, groans and grunts indicated a lively match, less a fisticuffs battle than an excited argument with waving and prodding hands. They must be disagreeing over the winner of the handwrestling.

As she approached the group, she saw that most of them were arguing on one side or the other about something that didn't seem to concern the contest at all.

"It's true," the red-haired fat girl yelled. "A slut. Pam's granny told Papa."

"You're a liar. A dirty little liar."

That was Jamie. Roberta hadn't believed the boy could show such anger. And more. The others who watched had stopped their partisan jeering at the beginning of the argument when Jamie scrambled to stand up. He now stood there looking tall and frightening, thanks to his heavy brace.

The gardener's boy, Gordon, joined in the shouting match. "The day she died, your Mam was making out she was going jogging. But she was really going to meet a man in an Italian car. Old Mac saw the car."

"It's nothing to do with Jamie," Merlina Camberson put in. "So keep quiet."

"It's not true. It's not true," Jamie insisted. He looked around, as if to find another witness to back up his argument.

As Will Brinkby and Roberta reached them Will tried to break them up. The red-haired girl he pushed to one side. His son he collared and swung around out of the circle. He did nothing to Jamie who was breathing hard and scowling.

"That'll do you," Will commanded. "Off wi' you all." He sniffed the misty air. The raindrops had begun to fall a little faster. They would soon be covering the area. "Looks like a hard rain driving in. Master Jamie, you go home. I'll have someone go along with you."

"I don't need anybody. I'm no cripple."

The fat girl giggled and Jamie swung around so suddenly his arm knocked the girl onto her posterior. One of the group unknown to Roberta helped the girl to her feet. She had stopped yelling and spent the next few minutes brushing her denims and complaining.

"He's a cripple and he just about broke my back."

"Your arse. Not your back," someone yelled, but she looked unhurt to Roberta who moved in quietly, hoping she would not be a new and prejudiced troublemaker. Roberta had been a teenager once, and had resented adult interference.

Although one or two brushed away raindrops, everyone quieted, curious to hear whether Roberta would take the side of Nick Demian's son when it was known to everyone that she was here to act against him.

She said in the most normal tone she could

summon, "Hello, Jamie. Who won?"

The boy's scowl, so out of place on his usually pleasant features, remained while he told her flatly, "You think I need somebody? I'm no baby. I don't need anybody. It was me that won the hand-wrestle."

"Is it true?" Will demanded of his son whose eyes narrowed as he looked at Will and then back at Roberta. The boy shrugged.

"Sure, it is. Hauling that thing on his leg everywhere —" He indicated Jamie's crippled leg and especially the shape of his cast, vaguely visible beneath his trouser leg. "It put the muscles to his hand." He added, trying to be fair, "He was always good at it. But red Meg here, she bet on me, and — well —"

"You know you're not to gamble. I warned you."

"But you —"

"I what?"

Watching them, Roberta realised that the boy was afraid of his father and of family discipline.

"N — nothing."

"I what?" Will repeated, shaking him.

"Only that you gamble."

It was hurriedly blurted out, which might be natural, but to Roberta's surprise, Will Brinkby acted as if he were relieved as well. Had the gardener been afraid the boy would say something else? If so, what?

Will Brinkby breathed deeply and nodded, although Roberta had supposed such an accusation would only anger him. Instead, he cuffed his son's head in a friendly way and chuckled.

"Well, now! I'm a bit older, boy. I know what I'm doing."

Except for Jamie, they all looked at each other and then there were belated titters of laughter. Half of them took the brookside path while the others went up to the square. Merlina Camberson waited for some encouragement from Jamie and receiving none, walked on besides the brook toward Demian House and her afternoon hours of work there.

"All's well now, Miss," Will Brinkby told her. "I'll get old Mac's ledgers for you. Shall I?"

"No. I think not, until Mr McQuarry comes back. Thanks, anyway."

The gardener gave her a salute with his fingers to his eyebrow and went back up toward Toby Teague's pub.

Jamie, too, moved away, adjusting his leg to the long strides he usually took, beside the brook. After a minute, and knowing she was not wanted, Roberta followed him.

"Jamie, did you know your friend, Mr McQuarry, left the hospital after we came away this morning?"

He nodded.

"But is it wise? With his bad shoulder?"

Jamie looked back at her. "He called us. Father went to help him, to persuade him to go back, if he needs more treatment." He set off again and Roberta headed back to the village. She had taken several steps through the mist with her jacket collar pulled up around her ears, and was passing the chemist's shop when Jamie's voice startled her. He had retraced his steps and was very close.

"I just wanted you to know. He doesn't hate women. Not the nice ones."

"Of course not." Then she added diplomatically, "We all have our likes and dislikes. It's just a clash of personalities."

"Father is — well, Father. He had a lot of responsibilities all by himself, what with Grandfather being like he was. He likes people or he doesn't. But he has good reasons."

It was a jumble but she thought she understood him. She said so. "I understand. I'm rather like that myself."

Jamie's serious face softened slightly.

"Whatever my mother did, she didn't make Father . . . dislike all women. He doesn't dislike you. I know he doesn't."

It touched her painfully when he added as she was continuing on, "I don't know why Mother never wanted me around when she jogged. I tried to keep up with her, awfully hard. I know she wanted Father's money and the property. But she must have loved him at first, or she couldn't have married him, could she?"

"Your parents loved you," Roberta said firmly, feeling a deep kindred spirit with him. "Or if one of them didn't love you as much as the other one did, well, you had the extra love of that one person. Like my mother. And your father," she added, remembering that they were not discussing her own problems and the boy would hardly be interested in anything but his devoted father.

"That's why I came home from the academy in Switzerland," the boy confessed. "I had this feeling that Father needed me. You know how you get a feeling sometimes . . ." Then he flashed a winning smile. "Besides, I was homesick."

"Of course. Your father might scold you for coming home without his permission, but I've seen him with you, and he's mighty glad you did come home. Always remember, you must never believe the gossip from people who have reasons to dislike your family. Be sure and consider the source."

He brightened. "I'll remember." He turned away, then came back. "Where are you going now?"

"I thought I might look over some bills and notes about the work of the villagers of Edenbrook through the years. It's only fair."

He considered, then confessed in a lower tone, "I think so too. I hope Father does right by them. I would, if it was me."

She saw that he didn't want to leave and suggested, "Would you like to help me with the bills and whatnot from the villagers' past history? At least, until this mist and rain lets up."

"Oh, yes. I would. I'm good at maths and things. And then after, you could tell me about how to put together the story about the ancient man they dug up in the Alps. How he lived and what he did and how he got to the Alps."

"We'll do that."

His father might not like it, but she hoped the villagers would see that the boy was, in some ways, on their side in the dispute.

Meanwhile, she had a puzzling matter to think out. The cruelty of Jamie's friends and companions in the village came from somewhere. They were too young to have known or witnessed anything about his mother. The story had begun with their parents.

Was it planted deliberately to shock and disillusion Jamie? What was the point, unless they wanted Roberta herself to hear about it and had staged this scene for her benefit? They might want to be quite sure she remained on their side.

Probably the whole ugly story had been true. Was his wife's alienation the sole reason for Nick Demian's anger at the world? Or were there more problems, as yet unknown to her?

Chapter Thirteen

Still under the overhanging roof of his pub, propped on two legs of his chair, Toby Teague had been watching her and Jamie. He seemed unaware of the heavy mist.

"Oh, good," Roberta said brightly. "You're still here. I wonder if you would be kind enough to locate some of the records and accounts for me. The ones concerning Edenbrook's growth and the work put in by the tenants."

Teague studied her for a moment, almost sleepily. What was he thinking? Perhaps wondering how friendly she was with the enemy's son. He suddenly emptied his pipe against the corner of the heavily reinforced door, making Roberta start in surprise. Then he got up, letting the chair settle back on its four legs with a crash.

"Glad to be of service, Miss." He made her a sweeping bow. "After you. And the lad, of course."

Roberta and Jamie moved ahead of him. She felt that the publican, his teeth shining with his grin, had almost swept them both into the dark little passage that smelled, not unpleasantly, of old, well-seasoned wood.

The lounge was empty and at this hour, late in the afternoon, only Elly Camberson was in the taproom, seated at the single table the room afforded. She was nursing a glass of lemon shandy while her left hand carefully traced the circle on the table made by the wet bottle from which the drink came.

She saw them pass and raised her glass to them, but before she saw Roberta's answering wave, she hunched her thin frame over the bottle as if deep in thought. Roberta wondered and glanced at Toby Teague who shook his head, ushering her and Jamie into the lounge.

"Whatever she had was before she came here," he said. "Poor Orin. It's hard to see the woman go to pieces like that."

Roberta resented this, though for all she knew, he might be right. "She must have been very pretty."

"Ay. Prettiest this side of Mincham. But that's all gone by. Here now." He swept his hand over a dusty pile behind the uncomfortable settle under the window.

She barely refrained from a groan when Teague thrust a coal scuttle full of miscellaneous papers in shoe boxes at her.

"You'll find a fair amount of receipts for the past few years. There's more in the cellar. A fine collection they are."

She sneezed from the paper dust and reached in her pocket for a tissue.

He watched her soberly, but there was a wicked glint of amusement in his eyes that suggested he knew he was upsetting this fancy American.

"We figured you'd be the very one for this work, Miss Fisher. You being so familiar with that Halloway female's papers and letters that you put together, and that."

She controlled her sneeze and said coldly, "There is nothing I like better. But I'd appreciate it if you would take this junk — er, material — up to my room where we can look through and tabulate it more comfortably."

"Seems fair. I'll just get my barman. He'll be happy to run you a favour."

Roberta realised she had made a mistake. It would not be well at this moment to let her tenant employers know she was beginning to have a few doubts. She became all charm and gratitude.

"Thank you. You've been so very kind to me, I won't forget it. I hope I can repay you by presenting the truth of this affair."

It was an equivocal statement but he accepted it.

"Just so. And it'll be appreciated, Miss. Believe me." He grinned at the coal scuttle. "Looks a sight, don't it? But you'll be used to that, eh, Miss? What with all the papers you must have looked through for the Halloway woman. Too bad this mess couldn't have been done on them tapes or disks too. Would have made it as easy as the Halloway thing for you."

He went off to find his lost barman, while Roberta murmured with a growing chill, "He seems to know as much about my Halloway tapes, notes and disks as if he had seen them himself."

Jamie had lifted the coal scuttle but she shook her head and he set it down. She started out of the lounge and towards the stairs with Jamie following. The thump and drag of the heavy weight secured beneath the arch of his foot made her hesitate but Jamie waved her on.

"I go up and down all the time. We've a heavy staircase at Demian House. It's no matter."

He said no more until they reached her room upstairs, but she puzzled him by the way she looked around the rooms and especially at the little round table in front of the window.

"Did you lose something, Miss Fisher?"

"Roberta," she corrected him. He nodded but still watched her.

"Is something missing?"

"I don't know. Some people here seem to know a lot about me and I just wonder how they got all the information. Also, people rummaged through my room in London and through Miss Halloway's as well. I can't help asking myself if there's any connection."

"Really?" He was excited but not, she thought, very worried. To anyone his age, the idea probably was more thrilling than annoying or alarming.

She picked up a lipstick, an eyeshadow compact, the usual unimportant items, including the hairbrush that had been replaced on the right of her dresser in Mrs Sloan's house. But it was here in its correct place. She opened the polished ebony box where she kept her imitation jewellery. The opal ring was still there, the stone with its curious flecks of fire and wine that almost seemed to reflect a face staring up at her.

Her own face, of course.

She couldn't remember if she had put it into the box with the stone upward, facing the soft, deep, velvety pile that lined the box lid. Or had she thrown it in carelessly, not wanting to handle it more than she had to?

She said to herself, "Well, obviously, no one has taken it."

Jamie reached in. "Could I touch it? It's funny. Like somebody's eye with little tiny spots in it."

To her own surprise it made her nervous to watch him touch the opal. She would gladly have let him walk off with it, but she found herself beset by the silly superstition. She wanted to take it from him, throw it out, anywhere. But Jamie seemed fascinated.

"I dreamed about this ages ago, when I was practically a baby. Isn't that funny?" He replaced it carefully.

She forced a smile but she was remembering something Sybille Halloway had said; that the man who had given it to her had intended to pass it on to his grandson.

Instead, probably short of cash for the moment, he had been forced to give the ring to Sybille Halloway as 'payment for services rendered' and undoubtedly, in the hope of keeping her mouth shut. It seemed obvious that the opal belonged to the Demians, but since Sheila Demian wouldn't take it, her brother Nicholas must be the owner.

By this time, Roberta would have been enormously relieved to get rid of it, but at the same time, she didn't want it stolen.

Meanwhile, Toby Teague's ageless barman, seemingly incurious as ever, set the coal scuttle in the middle of the floor and as he left, stopped with his liver-spotted hand on the doorknob to ask, "You wanting it closed, Miss?"

"Yes, please."

When he was gone, leaving the door securely closed, as Roberta noted, she sat down at the little table, with Jamie across from her. Together, they turned to the coal scuttle.

With Jamie's help she began to sort out the evidence of old expenditures. She frequently ran across pale, worn notes on ruled school paper, some in pencil, indicating carpentry and plumbing and an assortment of other repairs by the local residents themselves, most of these dated. The company receipts for payments of work were much less frequent.

Roberta remembered that Nick Demian and his family had supposedly paid many of the tenants' expenses, healthwise and in other ways. But she was supposed to be working for the tenants, and muttered, "I'd better not open that can of worms."

Jamie giggled at this remark. It was probably

too old and corny for his younger generation. But its significance remained, corny or not.

The evidence of the Demians' private support of the tenants would only be a point on the Demians' side in court. If Nick Demian had paid so much of their expenses, they were lying when they claimed that the various Demian properties should be turned over to their ownership by dint of their hard work and improvements. She found very few receipted bills paid for by them when serious work was done on the cottages or the town square buildings by outside companies. Certainly, the tenants had not paid for the cottages or other residences.

On the contrary, the hundreds of bits of paper remaining revealed little of any importance done by the tenants to the properties which they and their ancestors had occupied at nominal rents for nearly a century.

She knew there were many injustices in other places here and abroad, where tenants had to surrender the land or houses on which they had expended a lifetime of work that counted for nothing. But she was beginning to doubt that their kindly friend, Sir Arthur Laidlaw, knew all the facts.

Still, fair was fair. She could not understand why Nick Demian wanted to throw out all his tenants when the old leases ran out in the next couple of years or so. Unless he had a sale in mind that would make him an enormous profit. If so, the Demians would sacrifice a lot of her sympathy, even though they would be within their legal rights.

But why did Nick Demian have this vendetta against the people? What had they done to him?

With these thoughts in mind she went on sorting out the various 'proofs' of the tenants' work on the properties while Jamie stacked the notes and receipts by dates, frowning heavily over the writing.

He had a pile of them which he pushed aside to make room for another, when it slipped and scattered over the carpet. He tried to stop the trickle of paper but instead knocked off the ebony box. Upset and apologising, he scrambled to pick up everything, hardly hearing her remark that it had been bound to happen and not to mind.

The ebony box with its generally unimportant contents had received no harm but the opal ring rolled out across the worn carpet. He reached for it, caught it between the tips of two fingers and in a natural reaction, slipped it on a finger. Too big. He started to remove it when he and Roberta were both startled by a familiar voice across the room. The door had opened without them noticing and now it closed with a slam.

Jamie gulped and said, "Father! I didn't hear you." He didn't seem frightened but he was ashamed.

Nick Demian was wearing an old, none too fashionable raincoat, carelessly belted. His black hair looked windswept and wet, but he seemed oblivious of his dishevelled state. Most important, he had a Burberry across one arm and Roberta assumed it was for Jamie.

With his eyes on the opal ring in Jamie's hand Nick Demian said, "What the devil are you doing with that damned ring?"

Badly ruffled at having been caught unawares, Roberta snapped, "You might have knocked. I believe that is customary."

"I did knock." He came further into the room and put his cupped hand out to his son.

"Let me have it."

"It's awfully pretty, Father. Like a ring I dreamed about ages ago." With a slight show of reluctance he put it into his father's palm. Nick then put it back in the ebony box and set it on the table in front of Roberta.

She sighed elaborately. "It isn't mine. It was given to me by Sybille Halloway and I doubt very much if it was hers either."

His smile was grim. "No. That's fairly obvious. So she gave it to you. Now, I wonder why?"

She resented his tone. "Just her way of paying me for at least three months of unpaid work. She was good enough to tell me it was bad luck. That I don't doubt for a minute."

He surprised her by laughing. "Nor do I. I'm sorry Jamie finds it attractive. Bad luck or not, I don't like the thing."

"Father!"

But he was looking at Roberta. "Have you any idea whose ring it really is?"

"I suspect it belongs to your family. Your sister

Sheila recognised it. But she wouldn't take it."

He took the ring out of its case and then tossed it in the air a couple of times.

"I can believe that. She isn't much for rings, as poor Art has found out. Father gave that ring to my wife and then — being pressed for ready cash, as usual, as he was quite a gambler — he took it back and gave it to your friend Sybille."

"For much the same reason she gave it to me."

His smile was a big improvement over his expression when he came in.

"A debt paid off," he agreed. "Well, you may keep it. The Demians wash their hands of it. Veda was so insulted at having to return it that only a pair of diamond earrings would soothe the pain." Roberta didn't enjoy this mention of his dead wife. It seemed there was no love lost there. She was glad the boy Jamie hadn't taken offence at his father's remark.

She lowered her voice, glancing at the door.

"Does the publican know you are here?"

"Oh, yes. I complained about my boy being seduced by a London harpy."

"Good God, what will they think of me?" But she had to laugh. "I'm sure Sybille Halloway at her best never played out a melodrama like this one."

"I couldn't agree more. And now, I had better take this young rogue home to dinner. I promise you Jamie and I will leave the pub quarrelling all the way."

"Quarrelling?" Roberta understood and was

amused but Jamie was shocked. "Why, Father?"

"I think I know," she put in. "Your father will be furiously tearing me apart and you will be manfully defending me."

Jamie too became amused, getting into the spirit of their acting parts. He limped to the door after waving goodbye to Roberta.

Nick Demian lingered, taking her hand as if to anchor her. He bent his head and touched his lips to her palm lightly but very pleasantly, just about a quarter of an inch from her open and surprised mouth.

While she stared at him, he had another idea. "Look here, why not saunter down the brookside and just happen upon Demian House? In time for dinner?"

"That's a great idea," Jamie proclaimed. But Roberta brought them back to the business at hand.

"What? And ruin the war you and I have going so successfully?"

Jamie looked disappointed but Nick shrugged. She thought (or hoped) he too looked disappointed.

"Well, perhaps you're right. The Brinkbys live very nearly on our front step and they have busy eyes."

She went to the door which he had left ajar as they departed and heard the two quarrelling all the way down the stairs. She had a feeling that this serious and arrogant fellow was enjoying himself in this game they played.

Afterwards, she went to the window and looked out through the old, patched lace curtains. The rain was pouring now, and village men from the direction of Mincham Lane and locals up from the brookside, were converging on Toby's pub, all of them shimmering and unreal in the watery dusk. But apparently, the 'pub hour' was more important to them than the inclement weather.

Nick and his son came out of the pub, bundled up with their rainwear close around them. The villagers passing them reminded Roberta of two belligerent armies, most of them neither speaking nor acknowledging the Demians. Roberta thought there was some excuse for them; it was difficult to make out individual faces in this downpour. One or two of the villagers said something to Jamie who waved as they went by.

Roberta liked the way Nick Demian took long, casual strides that didn't appear to be coordinated to Jamie's ponderous effort with his foot. It was not difficult for the boy to keep up with his father.

Whatever the villagers thought of Nick Demian, he got full marks from Roberta for the way he looked after his son without seeming to do so, thus saving the boy's pride.

Nick Demian evidently had his car parked off Mincham Lane behind the shops of Camberson and his next-door neighbour who sold ceramic waterfowl for the tourist trade.

The Demians passed out of her sight beyond

the ceramic shop. They would now be crossing the flat stone bridge to Mincham Lane where the brook emptied into the watery ditch that ran beside the lane.

Sultana, Mr McQuarry's beautiful bay mare, had galloped along near Mincham Weir that fatal day ten years ago, destroying Veda Demian and crippling Jamie. By some chance, was that period the forbidden sector of McQuarry's records?

Roberta stepped back from the curtain and turned on the table lamp. She settled down to what appeared to be a sloppy paperchase, the receipted bills from manufacturers, in Mincham, and further west, as well as London's outskirts.

Two hours later she was working on the memos, reminders, and plaintive demands for payment from Edenbrook's tenants when an unknown voice which proved to be that of the almost mute barman, announced through her locked door, "There's dinner laid on in taproom, Miss. If you've a mind to." Then the taproom ghost was gone.

She got up, stretched, and realised that strange undercurrent of nervous ache inside her was hunger. She hadn't eaten since that delicious breakfast many hours ago.

Down in the taproom, with the rain still coming down in great curtains outside the taproom's single window, half a dozen men and two women, wives she supposed, were crowded around the semi-circular bar, most of them just finishing their beer and ale.

Will Brinkby looked over at her, toasting her with an empty mug and foam still forming a white moustache on his tough, friendly face.

"There's good smells from the kitchen, Miss."

Several others nodded before going back to their drinking.

Roberta thanked them smilingly, aware of their furtive glances after she lowered her head to make out the pencilled menu. She did look up once to say to Will Brinkby, "I don't see Mr Teague."

"No, Miss. The brook's rising where it runs under Mincham Lane, and he's out seeing to the lads at their work. They'll be digging out the mud and such to shore up the banks, such as they are, and removing the litter that's built up at the culvert."

Looking out of the window he frowned into the wet night.

"Looks to be breaking up 'fore long. But he'd want you to enjoy your supper, Miss, all the same. Found anything you can use for us in all them papers?"

"Oh yes, very helpful," she fibbed and went back to her menu.

From a choice of three courses she chose the grilled fish, roast potatoes and broad beans, and was not sorry. She liked English country cookery and was beginning to find unexpected advantages to this forced assignment. Besides, her active, screenwriter's mind was chalking up ideas, and certainly background, for future work.

But as she lingered over the warm, fresh apple pie and its sauce that had smelled so good when she entered the taproom, Roberta saw a shadow over all those dreams of work when she returned to Hollywood.

There would certainly be no Nicholas Demian in TV land. Nor Jamie Demian, whom she had come to like in a very short time.

She was knitting her brows over this when she saw a party of very wet local phantoms in rain-wear parading back across the square, just passing under the blue-white lamps whose high standards hung over the square at various points.

Several of the men and a dishevelled, white-haired woman were dragging what appeared to be canvas sacks, partially full. Roberta did not doubt that the sacks, dripping into the runnels of water across the square, were full of rubbish that had washed along the brook and jammed at the culvert under Mincham Lane.

Inside the pub many of the drinkers who had started their dinners dropped their cutlery with a clatter and got down off their stools to investigate. As the soaked and muddy group poured into the pub's dark passageway, illuminated by the lights from the lounge and the taproom, they dropped their bags on the stone-flagged floor.

There were several groans of relief but none from Toby Teague who had carried nothing and was now in his glory as he continued to issue orders.

He sent his taproom waiter off for towels,

sheets, rubber mats and anything else useful while he and the old woman whom he called Granny Perth opened the nearest bag.

"Found some odd ones, but finders keepers," Granny called out in a voice like a basso, but a trifle cracked. She had a rugged, heavily lined face and the profile of an eagle. She was undoubtedly one of those who peddled gossip about Jamie's mother to her daughter Pam. Roberta would not like to have bumped into her suddenly on a dark night.

Someone rummaging through a bag objected. "What do we do with them?"

But this didn't kill the interest of the crowd who began to open the other bags in which they had thrown the refuse gathered in the overflowing brook. Their noble deed in the clean-up might yet pay dividends.

No one had found a live fish at any rate, Roberta thought to herself. She wanted to go up to her room and read, anything that is but the papers from the coal scuttle. The truth was, however, she would much rather have been in Nick Demian's company. They could at least have had things to quarrel about.

She signed for her dinner, wondering if, in the end, she would have to pay for these meals anyway, and started out into the passageway. She was passing Will Brinkby when he pulled out what appeared to be a water-soaked cloth bag. Probably velour or velvet. He whistled.

"If it was dried out, this could be pretty. Might

give it to some lucky lass."

Granny Perth sneered. "What'll she do with an empty bag?"

"Not empty. Look here."

It couldn't be much, having probably been soaking away at the mouth of the culvert for sometime. Roberta edged her way through the eager crowd and started for the stairs. Will Brinkby looked after her for a moment and then broke the tie-strings of the bag in his powerful hands. He reached in, joking so loudly he attracted Roberta's attention again.

"It'd be funny if something inside here bit me."

By now, Granny Perth, Toby Teague and another man were caught. They stopped what they were doing and silently watched Brinkby pull out a square metal box, with a corroded little lock. To Roberta the box appeared to have been expensive once. The metal was probably silver but hopelessly tarnished now.

"There. What's to be said about this, eh?" Will shouted, raising the box in triumph, close enough to make Roberta shift away, out of reach of his waving arms.

There were excited murmurs but Toby Teague's put-down destroyed some of the euphoria.

"You thinking of biting it open? It'll have to be prised, or broken, and that'll take some of the worth out of it."

Ideas poured in and the argument became a free-for-all.

Curious in spite of herself, Roberta waited on the outskirts of the group but it looked like a long seige ahead.

"Got to take care," Will said, still looking his treasure over. "There's the thing. Slow and careful. The box is worth something. Like Toby says. Might get in a tidy little sum from those antique dealers that come down here off and on. Like tomorrow on the London bus tour."

Several voices, overcome with curiosity, objected, but Will Brinkby was still shaking the box in one hand and the cloth bag in the other. From the look of it, Roberta thought, they'd be here all night playing guessing games about the value of the soggy bag's contents.

Toby Teague reminded them, "Easy does it. Lay it away to be safe while we go through the rest. We'll get to it when I find me something that won't break the lock. May take half the night."

Roberta started up the stairs.

How good it would have been to know Nick Demian was up there waiting for her.

As for the mud-soaked remnant from the brook, she couldn't imagine how it would concern her anyway.

She had just put the heavy, old-fashioned key in the lock of her room when excitement broke out, either in the passageway outside the bar room or on the staircase she had left. There were several shouts from the men, but unless they had found a cache of money or at least a few jewels in the corroded box, she couldn't imagine what else had provided the excitement.

Nevertheless, the sounds of triumph below got to her. Succumbing to her curiosity at last, she went back and leaned over the wooden banister at the top of the stairs.

She couldn't resist calling to the crowd below, although, having escaped the sacks of rubbish, sticks, stones, grass and mud on the main floor of the pub, she was aware from this height that the odour from them had risen and was nothing if not pungent.

Chapter Fourteen

Jeers and laughing at the foot of the stairs did not sound too promising for the contents of the metal box.

"Serves me right," she told herself. "I should have minded my own business."

One of the younger men called up to her. He was one of those who had lugged in a bag full of muddy junk, along with enough broken branches to start a welcome fire in the lounge grate.

"You there, Miss, come see Will Brinkby's treasure."

"Have an ounce of manners, Sam. It's Miss Fisher to you," Toby Teague corrected the young man who clapped a hand over his loose mouth as if he couldn't stifle the giggles. He nodded to Toby, however, and Roberta noted once more that Toby Teague might seem lackadaisical but he and his pub were the heart of Edenbrook village.

She had come this far. Why not join them in their foolery?

"You got the metal box opened? What is in it?" she asked as she came downstairs. All of them except Toby Teague backed off. She was conscious of the fact that they were all staring at her expectantly.

"All right. What's in the box?"

Toby took the metal box from Will Brinkby's hands, leaving Will with the damp velvet bag that had held it.

"Here she is, Miss Fisher. What d'you make of it? Not something that's going to make old Will rich, I'd say."

The box lid had been prised open without damaging the little lock. She raised the lid and peered into the box which was lined with puffs and nubs of soft material. These obviously protected the contents: a slightly discoloured golden egg, maybe of vermeil or china, painted with delicate blue and gold designs and decorated with what were probably imitation pearls. The contents of the egg, like the box, were sealed by a tiny lock. Also gold, she thought. She had never seen an expensive object of this sort, but she knew what they were.

She looked up. "Have you opened the egg?" As she spoke her fingernail raised the upper half of the egg which was held to the lower by a gold ring and on the other side, the tiny lock that had come loose.

Granny Perth sniggered. "They thought it'd be a fistful of jewels inside. Maybe diamonds. Eh, boy? Eh?" She stuck Will Brinkby in the ribs with her bony thumb.

The gardener scowled but Toby Teague ignored any side issues.

"What d'you think of it, Miss?" He put his thumb and finger into the hollow egg. "Summat here. Paper. One's folded. Other — just a bit of scrap paper. Kind of a list. You can read it. 'De — june — ay . . . carrots, parsnips, broad beans . . . Diner — Dinner, I expect . . . How'd you say it, Miss?"

"*D'agneau.* Lamb. *Déjeuner* is lunch. Things that had to be ordered, perhaps."

It seemed ridiculous that someone, undoubtedly female, had put a piece of a market list in this ornamental 'egg' that should only be used as an evening bag, or decorating some cabinet of small treasures.

Will Brinkby asked, "Ordered by who? One of our females? Nobody talked of losing this thing."

"Maybe someone from the tour buses," a woman suggested but Toby scoffed at this.

"What'll they be doing making lists of food and whatnot? Our tourists come from outside. They're not planning to cook dinner and lunch when they get back to London. Not even Eyetalians."

"*Déjeuner* isn't Italian," Roberta said. "It's French."

"Well, it still don't make sense."

Roberta reached for the other piece of paper, folded in quarters. It was a small, lightweight sheet, torn from a notebook, the paper lined in blue grid style, like so many inexpensive French notebooks. Something hastily written, no doubt. Perhaps intended to be rewritten on letter quality paper.

Several men and one of the women crowded

around Roberta, trying to read the little notebook sheet over her shoulder. Feeling guilty and ashamed at reading something so private, Roberta still could not resist. She did, however, read it silently in spite of Toby Teague's insistence.

"Out loud, Miss. We're all cravin' to hear."

Chéri, (it began)
Je vous embrasse affecteusement, comme toujours.

You know that? *Eh bien,* it must be in English now. Good for you.

Do not say you hate me, *mon cher.* There are bad people in every village. Tongues of wickedness.

Soon, together, we will give them all the back of the fist, eh? I will show you how much I —

The writer must have been interrupted, or perhaps stopped to consider what next to say. Who had written this? A woman. The writing was spidery and small, some of the ink water-stained. The phrases sounded feminine to Roberta, and the word 'cheri', used twice, definitely referred to a man. Unless, of course, the writer was homosexual, in which case Roberta's deductions meant nothing.

She gave the note and the once-lovely egg to Toby Teague who was closest and had taken the box in his palm. Will Brinkby, having read the note aloud in a monotone, objected plaintively.

"A love letter. Nothing but a love letter. What of the egg there? Are those stones worth anything?"

"They may be," Roberta ventured. "If this is gold leaf and if the stones were carefully polished. But the pearls still may not be worth much."

"I've heard of those Russian ornamental eggs," Toby said, toying with the hinge and hanging lock. "Not real ones," he added, seeing puzzled expressions on the faces around him.

Roberta was still examining the egg. "I don't think this is a Fabergé egg. These are used as evening purses by women. Fabergé made egg-shaped treasures. Only they were too valuable to be carried. I never saw one used as anything but an ornament on display."

There was a good deal of disappointed murmuring and jeering, and as Roberta started upstairs again she advised Will Brinkby, "See some jeweller as soon as you can. The egg itself may be worth something. But be sure and let the rest of the village know what you've found, in case it belongs to one of them."

Will's eyes widened. Conveniently, he skipped over the advice to look for the rightful owner. "Think it may be worth real money, Miss? I'll do that very thing. Meanwhile, Toby, you got yourself a prize. I'm giving over the grocer's list and lover's note to you."

More jeers. But Roberta was on her way to her

room, sleepy and no longer very interested.

The sight of all that paper junk in and out of the coal scuttle was enough to give Roberta a headache. She refused to spend the remainder of the evening correlating the expenses nobly paid by the villagers or, as she had been discovering before dinner, billed to the village and presumably paid by the Demians. Very few of the large demands for payment had any evidence of being paid by the tenants.

After soaking for a while in the old, claw-footed bathtub, she made her way down the hall under what seemed to be no more than a child's night light. As she opened her door something surprising occurred to her. Not a sound came from the bar room, the passage or the lounge below. Had that noisy crowd vanished so quickly?

She went out to the banister and leaned over, getting a vague, shadowy view of the passage and open bar room doorway below. A dim, blue-white light came from the bar room but she was sure the whole ground floor was deserted. Even the comfortable lounge was dark. All that boisterous village crowd had vanished in a matter of ten or fifteen minutes.

She shivered and went into her own room, locking the door behind her. It was a puzzling phenomenon. In her experience, a dozen people or more didn't become silent and vanish all at once. There were always giggles, stifled laughs, little noises, as the last stragglers of such a group broke up and went on their way.

She hurried to the window. Through a wet world drying off in a kind of foggy mist, she made out the chemist McQuarry's shop. A man and woman moved along, probably towards their cottage, and in the northeasterly direction beyond the square a solitary youth hurried along past Camberson's closed and darkened shop, turning toward the culvert and Mincham Lane. The rest of the village must have retreated out of sight already, into their own cottages.

Roberta watched this silent, now motionless scene, hypnotised by the unreality of it. She was more aware than she had been when Mrs Peavis first mentioned her going to see these people, that there was something peculiar about her presence here.

Surely, anyone from Mincham, or an old acquaintance from the Cotswolds, would be far better suited to whatever purpose she was really serving here? The ancient village seemed to be cut off from the rest of the world.

She wondered suddenly if tonight's find had been a set-up, staged just for her, as if she might be used as a witness for the discovery of the contents in the jewelled egg case.

But if so — why?

She left the window and rummaged in her handbag to locate two aspirin tablets, which she drank down with a glassful of water. Since she didn't often take them, they worked quickly to remove her headache and enabled her to sleep dreamlessly, so far as she remembered, until she was awakened by another of those golden autumn mornings.

Yesterday's pouring rain was gone, except for a muddy puddle or two and still-dripping eaves. It was impossible to feel scared or let her imagination run riot on such an autumn morning.

She had just returned from her bath when Toby Teague knocked his knuckles on her door unexpectedly hard. Yet he didn't seem angry after she unlocked the door, but there was a wary look in his eyes and in his slightly twisted grin.

"Telephone, Miss Fisher."

She started past him, tying the sash of her robe more securely. He stopped her.

"No. No. Wait. He's rung off. Just left the message: 'Send that female to Demian House at once, and tell her I want no delays.' He wants to settle something with you about his boy."

"What does he think I'll do, contaminate Jamie?"

"Well, he gets these ideas. He likes ladies one day and the next — forget it! They're poison. He can't get away fast enough. Talk about women-haters!" He took a deep breath. "Sorry. I just don't like to see a lady talked about like."

"What have I done to him?"

Toby shrugged. "You're on our side, Miss. That's an even worse crime than the others."

She certainly hoped this was Nick Demian's idea of a game he was playing against his tenants. Judging by last evening when he and Jamie were leaving, he was on her side, she hoped!

But taking her cue from Toby Teague's attitude, and especially his wary eyes, Roberta gave him a haughty stare.

"We'll just see about that, especially after he insulted me when he came to get his son yesterday." She wasn't sure he altogether believed her, and she was certain he was just sussing her out, lying to see whether she would defend Nick Demian, so she pursued the matter in a hush-hush secretive way that she thought would have been worth a screen test for a character in one of her own scripts.

"Look here, Mr Teague —"

"Toby."

"Right. What's that man's game? I know he dislikes me. So why must I go clear along that stupid brook and see him now?"

She really had him confused. She was convinced of it.

"I couldn't say, I'm sure."

"Unless," she pursued her play-acting, "I can find out how he hopes to defeat these decent people who have been his hard-working tenants for so long."

He brightened. "Just so."

She didn't want to appear too stupid about all she had discovered in those papers she had found in the pub's coal scuttle, so she gave him a hint of an explanation that would show more directly why she was to be seen in the 'Enemy's' company.

"Maybe he feels those papers in the coal scuttle

are more helpful to your case than he thought. That would explain —"

His shaggy head nodded. When he looked up he did not seem as unperceptive as she had hoped. To Roberta this whole pretence of dislike between her and the Demians was a questionable idea, but she had come this far and might as well see it through. She certainly didn't want to lose all contact with the Demians.

She sighed. "It does seem silly, doesn't it?"

He hesitated. She knew he was studying her and she tried to retain the thoughtful, determined look of a foolish woman who was convincing herself, despite its unlikelihood.

She wasn't sure whether she could successfully 'simper' but she tried it now, saying, "You mentioned, as I recall, that Mr Demian hates woman, although you said he may give them the impression that he is attracted to them. Was that it?"

"Well, in a manner of speaking, it's about the way he has been."

She pursed her lips and smiled what, she imagined, was the nauseating smile of a woman who thinks she is more attractive than in fact she actually is.

"I think I've taken the wrong tack with him. I should exercise my womanly wiles, if you'll pardon my conceit." *(If he swallows this performance, I've been in the wrong profession!)*

He didn't seem to find this as amusing as she did.

"Very good idea, Miss Fisher. And then, we

can get to the bottom of whatever he's planning. And a lady with all your good looks," (Oh, brother, is he laying it on thick!) "well, she ought to be able to handle it as well as any female. Be she cook, housekeeper, stranger, or — like you — a TV lady writer."

"How sweet you are! If you'll pardon me, I'll hurry and dress for the occasion, as you and I would say. By the way, it might be as well to keep this a teeny-weeny secret from the rest of the village. They may not approve of this devious means to extract information from Mr Demian."

He nodded conspiratorially but, she had a suspicion he would rush to tell someone, any of his confidants, as soon as she'd left. She wanted him to.

Roberta watched him go down the stairs and finally closed the door, smiling to herself.

While she dressed, taking some pains to look her best (after all, Toby Teague would expect it of her) she tried to unravel what was going on here.

All that gossip he had told her was pure bilge, about the Man Who Hates Woman. She thought back to the hard, warm strength of Nick Demian's mouth on her palm. The excitement his touch had stirred in her remained even now.

Hate women? Ridiculous.

"He may give them the impression he is attracted to them," Toby Teague had said . . . Well, he certainly had done that recently.

But Toby and his friends had a motive; what

her greatgrandfather had called 'an axe to grind'. They didn't want their landlord to call in the leases their families had held on this land since time immemorial.

She banished her mental monologue while she finished dressing, careful to wear flattering high heels that enhanced the shape of her legs in the narrow-skirted green suit with its deep pink blouse.

"If it rains again, I've had it," she reminded herself as she slung a smaller-than-usual handbag over her shoulder and started down the stairs.

She had felt perfectly comfortable with herself until she went through the passageway outside the bar room and found Will Brinkby in her way as he lumbered in for breakfast. She greeted him with a smile but he raised both huge hands and for an instant his stance appeared menacing.

"You'll have a care, Miss, now, won't you?"

"Of course. Care for what?"

He dropped his hands and smiled sheepishly.

"Old Toby, he says Mr Nick went and ordered you to go to Demian House."

"That's right."

"You will have a care? Toby says you must."

"Toby ought to know," she said sweetly. "Excuse me. You are in my way."

"Oh. Sorry." He shifted his feet.

She passed him wishing, when she got out into the sunlight, that she hadn't shown her annoyance so clearly. These medieval characters really would stoop to anything.

"You'll have to get up pretty early in the morning to fool me," she told them all. But silently.

Toby Teague had talked a great deal of rubbish and more than hinted about Nick Demian and other women. But Roberta was perfectly aware that the intention of these villagers was to make the enemy, Nick Demian, look as bad as possible.

The origin of this misogynist thing that Toby seemed to have on the brain was the death of Nick's wife and that death could hardly be laid at Nick's feet. Even if he were fiendish enough to plan his wife's murder by feeding McQuarry's mare some deadly weed, that would have been a highly imponderable method. A dozen — make that a hundred — things could have gone wrong.

But most important of all, he would never have risked Jamie's life.

The enclosed little village did fascinate her, ominous or not. It was a selfish truth, but as an outsider, she might be of help in unravelling their problem. After all, the danger here, if danger existed, was towards either the Demians or the villagers. Not to herself.

Chapter Fifteen

Just as a bus beside Granny Perth's shop was loading up village youngsters for school in Mincham, Roberta started down past the chemist's at the turn of the brook. Here the water, now rippling thinly again over its pebbles, drifted past the Old Mill. Its west side, facing her, was still in morning shadows. A small channel of the brook flowed around the mill, as well as the useless mill wheel and the unlucky vegetable growth under the mill's north face. This channel had turned to a small, swampy patch when the vegetables failed to materialise.

She walked on, careful not to get her heels caught between the stones that had washed over the uneven path along the brook. The cottages that lined it, though set back twenty and sometimes thirty feet, were spaced a distance apart, particularly on the north border of the brook. Roberta wondered that so few people in such a small number of dwellings could still arouse attention enough to warrant Sir Arthur Laidlaw's sympathy and action.

Today, excursion coach day, saw the women outside their picturesque cottages, armed with brooms to sweep down vagrant webs and dust from the eaves, or cleaning windows whose shutters were decoratively open. Roberta recognised them only by sight. She smiled and nodded to them but wasn't surprised when they ignored her. It had been like that back home in some isolated western desert towns.

But she was very much aware of the looks that followed her as she passed beyond each hard-working housewife. At first, it made her uncomfortable. She was sure they all had guessed she was betraying her 'employers' and meant to sell them out to Nick Demian. Maybe. Maybe not. She wouldn't make up her mind until she judged Nick Demian's true feelings and motives for herself.

She was relieved to get to Demian House, near the east end of the village, where trees closed in the tiny brookside settlement and if she listened carefully she could hear a 'lorry' rumbling along the distant highway, either to or from its turn into Mincham Lane.

Beyond the two-and-a-half storey Demian House that loomed somewhat above its two neighbours, Roberta noticed old Samson Brinkby mopping the crusted mud off the stepping stones in front of the gardener's cottage.

He acknowledged Roberta and she had a pretty fair idea he had been watching her as she walked beside the brook from the time the little stepping stone path turned eastward beyond the chemist's shop.

When she was close enough for him to get a good look at her face she shook her head, showing as much disgust as she could muster up, and pointed a thumb at Demian House.

"He orders me about as if he had hired me. After all, my employers are the villagers."

He grinned, showing his toothless gums, and said "Ay!" like a character in a bucolic play. Though she wasn't sure he knew what she was talking about.

She gave up and walked up to the front door of Demian House. He surprised her by loping along so close behind her she was startled.

" 'E's a good lad. Maybe a bad leg but a fair good lad." It was hard to understand him but she got the drift of his remark.

She nodded. "Jamie Demian is a very good lad. I like him. But that's easy to do."

Samson grunted. "For some." He tilted his head, his grey, windblown hair flying around his cheeks, as he indicated Demian House. "Not all. No Miss. Not all."

She stiffened apprehensively, wondering if he meant Jamie's father. Surely not!

She expected Elly Camberson's daughter, Merlina, to open the door but Sheila Demian did so with her usual calm, friendly, but not too effusive manner.

Good heavens! Maybe *she* was the one Samson Brinkby had been talking about.

"My brother is expecting you, Miss Fisher. Do come in." Her cool features broke into a grimace. "I only hope you can take his mind off the sketch he is working on. He's not going to be very popular with our prime minister."

Roberta laughed. She hoped she was expected to. "I suppose politicians are used to it."

"They are used to Nick, that's certain. Come along. I understand he's very angry with you, but you musn't mind that. It happens all the time."

They were going up the wide, oak staircase which, to Roberta, seemed to hang over the heads of whatever luckless individuals moved from the lobby, under an archway, into the big ground-floor lounge. She paused to take a sneaking look over the banister into this room below. It looked surprisingly comfortable, probably because its two long French windows opened onto the autumn garden. This attracted a great deal of sunlight to the evergreens and some late-blooming pink flowers that looked like roses from Roberta's position on the landing.

The landing itself was wide enough to accommodate a round tilt-top Hepplewhite table in the corner. On its surface was an electric lamp, its too-long cord coiled neatly underneath at its foot.

"Coming?" Sheila called, looking down at Roberta from the top newel post of the staircase on the floor above. She didn't sound angry or even impatient. Her attitude seemed to be one of faint surprise that a simple staircase had taken Roberta so long.

Talk about efficient, Roberta thought but she hurried a little. She remembered the scene upstairs on the night she arrived at Edenbrook, the night when Elly Camberson had behaved so oddly and fainted over nothing, at least so far as young Merlina, Sheila and the stout cook seemed to feel. Roberta still couldn't figure that one out.

Meanwhile, she followed Sheila Demian like the little white Maltese terrier who followed at her present stepmother's heels all day, yapping with every dainty step of each paw. The difference, aside from hair colour and size, was that Roberta was too impressed to bark.

She kept asking herself what she was doing here. But she no longer wondered why the Demians aroused so much animosity in their neighbours. They were just a tad overbearing. No. Make that 'sure of themselves'.

At the far end of the hall upstairs Sheila knocked on the closed door, announced inelegantly, "She's here," and made a gesture of ushering Roberta past her into what was obviously Nick Demian's office-cum-studio. It was an inviting room to Roberta in spite of, or perhaps because of, its messiness. There were piles of books here and there, canvases unframed, an uncomfortable-looking bed made up with linen and a heavy souvenir wool blanket that proclaimed: "Welcome to Blackpool".

Nick Demian, in shirtsleeves and slacks, sat at his big 'desk' that was hardly better than a kitchen table. This was loaded with sketchpads and bottles and glasses of pencils, pens, brushes and a letter-opener.

There seemed to be no model for the prime minister's sketch he had before him; more of a caricature than a sketch.

Nick had already stood up at his sister's knock and came forward to meet Roberta with an expression that flattered her by its pleasure.

He took her hands in his and held them to his chest as he leaned forward and kissed her cheek. She felt warm and wondered if she had blushed. At her age? Make that flushed. The day was reasonably hot.

While she laughed and put on a fine pretence of accepting this as his standard greeting, his sister said in the doorway, "I can see I'm not needed here. But do remember that breakfast will be ready soon. Miss Fisher, don't let him starve you while he chatters."

For the sake of politeness Roberta almost said, "I've eaten." But honesty and appetite got the better of her. "I'll do that. Thank you."

"Good. I'm expecting a London call but you just come down as soon as you like. Cook will be ready for you."

Nick called after her, "Is Art still making a pest of himself with his calls?"

Roberta knew from Mrs Peavis's gossip that Sir Arthur Laidlaw was more or less pursuing Nick's sister long distance. Perhaps between wives. Apparently, there wasn't anything passionate. Sheila Demian laughed.

"Why not? It's good for my reputation. Besides, think how disappointed Mrs Peavis would be if I turned him down." She left the room and closed the door, ignoring their laughter.

Roberta remarked, "Sir Arthur seems charming. Doesn't your sister like him?"

He shrugged. "Sheila would wear Art down in a week." He saw her eyebrows go up and added, "No. Not that way. Simply by being her ambitious self, always on the move."

He did not let her hands go until he had seated her on the bed and pulled his stiff, ladder-backed work chair over to her.

"Was I too much the lord of the manor on the phone this morning?"

"Rather like your sister, I would say. You impressed my landlord and the village gardener. Of course, you didn't win any friends."

"Not even with you? I thought you'd appreciate it. You know. Acting. Hollywood, and all that. Maybe Jamie is right. He's afraid you will take all my growling seriously. Poor Jamie."

"Why Poor Jamie?"

"He shows all the signs of being in love with you."

She pretended to bristle. "And that strikes you in the same way Sir Arthur's wooing of your sister strikes her?"

She could hardly argue with his mischievous smile which lit up his dark eyes and in many ways made him even more attractive to her.

"Ah, but you see, Jamie's passion makes him my rival."

There it was. Toby Teague's warning. Nick Demian led women on. To their ruin?

Oh, come now, Roberta. You're a big girl.

232

She smiled back but broke the spell by reminding him, "I am curious to know why you asked me — ordered me — to visit you here this morning."

The grin remained on his lips but the excitement vanished from his eyes. "Nothing easier. I returned to Mincham yesterday and after getting old Mac safely back to the hospital, I had a little talk with the lady who collided with him on the approach to Mincham Bridge."

She leaned forward. "Did you find out anything? Surely, it was an accident!"

"Oh, yes. Mac is satisfied. And so am I. Mrs Seddley is quite innocent. A pawn, in fact."

"Then, what — ?"

"On her part. This woman, Mrs Seddley, tells me she is seventy-eight, has lived in Mincham and Exeter before that, all of her life, and never been involved in an accident. A matter easily checked." He slapped the bed beside her. "But you see, she believes that someone behind her simply ploughed into her car pushing hers forward."

She stared at him. "You mean, someone wanted to hurt her?"

"Or the person she ran into."

"But who would want to run into Mr McQuarry?"

"Who can say? But it isn't a nice business, any way you look at it."

"God, no! How can I help?"

His smile returned, gentler, almost humorous. "Mrs Seddley got a vague glimpse of the driver.

Not, unfortunately, the number plate. The sunlight was reflected off his windscreen and blurred her vision of the man himself. She thinks it may have been a man but isn't sure. Of course, it all happened so quickly, and a traffic pile-up followed. But I'd like to get some pictures to show Mrs Seddley."

"You think the person who ran into her might be from this village?"

"Who knows?"

He sat down beside her on the bed, saw her look at it and was amused.

"I agree. This is quite a mattress. I don't spend every sleeping hour on it. But it has one great advantage." He looked at her, seemed hesitant. Then he said rapidly, "I've always found moments of privacy necessary. To think. And to work. Does that seem at all understandable to you?"

She found it curious that she couldn't remember anyone saying this to her before, and yet, it described her own life so exactly. Even in what had been called 'The Steno Pool' in Hollywood studios, surrounded by other typists and would-be scriptwriters, she had felt the necessity for the privacy he described. She had always been a loner.

Nick was watching her face carefully. "What are you thinking? That's an odd look."

"I ought to know what you mean. I was born a loner and a part of me won't ever change."

"Good." He slapped her hands lightly. "You

would be surprised how few people do understand us. We have to treasure each other."

She laughed at that. "I'm honoured to be included."

He seemed to think everything was settled between them. She had no idea just how much this entailed. He said, "Well now, to get to the matter in hand."

She sat up straight. "Aha! I knew there was a catch to all this loner-meets-loner bit."

He ignored her teasing. "Americans in Britain are usually loaded down with instant cameras."

What on earth had that to do with anything? "Not all Americans. Me, for instance."

For some reason this was upsetting news to him. "You don't? But it's easier to explain one of that type. People would expect it, where you snap everyone you see and it's developed in no time."

She shook her head. She still wondered if this wasn't a peculiar Demian touch of humour. "I have a good little German camera. Quite old. But it's filed away with the rest of my stuff in London. Why? Did you want your picture taken?"

He tried to regard this with a short laugh but brushed it aside. "Nothing like that. I wanted to borrow it to show the Seddley woman colour photos of your friends, the villagers. To see if any one of those faces resembles whoever she saw or didn't see in that car behind her."

She could hardly believe that any of the Edenbrook people she had met were capable of running into a seventy-eight-year-old woman deliberately in the hope of hitting McQuarry, which must be what he was getting at. For what reason? She asked the question aloud.

He reminded her, "Mac was sitting in the passenger seat struck by Mrs Seddley, accidentally, on her part, I am convinced, but it would normally have been occupied by Jamie . . ."

She caught her breath, beginning to find this suspicion evidence of Nicholas Demian's pathological hatred of his tenants. She tried to calm what she considered a dangerous imagination.

"But surely, there isn't any proof that these people want to hurt Jamie. Why?"

He was probably disappointed that she couldn't fall in with his preposterous notions. He was silent for a moment, taking his eyes off her and looking out of the window at the woods that surrounded the garden below.

"You are probably right. But I want to satisfy myself in any case. I'm afraid I've aroused Mrs Seddley's curiosity, and of course, Mac has always believed . . . However —"

"Would you like me to take snaps of the people I see every day around the pub?" she asked, hoping to mollify him. "I could think of an excuse easily enough."

"No. I had thought of Jamie using the camera. A kind of childish gesture, taking pictures to carry back to Switzerland with him." She opened her mouth to offer again, rather than involve

Jamie in the conspiracy but he shook his head.

"No. I've involved you too much. It isn't fair to you. If you had already a camera it might have seemed natural."

He reached over, smiling again, but his eyes questioned hers, studying her face for clues, she thought.

"I can buy one. Say I'm going to spice up the evidence of your hard-working tenants with pictures of them at their endeavours."

He laughed at this. "No, thank you. You've done quite enough for Jamie and me. If anything happened to you, I'd never — Jamie would never forgive me." He squeezed her fingers between his. "Nor, if you want the truth, would I forgive myself. But I think I've taken up quite enough of your time when you must be starved. Shall we go down and see what Mrs Schramm has to offer us?"

He got up, held out his hand to her, and there was nothing to do but accept the fact that he did not quite trust her yet. Unless, of course, he really did care about her and was afraid of endangering her. She found it hard not to believe him when she wanted to so much.

On the other hand, the more she thought about it, the more terrible it seemed for a grown man to have such suspicions about tenants whom he had known from his birth. And what had he meant by his questions about the car that ploughed into Mrs Seddley's car? Why would an accident to a respectable but unknown lady of seventy-eight have anything to do with McQuarry? Or with Jamie? She had a strong feeling that the danger to him was at the bottom of his father's concern.

It was unnerving to think of a man with such deep hatred that he could suspect unimaginable crimes.

Chapter Sixteen

Like Roberta, Nick Demian must have found his spirits lifted by Mrs Schramm's excellent breakfast. When she remarked on the plain but deliciously cooked scrambled eggs and apologised for having been caught trying to speak with her mouth full of crumbling buttered rolls, Sheila Demian, who seemed so casual about almost everything, confided in a dream that surprised Roberta.

"I heartily agree. Do you know what my dream is, Roberta?" (The formal 'Miss Fisher' was gone, which satisfied Roberta.)

"Here we go again," Nick said with some amusement.

His sister said, "Quiet! I see Schramm and myself setting up a bed and breakfast place somewhere."

"In the Cotswolds?" Roberta asked. "Or that lovely area you call the New Forest? I drove through there once."

But Sheila had other ideas. "Nearer London. Not so touristy. For Londoners themselves, tired of the week's whirl. A place to relax for a day or two, but not overstay their welcome. Above all, a place where I have the last word."

Her brother remarked, "That was for my benefit. But it's an idea, if we didn't have the responsibility of this stately pile."

Sheila wasn't offended. "Well, someone needs to take these things into consideration and the place I have in mind is just the answer."

Roberta laughed but had to admit, "I can think of dozens in Hollywood who are in and out of London every season. I could recommend you."

Sheila rolled her eyes. "Thanks, but not in my style. Or Schramm's, when it comes to that. No Hollywood types."

Feeling rebuffed and perhaps with reason, Roberta forced a smile and kept her mouth shut afterwards.

When she was leaving after Sheila had gone back to the kitchen to see what supplies were needed, Roberta said to Nick, "I think I offended your sister at breakfast. That stuff about sending people to her place. Actually, it was just a silly remark."

He raised her chin with a bent forefinger.

"Sheila is just Sheila. She doesn't mean to be rude. I'm sorry. That's not true. She just doesn't care. But that doesn't mean she dislikes you. Matter of fact, she likes you."

"Good heavens, why?"

He grinned. "She claims you and she are alike. You understand each other."

That did make her laugh. "This is my cue to go. My employers at the pub will think I've sold them out. I suppose I have."

He looked over her head, through the window

by the front door, and along the brook towards the chemist's shop and the Old Mill straddling the water in the distance.

"Yes. I suppose so." He studied her face and suddenly said, "Don't mention this to them, the villagers."

She was puzzled by his sudden seriousness. "If you wish. What?"

"While I was in London I had a call from Zurich. One of Jamie's surgeons. He had just returned from Boston in the States. While he was there he discussed Jamie's case with an American specialist. Showed him the case history."

She felt as excited as he must be. "Oh, can Jamie's leg be treated?"

His expression softened. "Treated? Jamie's doctor believes the very least we can expect is a definite modification of the brace. It would make an enormous difference. And there is a chance for even more improvement."

"How wonderful!" She caught herself. "They really mean it? It isn't just for money or something?"

"Money?"

She backtracked. "They told me that about Mom. But it wasn't true. It was the money. I'm sorry."

Thank God he hadn't been affronted. Instead, he said gently, "It isn't that way this time. They are both eminent men. The American is one of the foremost in his field."

She breathed more deeply. "Thank heavens!"

He leaned forward and his lips touched hers, lingering there. Her heart was thumping so hard he must surely sense her excitement. She returned his kiss, feeling drawn into the warmth and strength of him. Her arms reached around his shoulders, as if to pull him closer, but she need not have tried. She was so close in his own arms that at the moment there was no way out, a fact that gratified and enthralled her. She felt the enormous comfort of his own arms holding her to him, even when she became breathless and the heat of his mouth was removed from hers. An instant later she missed that heat and contact, which she realised she had so desperately needed for longer than she could remember.

Freed of his clasp, Roberta backed away, laughing on a slightly hysterical note. She made the joking remark, "I needed that!"

Fortunately, he understood her and laughed too.

"We both needed that."

"Not when you met me the first time in Sir Arthur's office."

"Perhaps not. Though I wanted to kiss you that same night when you scrambled out of my car."

"Liar." But her fingertips touched his lips softly, adding, "When I'm wading through all that evidence of your tenants' good faith — if any — I'll keep warm remembering this. Thank you."

He grinned again, brushed her forehead with

his lips, and opened the door for her. After looking around the brook and the cobblestones, she slipped out and started back along the brookside toward the village square.

No one seemed to be at home in the freshly cleaned cottages she passed for the second time, but things began to look more promising as she turned up the little slope opposite the mill, with the pub on her left and the square on her right at the top of the slope.

The coach they had expected had become three, two of them from London. They stood empty now on the west side of Orin Camberson's shop, from which establishment emerged more than a score of people, some carrying canvas shopping bags and two carrying French string bags. So far as Roberta could see, most of the bags were jammed full of souvenirs already, plus bric-a-brac and oddments that stuck far out of the bags, as did two samplers in wooden frames.

Toby Teague was in the open doorway of the Camberson shop with a stout, fortyish female, pointing her towards a rack of postcards and a counter where a small line of customers waited to buy stamps. Toby turned, saw Roberta and came out of the shop, obviously curious over her bout with the Demians.

"Mr Nick make his excuses for calling you in like that, Miss?"

"Excuses! That man is a real woman-hater like you said. He's been haranguing me for the last hour about what he calls 'betraying him to his enemies'. What enemies? The man must be mad."

She hoped her performance satisfied him but sounds began to gather around them. Chattering voices, giggles, cries of: "I've got to get a few feet of this. Madge, say something. Keep walking while you talk. That's it."

There was more of the same, including an occasional very American male voice.

"Phyllis, for God's sake, enough is enough. You've got enough rolls of that cockamamie film to paper a privy."

"Don't be coarse, George."

Toby Teague looked around, seeing a group of six get out of the third coach and troop into the pub. Several other tourists were being escorted down past the closed chemist's shop to the cottage of one of the women tenants.

Toby made a tired gesture with his big hands, telling Roberta, "I best tend to business. I'll just be standing outside the open door, pipe in hand, nodding to them as looks to come in for a dram or two, so to speak. They like rural characters, you know. I may be the star in some Yank's parlour movies."

He started over to his pub to show himself, the first of the 'local characters', while Roberta glanced around at the tourists, some of the men in old-fashioned Aloha shirts plus loose and baggy slacks.

Like the men, the women were chiefly in their forties and fifties, several smartly dressed, some of them limping, due to inappropriate sandals and pumps.

Roberta sympathised with them. She had often been caught trying to look glamorous in an unglamorous situation. Like now, in her high heels and narrow-skirted suit, she thought wryly.

She knew she should go back to her room in the pub and work on the contents of the coal scuttle, but the chattering crowd already in the pub put her off. She would spend a few more minutes studying the make-up and age of the village centre.

The pebbled square caused the problem that troubled most elegantly shod females. They kept slipping on the stones and as they did so they would lose their paper or canvas bags full of souvenirs. Also, they had to put in considerably more effort than those merrily scuffing along in jogging shoes.

Two girls, blonde and brunette, both of them attractive, headed down to the little wooden footbridge that led across the brook to the old flour mill. There were still smudges of mud from last night's rain and overflow, but the picturesqueness remained and Roberta had no doubt that the tourists would love it. The two girls were photographing the graffiti on the big, grey westfacing side of the mill with its one tiny window embrasure near the roof. The other windows had been nailed and boarded up to prevent looters and mischievous youngsters from using the place to sleep in or take drugs. The ground floor was obviously locked when not in use as a cinema or Saturday night theatre.

Roberta could see the girls try the door, and failing to budge it, walk around the body of the big mill. Curious about the grounds of such an ancient building, Roberta walked down to the footbridge and crossed, hearing the heels of her own shoes clattering on the loose boards. Behind her she heard a heavy echo. Toby Teague was stomping along, more or less in her wake.

He seemed pleased by her sightseeing but reminded her, as one would a well-meaning but daring tourist, "Have a care, Miss. Excuse the liberty. I wasn't on the prowl behind you. Actually, we want to make sure the tourists don't have any nasty accidents."

Had he been watching her from the pub? She slowed her pace. "Good heavens! Is it dangerous around here?"

"Not dangerous generally, although it would have been last night with the brook waters all over creation. But if you was to slip on one of them pebbles, you'd land in that muddy grass. That's where a rivulet from the brook runs into the vegetable patch now and again. Like last night. You'd get your pretty suit all wet and muddy. Elly Camberson, she slid right in one night. Broke her ankle, she did."

"How awful! But she's all right now?"

"In a manner of speakin'. Elly's a wee bit — what you might say — apt to lose her footing at times."

Nicely put, but obviously covering Elly Camberson's drinking problem. Roberta said no more. She felt for anyone who might be under the control of an unpleasant husband like Elly's.

Ahead of her the two girl tourists had vanished near the waterwheel and Toby pushed past Roberta in that direction.

"Take care, ladies," he bellowed to the two girls. The blonde was trying to move the waterwheel while the other snapped instant pictures of her.

Hearing him, they looked back. The blonde at the wheel wrinkled her nose at Toby. She had prominent front teeth that dominated an otherwise attractive face. She looked as if she might remain by the wheel, largely escaping a drizzly trail of water that seeped around her sandals, but the girl with the camera and the jogging shoes started back to the path, passed Roberta and Toby with an impertinent smile, and circled towards the east wall of the mill.

Toby said, "I give up. They don't usually come down here. If they get their silly shoes wet, we've got to pay, else there'll be nothing but complaints and then we're off the tour list."

He had no sooner ended his protest than the shrieks began. Roberta winced at the shrill noise which was surprisingly loud, considering the girls were out of sight already, but Toby went into action at once, muttering, "Damned females!" He bounded off along the little path in the wake of the two girls who had disappeared around the east side of the mill.

Half a dozen tourists came out of shops in the square and looked idly down across the brook to the mill and its east bank.

No help there. The tourists were too far off. Roberta tottered after Toby Teague, although she knew what to expect — girls with muddy feet and bad tempers.

Toby had waded in around roots, mud and water by the time Roberta reached the east wall of the mill. The muddy water almost reached the top of his boots but he was not a man to worry about trifles. The brunette had slipped into the mire and then lost her balance in the dirty water, and rotting, wild vegetation. Trying to save her camera which she held over her head in both hands, she couldn't provide a hold for the blonde and Toby to get her up to her feet.

With her own high-heeled feet spread apart to anchor herself, Roberta reached over to get one of the girl's wrists but only succeeded in grabbing hold of the camera. The girl's rescuers, Toby and the blonde, now got a better grip on the brunette's arms. After that the rescue should have been simple but the brunette kept up her panic-stricken complaint.

"There's a horrible creature under my left foot. I can feel it move. It grabbed my ankle. It's soft and — ugh!"

The blonde scrambled to safety on the path and after a glance behind her, started on a run to the rickety little plank bridge dripping mud and water and yelling, "Help, somebody! Help!"

Meanwhile, Roberta tried to pull the brunette up with her own free hand as Toby's fingers lost their slippery grip. The girl was now hip deep in the mire.

"What the devil is going on?" a familiar voice asked Roberta and she was bodily lifted to one side by Nick Demian, who then knelt at the edge of the path.

Squirming and wriggling in the engulfing muddy vegetation, the brunette cried, "There's something under my feet. An animal. I know it."

Seeing the pub owner's failure to get the girl out, Nick reached out over the water and tangled plants to take one of the brunette's arms while Toby reached down again after the other.

Together, the two men pulled up the now-sobbing brunette, setting her on the path to shake off mud and tendrils of decaying vegetation while Roberta scrubbed the filth off the girl's feet and legs.

Toby looked back into the water, watching Nick who had reached down under the debris and was drawing up a solid object dripping muddy vines and leaves.

Toby grumbled, "Like as not, the girl got tangled up in rubbish disposed of illegal-like. But anything to make the visitors happy, they say. Is it rubbish, Mr Demian?"

"Not exactly. No." Nick's voice sounded hollow with shock, Roberta thought, and she stared at him in growing horror. He began to pull the mud-encrusted thing out of the water.

Roberta wet her lips. "What is it?"

Toby's eyes opened wide, and choked, "Well, Mr Nick, I'd say you've just raised up a human limb. Seems to be still connected with the body too . . ."

The unfortunate brunette stopped scrubbing her body and began to scream again.

Beside her, a badly shaken Roberta wished she could do the same.

Chapter Seventeen

While Nick and Toby Teague removed the body from the watery vegetable patch to the path, Roberta began to recover the initiative she had always used during accidents and emergencies at the film studios in Hollywood.

She hurried the brunette to the mill bridge. Here they caught up with the blonde who had slipped on the mossy wooden planks of the bridge and was now picking herself up, cursing.

Roberta wanted very much to know who the drowned victim might be, but she could be of more use elsewhere. After staring back at the two men hauling the body slowly out of the mire, Roberta suggested to the two soaked, mudstained and weeping tourists that for their own protection they should not give out any tales about the dead body to the villagers.

"They're sure to make trouble and delay you for hours when you begin to describe your accident. They'll say, like as not, it's your fault. You were where you shouldn't be. Not that it's true, of course. But you must be discreet."

The brunette, trying to keep her bra and sweater from sticking to her breasts, immediately latched on to this with the sobbing protest, "I told you we shouldn't have wandered over that

251

awful old dump! Didn't I tell you?"

The blonde was eloquent if not dainty. "Oh, shut up! You've been a party pooper ever since we came on this damned trip."

The brunette was sobbing, "I'm a mess. A mess."

But the blonde agreed with Roberta.

"I'm for getting back to London. I certainly don't want to be caught out here in the sticks any longer than I have to." Then she demanded of Roberta, "Where can we get cleaned up?"

The handiest place Roberta could think of was her own room at the pub.

It took both her and the blonde to get the badly shaken brunette up the slope, through the milling crowd on the square and into Toby Teague's pub. Even here there were problems. Toby's handful of customers probed them to know what had happened.

Roberta urged the two girls ahead of her up the stairs. Following the two uncomfortable and still dripping girls, she gave one answer to all questions on the ground floor below her.

"The young lady fell into the brook. Her friend got her out."

It only half satisfied them. Most of them went out to seek more information. Only one person tapped Roberta's shoulder. It was Orin Camberson.

He was scowling, his small, pale eyes angry as he demanded, keeping his voice low, "What the devil is going on here? Where is my wife?"

"Your wife, Mr Camberson, is not here. Why don't you go and find her?"

She decided to let Nick Demian make the explanations. This was a village affair. She hadn't the faintest idea whether the body in the mill garden had been an accident or even a murder. Either way, it was no concern of hers. She had been mixed up with one accident in London and had no desire to be the object of more questions, by the police, or the villagers.

One of the tour party, a stout, eager little woman, came rushing in from the square.

"It's a body. Did you ever? Ethel, a real, live — I mean dead body. They didn't promise us this on our tour. Do you suppose it's a gimmick of some kind?"

Whoever 'Ethel' was, Roberta never discovered. The pub cleared out as if swept into a vacuum cleaner, one woman throwing a camera bag off her shoulder and getting it ready for shots on the way.

The two girls were in the upper hall, waiting for her, the brunette looking lost and scrubbing her skirt obsessively, further working the encrusted mud into the fabric. Her blonde companion was trying various doors, all of them locked except the bathroom, next door to the little WC. The blonde's American Levis clung to her hips and abdomen like moist skin playing up her sexy look.

Facing up to her self-appointed job, Roberta said briskly, "If you want to wash up, help yourselves. I'll get you bathrobes. Then you can try on something of mine. We aren't too far from the same size."

The blonde said, "Ha! You'll never get fatso Barby into anything you wear."

Barby, the brunette, was too upset already to take further offence. "Same to you, giraffe! I get the bathroom first."

As Barby passed the blonde and pushed her way into the bathroom, slamming the door and turning the key noisily, the blonde looked at Roberta and rolled her eyes.

"Jesus! What did I let myself in for on this trip? I'll tell you one thing. I'm not about to stay a minute longer in this hole than I have to. I'm Thea Ewert. Phoenix, Arizona. You live around here? If you can call this living."

"Temporarily. Roberta Fisher."

Roberta unlocked her door and the blonde followed her in muttering, "You don't sound like a limey to me. Well, what do these people do, set traps to catch us dumb tourists?"

Roberta didn't bother to remind Thea that it was 'fatso Barby' who had done most of the stupid things like prowling around the mill where it was dangerous, and slipping into the mire where she had no right to be!

Roberta thought the sooner she got rid of these two nitwits, the better.

She was aware of a persistent nervous trembling in her body and tried vainly to calm herself with the thought that accidents happened everywhere, and at any time. Look at Sybille Halloway's accident. She had drunk too much brandy and a rug went out from under her on a slippery floor. So far, no one had seen anything about the drowning in the mill garden to classify it as anything else.

Or had they?

She hadn't the least idea what they had discovered about the woman's body. Or even her identity.

The blonde, Thea Ewert, held up a pair of slacks Roberta threw to her.

"No way, kid. Any jeans handy? I can get away with wearing them skintight."

Nervous as she was, Roberta found it amusing to be called 'kid' by a girl several years her junior. She found a pair of faded jeans in the oak wardrobe and the blonde was satisfied.

"Never had any complaints over 'em being too tight. These will do." She began to peel off her soaked Levis, meanwhile tossing out a careless "You're bound to be reimbursed for the loan of this stuff. Sue the damned city."

"City?"

"Well, this creepy little dump." She wore little under her skintight trousers and had to scrub off her bare, pallid skin with the towel Roberta threw at her. She had a surprisingly skinny torso, all bones, with an underwired bra the likes of which Roberta hadn't seen in some years, but once she shook off her boots and slipped into the borrowed jeans, she once more assumed a sexy persona.

Barby, the brunette, would have to be attended to. Roberta took an old towelling bathrobe and went down the hall to the bathroom. Eventually, it was opened a few inches and the brunette dragged the robe inside, then came out a minute or two later, barefoot, wrapped like a mummy in the robe and carrying her sodden clothes by two corners. These she thrust into Roberta's hands and shuffled down the worn, faded carpet to her host's room. She had pushed her way in when Roberta heard footsteps on the stairs behind her.

She had never been so glad to see anyone as she was to see Nick Demian. She was flattered and pleased by the lifting of his own troubled expression as he caught sight of her.

"Thank God, you're all right. Old Toby said you came in with those two idiot tourists." He took her shoulders. His hands, jacket and shirt-sleeves were wet, but she was too grateful to let that worry her.

"They'll be all right. According to them, they don't want to hang around this hole any longer than they have to. I'm quoting Miss Thea Ewert of Phoenix."

"This hole?"

"Edenbrook."

His frown remained but he laughed. "Well, that's a relief. They will be needed at the investigations in Mincham, however, but at least they won't be in our hair for the moment."

He put an arm around her and was about to open the door of her room when she asked, "Excuse me, but do they know who the dead person is? Was? And how he or she got there?"

She sensed Toby Teague before she saw him looking up at them from the main floor below. Before Nick could answer her Toby called up to them, "Something familiar about the corpse, wouldn't you say now, Mr Nick? I can't quite bring it to mind, but she's known here. I'd swear to that."

Nick's voice was chill and clipped. "Very likely. Samson Brinkby and I believe it was possibly the Frenchwoman, Mrs DeVrees."

"Really! Well, then." Toby nodded wisely. "My very thought."

Someone called to him from the bar and he went sloping off.

Roberta took a long breath, trying to still the jangling nerves inside her. She tried to avoid the tragedy by remarking, "Our friend Teague seems to have more curiosity than sympathy."

"Yes. Toby enjoys horror. And death," he added, his thoughts perhaps reverting to his own wife's death, Roberta pondered.

He squeezed her shoulders and for a minute she felt his lips against her cheek. "I don't want you in this more than necessary."

She puzzled over what that meant. Was it purely concern over her nervousness? Or — good God! Did he think her reputation was so bad after Sybille Halloway's death that the police would wonder about the Frenchwoman's accident?

I'm imagining things, she told herself, trying to

induce anger to take the place of fear. She pretended to take his remark at face value.

"I know she had given up her post here, but why wouldn't Mrs DeVrees just get that Mincham lane bus they say goes by the Edenbrook bridge?"

"Probably because most villagers caught the bus over by the culvert there, close to the square."

"How unprofessional of her not to let your sister know. Sheila told me the woman gave no notice."

"Yes. Frankly, I've never been satisfied by the whole matter. She must have had some trouble locally. A quarrel, or even some matter in France that needed her attention. No one ever gave me a straight answer as to why she quit her job."

He looked at her, saw her troubled expression and relieved her anxiety by dismissing any concern she might have. "Anyway, no need for you to be upset about it. You've only just arrived and according to the doctor Constable Ackroyd brought from Mincham, Mrs DeVrees has been dead for a number of weeks."

"Since she gave up her job."

"It would seem so."

She shuddered. "What a horrible way to go!" She thought of Miss Halloway. "Did Mrs DeVrees drink?"

"I shouldn't think so. She liked a small glass of sherry before her dinner, Sheila says, but that was all."

Demian opened the door of the room Toby Teague had assigned to Roberta and was met by shrieks and rustling from Barby, the brunette. He muttered, "Damn!" and Roberta entered first.

Barby dropped Roberta's best suit skirt that went with the long, slim jacket, and wrapped the towelling bathrobe more tightly around herself. Roberta picked up the jacket, saw that one of the four buttons had been pulled off and felt like kicking the girl.

It was Thea Ewert who looked over Nick Demian with interest, a definite light in her eyes.

"We really have to be back in London tonight. I just know you can use your clout and cut the red tape." She strolled across the room towards Nick with what was probably her practised smile. Certainly, her movements were enviable to Roberta.

With great satisfaction Roberta noted Nick's refusal. "I'm afraid that would be out of my hands, but the young constable from Mincham is down in the parlour. He's the man you should see. You and —" He glanced at the brunette. "You and your friend."

The blonde's full lips twisted a little, spoiling her pout, and 'Barby' began to complain, "I can't go anywhere like this."

Nick took everything in his stride. "You will be driven in to Mincham with your tour guide. I'm sure you will find everything you need at

Windrowe and Beverley's. At our expense, of course, ladies."

"Well, that's more like it." Barby motioned to the blonde who looked back once, no doubt hoping Nick would go along, but getting only his polite dismissal. She hastily slipped on a few of Roberta's clothes behind Nick's back, and followed her companion.

Roberta, who was used to the easy, shallow reactions of many males in Hollywood, was more than ever impressed by the fact that Nick Demian could turn down all the glamour and tight, rear-end appeal of the blonde.

In spite of everything that had gone on today, Roberta couldn't forget the passion and heat of Nick's mouth on hers and the firm strength of his body pressed so hard against hers. There was none of the fumbling or persistence of the egotist trying to show off in that kiss, which promised a physical union so much deeper. Where she came from, much of the emotion she had seen, witnessed or been a part of, was almost mechanical. It was as if, in the back of everyone's mind was the thought of an invisible camera recording every motion, every reaction.

With the two girls gone Roberta was gripped by the real tension of the last hour. She felt for the edge of the little, round table and saw Nick studying her with the warm concern she had noticed before and which made her care so much about him. He reached across the table, took one of her hands.

"My poor darling, I couldn't blame you if you never wanted to see this hell-hole or anyone in it after today." He shook her hand gently. "I only wish you would stay just a little longer. Not because of the silly business Art Laidlaw got you involved in but just because we need you, Jamie and I. And Sheila, too, if you want the truth."

She blinked, feeling the painful stab of tears behind her eyelids.

"Funny. I don't think anyone ever said that to me before. Except maybe my mother. And she's long gone. You don't mind being compared to my mother?"

He laughed tenderly. "Not if it keeps you near me. Promise?"

"I promise."

Then he was gone.

It was appalling that Nick should be troubled by all this business merely because his family had looked after these feckless villagers for hundreds of years.

It wasn't fair. He hadn't even been in Edenbrook when the housekeeper decided to leave Demian House without giving notice.

What was it Roberta had overheard Toby Teague and the awful Camberson say about Nick's treatment of women? And two male gossips had mentioned the housekeeper who evidently couldn't make Nick fall for her wiles, so she left the household high and dry. Nick hadn't fallen for her any more than he had fallen for Barby and her blonde friend today.

261

High and dry. Roberta winced at her mental description of the body they had found. Nothing 'high and dry' about the death of the poor woman in the mill pond.

Chapter Eighteen

It was a long wait.

To take her mind off whatever was going on in the kitchen of the pub, Roberta went to the window, hoping to calm that turbulent nervous state that made her feel so shaky. She kept imagining what it would be like to find herself slipping into the thick oozing mud and tangled vegetation, undoubtedly at night, and finding herself sucked beneath the water, unable to find a purchase on the slippery depths below the vegetable patch.

From the window she got an all too clear view of the civic excitement that spilled out over the Edenbrook square, down to the brook and beyond it to the horrible and deadly mill site.

An old, joking phrase flashed across her brain: 'Did she fall or was she pushed?'

Good Lord, how hideous to find anything funny in what happened to the unfortunate woman.

And just what *did* happen to her . . . ?

Across the room behind her the door squeaked open. She jumped, then remembered it would be Nick Demian and was enormously relieved.

It wasn't, though. It was Elly Camberson, looking haggard as usual, not drunk exactly, but her white-gold hair fell uncombed across half her delicate face and her eyes were nothing if not haunted. She carried a tray covered by a tea cloth that had seen better days, though it was clean.

"Mr Nick, said you was expectin' this, him being in the hands of the law, and that."

Roberta came away from the window. She didn't believe for a minute that Nick Demian was literally in the hands of the law and she resented the occasional remark in the village that he and his family were regarded as oppressive and feudal. She dismissed Mrs Camberson's manner.

"He said he would send up a sandwich or something. Thank you. I suppose he and Mr Teague are explaining how they got the woman's body out of that place?"

"Just so, Miss." The woman looked almost transparently thin and this caused her eyes to bulge. Her stare made Roberta more nervous than ever, so she kept her attention on the wooden tray which she took from the woman. Mrs Camberson watched her every movement.

When Roberta uncovered the sandwiches she smiled at their thickness, but the bread was home-made, smelled delicious, and the slices of lamb were still warm, still tender and giving off a savoury odour of mint. Although after two meals, she was hardly this hungry, she thought the offering was worthy of any place she enjoyed at home and better than most. She thanked Mrs Camberson.

The woman flashed a quick on-and-off smile. It looked quite genuine, but frightened as usual.

What was the matter with her? Surely, this couldn't all be a fear of her husband's iron fist! Somebody ought to give that man a dose of his own medicine.

"Coffee's hot," the woman pointed out suddenly, as if she had just remembered her lines. "You being American, Mr Nick said you were to have hot coffee. And the cherry tart, too. Most particular, he was."

Roberta looked up. She had already noted the big, steaming coffee mug with its covering saucer. How kind he had been! She sipped the coffee and over the rim of the mug remarked to Mrs Camberson, "You are kind. Miss Sheila Demian said you and she had been girlhood friends."

Elly Camberson brightened. "Those were good years, Miss Sheila and me were friends for ever so long. Real friends." She cleared her throat, covering her mouth. Her fingers shook. Odd, Roberta thought, then realised it must be because of the woman's next words.

"The — ah — doctor from the Mincham police is here. But he is seeing to the body. It's the constable wants to see you soon. He's in the lounge. The parlour off the taproom, talking to Mr Nick and Toby Teague."

"Does anyone know just how the poor woman died?"

Mrs Camberson seemed positive on this one subject. "Drowned, they think. Something about inhaling water, you know. Getting the mud and water and maybe a leaf or something stuck in her lungs when she was forced to breathe under the muck."

Roberta shuddered, and then was astonished and ashamed of her own reaction. She asked herself: *Why the devil am I relieved? What else could it be?*

She glanced out of the window at the square. She could still see the front of a coach parked beside Orin Camberson's post office-cum-tobacco shop. The driver was behind the wheel while the flippant tour guide helped various members of the tour up the vehicle's steps. There was a slight delay for each tour member as the guide, with a knowing air, confided various information on what Roberta supposed must be 'the accidental drowning of a local woman'.

Accident or otherwise, everyone seemed to accept it in their stride, almost enjoying the excitement.

Elly Camberson cleared her throat again. "You'll be done with that mess?"

Roberta turned back to her luncheon tray. "Mess? It's very nice. More than I can eat, of course. But I know I'm taking up your time. Why don't I get this downstairs myself and maybe have the sandwich wrapped for later?"

Mrs Camberson pointed to the cherry tart. "Aren't you going to eat that? He'll be ever so cross if you don't."

Surprised, Roberta asked, "Mr Demian?"

"Oh, no. Orin. I mean, my husband."

"But why should he be? Oh, never mind." She

got up and reached for the tray.

Mrs Camberson looked as if she might also be ready to return the tray downstairs but was startled by a knock on the door. The door opened immediately and Nick came in. He looked angry, his mouth set, and his eyes had an angry light she had seen several times, though not directed at her, thank heaven!

"I'm sorry, Roberta. We have a new young constable in Mincham. Very new. And very young. He wants everything done in triplicate. First, our story. Then the two young tourists. I'm afraid there was more babbling than sense there. And now you, though your story is certainly a duplicate of Toby's, according to him."

"I understand. I don't mind."

Although the idea of reliving those few awful minutes was nerve-racking, Roberta hadn't lived in crime-ridden cities for nothing and acknowledged the situation. She added with a grin that was half grimace, "Makes me feel quite homesick."

Elly Camberson's pale eyebrows raised and then almost came together as she puzzled out this half-humorous reply to what must prove an unpleasant interview, but Nick liked it and offered her his arm.

"Come, duchess, we'll beard the mighty lion together."

He explained as they went downstairs, "I understand our regular Constable Pilsbury is down with a broken tibia. Poor devil was chasing some youthful apple thieves over a stile into Forly's sheep pastures."

Priorities seemed to be strange in these little-known villages. Roberta shook her head. "A woman dies a horrible death and the investigation is less important than boys stealing apples."

"Very true. But you see, Forly's pasture is a distinct no-no in Mincham country." He saw her face and apologised. "I know. At heart, I suppose Edenbrook and the Demians still belong to the Middle Ages."

"So it would seem."

She was surprised that he appeared to be so concerned over her reaction. Maybe, in some odd way, he would begin to see that even the Demians were a little like their medieval villagers.

"Anyway," he added on a joking note, "we have Arthur Laidlaw coming to our rescue. The locals are fond of him, for obvious reasons. But also — he was once one of them."

She didn't know whether she was glad or sorry. Sir Arthur might resent the little she had done for the 'poor, put-upon villagers'.

She tried to banish another feeling, the very matter that worried her companion. What questions would the 'new young constable from Mincham' ask her that Nick thought might trouble her? She knew what she had seen, what had shocked and terrified her, and she would simply tell the young constable so. It would be much the same as Toby Teague's testimony. How could it be otherwise? They had seen and been a part of the same episode at the mill pond.

It occurred to her belatedly, however, that her recent experiences in London, her questioning by the authorities and the necessity for Sir Arthur to speak up to the police about her (once again?) just might seem a bit excessive.

Why had these things sought her out? Mrs Halloway's accident and Roberta's discovery of her poor body only minutes later were coincidences that could have happened to anyone. As for this unfortunate dead woman in the mill pond, she must have been dead for weeks. Anyway, the first to discover her body had been the two girl tourists and Toby Teague.

And Nick Demian, of course. The girls were too hysterical to think about retrieving the woman's body; the brunette couldn't even get *herself* out. Even Toby was floundering at the job before Nick Demian arrived.

Roberta and Nick went down the stairs closely, both ignoring the effect this would have on Toby Teague and the villagers. Just before they reached the dark little passage at the foot of the stairs, Roberta asked, "How did you happen to find all of us at that awful spot?"

His answer was perfectly sensible. "The noise. That brunette with all her wailing. And the blonde running across the little mill bridge. Even you were understandably calling for help."

"Come to think of it, I was." No doubt of that.

He reminded her, "I was on my way to tell you Art would reach here before dinner. I had a nice little performance worked out, warning you that neither he nor you would get me to do my duty by the villagers. That secretary of his, Mrs Peavis, made that clear. But by the time I reached the square an hour ago all the play-acting blew up. That poor creature . . . Could she have been drinking and lost her footing? I can't think of any other cause for her slipping into that damned pool of slush."

She reminded him quietly, "Our little game seems to be over. It's so ghastly, the way the woman died."

A crowd of onlookers, most of them villagers, watched from the taproom as she and Nick passed the open doorway. She felt uncomfortable, hoping the police wouldn't bring up the subject of that other woman who had died and been discovered by her. A childhood protest of hers: "But it's not my fault", would have been stifled by her understanding mother's gentle question — "Then why are you dwelling on it?"

They were ordered into the lounge across the hall by the upheld forefinger of what could only be Constable Ackroyd, a thin man in his early twenties with a prominent Adam's apple, a wispy tan moustache, glasses that caught the light from the south window, and a voice that matched his juvenile moustache more than his manner.

Roberta didn't dare to laugh but his voice did give a hint of adolescent changing. Maybe this was just nervousness, or then again, maybe he was younger than he looked.

"In here, if you please, Miss —"

"Fisher," Nick put in.

The young man frowned. He looked behind Nick Demian. "As I was about to say. Mr Teague, will you please order those persons away from the door?"

"Ay, sir."

"And close the door behind you."

"Ay, sir. Just as you say, sir."

Roberta caught Nick looking at her and was afraid he might make her laugh, so she avoided him carefully. But it had been ridiculous to see how obsequious the eavesdropping publican behaved to his lanky and vaguely absurd official guest. Roberta was sure it was all a put-on. The real Toby Teague hadn't been in the least impressed. He seemed to be enjoying all the respect he pretended to show the young man.

The constable with the wispy moustache waited until Toby had gone out, closing both lounge doors behind him. Then the young man turned to Roberta who had sat down without being given permission. Nick stood behind her, one hand on her shoulder. She felt its strength and was grateful.

"Now then, Madam," the young man began.

Roberta looked around but there was no question. He meant her. "I went out in the square to wait for Mr Demian."

"I had invited her to lunch," Nick explained. "I wanted to scold her for taking on the case of my wretched tenants."

The young constable raised his hand, palm up. "The young lady can speak for herself, sir."

Roberta was secretly amused. Much as she cared for Nick, it might do him good to discover that even he must wait upon the law. She hurriedly took over.

"Toby Teague and I both saw the two tourists fooling around the Old Mill. The brunette was taking pictures of the blonde. Mr Teague was going down to warn them. It was slippery, you know. He said the local ladies planted vegetables there but when the brook overflowed its banks occasionally they lost the plants and the mud spread. Anyway, the girls paid no attention and first thing I knew, we heard a scream. That was at the back of the mill."

The constable nodded. "The young ladies had slipped into the swampy vegetable patch." He took off his glasses, rubbed the lenses on his coat sleeve, and put them on again. There was something disconcerting about the gesture, as if four piercing eyes now stared at Roberta.

"That is your story, madam?"

She drew herself up. "Certainly, it is." Nick had been about to interfere but she didn't want any more trouble. She pinched his hand to stay him.

Constable Ackroyd said, "You claim that this Toby Teague is responsible for your being down there on the path where the young ladies were permitted to fall in?"

"Permitted! I had nothing to say about the

matter. We both heard the commotion and —"
What was he getting at?

"Because, Madam, this Toby Teague tells me you were already there when you summoned him and he came down from the square afterwards. You alone were present when the young ladies fell in and almost drowned."

"This is ridiculous," Nick said sharply. "Ask Toby directly. But first, I advise you to make certain how and why the dead woman fell into the mill pond. And when. How long ago?"

Ackroyd flushed. "I had intended to do just that, sir."

He looked around, hesitating a moment, which gave Nick time to get to one of the doors, open it with no nonsense, and beckon to Toby Teague. The publican was embarrassingly close to the doors. Roberta did not doubt that he had been trying to overhear the conversation through the thick, oak doors.

He recovered quickly, however, with his famous big grin. "Ay, Mr Nick. You're needing me? How can I be of assistance? A bito' a dram, maybe?"

"Never mind the dram," Nick began. He had never pulled rank with Roberta since London but she felt the 'lord of the manor' affection was still much in evidence here in Edenbrook. It amused her but it wasn't very wise. "What really happened out there?"

Toby looked around at every accusing face. He seemed suddenly astonished. "But I thought —

273

I mean — what does the lady claim?"

"Claim?" Roberta echoed. "You and I were practically together. After the first girl fell in and the second was trying to rescue her, I reached for the camera which was hindering Miss Ewert from pulling the dark-haired girl out. But you, Mr Teague, you were in the mire, trying to rescue —"

"Quite right," Toby agreed blandly, almost too eager. "Like you say. I was doing my poor best to save the young female. But — well, Mr Nick here, he knew just like that —" he snapped his big fingers, "how it was all to be done. A real authority on brooks and mires is Mr Nick. Knows all the ins and outs. Many's the poor lamb he's rescued. Nobody knows better how to do with bogs and mires and that."

"Oh?" Constable Ackroyd said and looked at Nick speculatively.

Toby just couldn't stop apologising. "Now, see here, Constable Ackroyd, I've no wish to get anyone hereabouts in trouble. You can't call all that rubbish in the brook evidence, and who's to say it had anything to do with Demian House? An egg, they call it. Not a thing more. A jewel egg."

Roberta stiffened nervously. What was this? What had Nick Demian to do with that designer's egg, a woman evening case that the men had found last night among the brook debris?

Toby babbled on, all innocence.

"If Mr Nick wants it the way him and the lady

274

says it was, then that's how I'll see it. There's none will say different. Is that all, Mr Nick? Constable Ackroyd?"

"For the moment, perhaps," the constable said primly, having apparently taken the 'rubbish' in the brook as referring to the dead woman's effects. Which indeed, might be the case. "Of course, there's quite a bit of a rigmarole to be gone through. Constable Pilsbury and I may be in contact with London. Some connection with the Yard. But that'll depend on Constable Pilsbury's health and the — Shall we consider a post-mortem the next matter of business? In Mincham, of course."

"Then the matter may be more than an accident?" Nick asked.

Roberta felt edgy about the question and did not fail to notice Toby Teague's interest. He cut in with his hearty manner.

"Fancy, now. I wouldn't've thought it. Such an innocent-looking business. And so much else aside from that egg being found."

He was certainly working hard to press the discovery of the jewelled egg case and the half-completed note washed out in last night's storm.

To Roberta's surprise and her secret relief Constable Ackroyd dismissed Nick's question.

"No reason to believe otherwise, as yet. It's just a matter for discussion. All that talk by the young tourist lady who slipped and got herself ensnared in those roots. Kept insisting the body made a grab for her feet. Entangling her, as it were."

Roberta turned away, feeling sick, but at least Nick, with his hand on her shoulder, had seemed to find nothing familiar in the debris found last night — or perhaps he hadn't heard the full description of the jewelled egg. Instead, he objected indignantly to the constable's animation of the body.

"Must we talk as if the unfortunate woman was a — a —"

"Ghost?" Toby Teague suggested. "More like one of them things that rise out of the sea, so to speak. Nothin' like that, is there, sir?"

"Certainly not." Ackroyd looked at the publican with a stern rebuke. His bad taste, or peculiar sense of humour had turned the constable against him. Ackroyd asked Nick, "I'm told a Mincham gentleman once known to most of us is expected today. Sir Arthur Laidlaw."

How had he learned that, Roberta wondered.

Ackroyd went on. "You being a friend of Sir Arthur, Mr Demian, you'll no doubt welcome him helping us in our enquiry. Get it all sorted and slipped into the right drawer."

"I understand. Anything we can — that is, I can do."

Roberta wondered if Toby Teague had been responsible for spreading the story of Sir Arthur's expected arrival, emphasising that 'their champion' would be sure to speak for them. Yet one more attack on Nick Demian. This time, more insidious.

Ackroyd ignored Toby and turned to Nick. "It would be in good taste if this fellow clears his premises of them that doesn't belong. They're already sticking heads in, like they'd nothing else to do but gape."

Toby put in, "Sorry, I'm sure, Constable Ackroyd."

He slid toward the doors of the lounge which were still ajar, making motions to shoo away the grinning, toothless old ex-gardener, Samson Brinkby, as well as his grandson Gordon, who usually hand-wrestled Jamie Demian, and narrow-eyed Orin Camberson. Behind them, Roberta saw the heads of women, some of them springing up on their toes for seconds at a time in order to get a glimpse of the goings-on in the lounge. When Toby Teague gestured, they all dropped back reluctantly.

At least, the tourist coach must have taken off with its cargo on the way to Mincham.

"You may go." Ackroyd ordered the publican in a lordly way that didn't at all match his voice. When he was alone again with Nick and Roberta he seemed more willing to rely upon the opinion of the man whose family owned Edenbrook.

Roberta found it interesting, if not very democratic, that Nick accepted his responsible position with so little humility. Obviously, he and his family were used to the role and its associated power.

Ackroyd opened a little typist's notebook and jotted down a couple of pot-hooks which Roberta recognised as from her own school of shorthand.

"I'm told, Mr Demian, that the body may have been that of a woman who left your employ? That would be —" He glanced at the figures on the back of the notebook. "Over six weeks ago."

"If it actually is Mrs DeVrees. I only met her a few times and very casually. But I signed the salary cheques."

"Of course. And this lady here?"

Roberta began, "I never —"

Nick said, "Miss Fisher never met Mrs DeVrees."

"Just so." The constable studied his notebook. Roberta didn't think he was looking there, merely thinking or making her worry, for some reason. "Miss Fisher. Roberta Fisher. Recently interviewed in the matter of a Miss Sybille Halloway's death?"

Roberta took a deep breath; reminded herself that she was innocent of any wrongdoing. But there was the undeniable fact of her presence where two dead women had been found.

She saw that a frowning Nick was about to speak and cut in ahead of him. "My employer died recently in London and there was publicity about it. I had been working on Miss Halloway's autobiography. Then, Sir Arthur Laidlaw asked me to write a report on the contributions made by these villagers to the maintenance of the Edenbrook properties. I never saw or knew the woman who died out there beside that mill. Whoever she was."

"That should settle Miss Fisher's knowledge of this business," Nick put in crisply. "I myself want to conclude some business in Mincham with a Mrs Constance Seddley. About a car accident yesterday. If you like, I can accompany you, constable."

The young man's eyebrows raised. He was obviously more impressed with 'Mrs Constance Seddley' than with Edenbrook's Demians.

"A fine, charitable woman, that Mrs Seddley. Be happy to drive you in, sir. We can call upon Sir Arthur's advice later."

"Excellent." Nick seemed perfectly happy, but as Ackroyd prepared to leave, Nick took Roberta's hands in his. Her hands were shaking and she welcomed his warmth. "Art will be arriving any minute and Sheila may not have heard about this business here at the mill."

Anxious to be of help, she volunteered, "I can tell them if you think best. I'll go at once. But what about our 'friends' here? Thanks to Toby Teague they must know by now that we aren't enemies."

"No. Bosom friends." Under the curious and interested eyes of Constable Ackroyd he lifted her chin and kissed her. Perhaps out of sheer bravado. His heated kiss took her breath away, but though she had to grab for his jacket lapels to get her breath back, she loved the excitement of his mouth on hers and the desire he aroused.

Then he left the lounge, following Ackroyd with two long strides. Roberta waited a minute or two, her head whirling with ideas, good and bad. Then she went to the door after them and almost fell into Toby Teague's arms. The publican grinned, showing all his teeth, though he pretended to be concerned over another matter.

"Ah, now. And there's me missing the police officer like the clumsy fellow I am. I thought I might let Constable Ackroyd check the things washed along in the brook last night. Do you suppose the constable knows any French?"

"I'm sure I couldn't say." He hadn't touched her but she felt as if he might and was repulsed.

"True, Miss. It's you that knows the language. You and that Mrs DeVrees." He must have sensed her start. He went on pleasantly enough, "But her being gone and all, we can wait."

Trying to recall exactly what the half-finished note in the jewelled egg had said, Roberta managed to dismiss the matter with a suitable indifference.

"Probably. Excuse me. I'm off to see your very good friend, Sir Arthur Laidlaw. He's awfully interested in the affairs of the village, as you know." She punctuated this with a short laugh. "Who knows better?"

She could tell that her manner puzzled him but by the time he thought of a reply she was halfway down the square and passing the chemist's shop.

Chapter Nineteen

Before Roberta reached the turn in the brook and the stony path she saw Will Brinkby's son, Gordon, the handwrestling opponent of Jamie's, wandering along the side of the chemist's shop. He appeared to be examining the weathered wooden exterior, looking for something.

A way of entry?

Had his father returned his own key to McQuarry? How had he done so, and when, unless he had been to Mincham and back.

Young Gordon saw her, but his eyes looked shifty to Roberta and he certainly avoided her. He moved across her path to the brook, moving along over wet pebbles toward the east end of the double set of cottages. Going home, obviously. The Brinkby cottage was within fifty feet of Demian House. Roberta slowed her own pace to keep from walking beside him. He found a branch broken off by the wind and rain the night before, and dragged it along through the shallow water. This slowed him still further and caused Roberta to stop in her tracks.

She looked around. All the attractions of a crime scene still held some tourists and a few locals around the square or crossing the little mill bridge. No one seemed to be interested in her.

Toby Teague and his pals must be talking things over in the pub.

Roberta moved calmly off the path, acting out some of Gordon Brinkby's curiosity over McQuarry's shop and its setting. A few bushes gave the side and the rear of the building a look even more rural than the rest of the village. In the case of McQuarry's house it also appeared almost sinister, with every window on this side shuttered and forbidding.

No matter, she told herself when the back door suddenly opened under her hand. She knew Nick had closed and locked it yesterday before he left with her on the drive to Mincham. Since Will Brinkby's son had just left the building it seemed likely to Roberta that he had unlocked the door, and with a key presumably given to his father by McQuarry for whom Brinkby worked. Hadn't McQuarry mentioned the man when he permitted Roberta to use some of his daily records, if they contained facts helpful to the villagers?

She opened the door and slipped in, looking around what had once been a kitchen and as she remembered now, contained some of his pharmaceutical items.

But why should Gordon Brinkby be sneaking around the place? It was unlikely that he was sent by his father, who would very probably prefer to find whatever he wanted to know, himself. No prowling around was necessary. Why then had the son been so furtive as he slunk around the outside of the shop?

Roberta studied the kitchen and to the best of her knowledge found nothing out of place. One of the old-fashioned window shades in the kitchen was raised, but that only made it more natural. She remembered that it had been raised yesterday. Through the open doorway into the front of the building daylight illuminated the centre section of the front room with its counter and wall displays of well-known non-prescription drugs.

It was in this room that Roberta became conscious of a sudden memory; a smell she associated with sweets, when she was a child. Liquorice. Every child she knew, except Roberta herself, loved it. There were proud displays of the Italian confectionery tasting of and smelling like liqueurs, after-dinner drinks, anisette. But it was liquorice, not anisette. She had smelled it yesterday when the teenagers came down the brook to watch the 'Great Hand-Wrestling Championship'. She had caught a whiff of it as Gordon Brinkby passed her on previous occasions. She hadn't particularly noticed it today but it was clear that he had been in this room.

Everything seemed to be in order at first glance. She walked around the room, peering into shadowy corners, and all looked fairly in order. It was not until she reached the area beside the exhibit of non-prescription drugs in a glazed cabinet that her shoe scraped up a piece of paper and she reached down to remove it from her sole.

Her footstep had torn it and she was about to

leave the lined paper, about three inches long, on the shelf before her. But as she opened the glass door she recognised that the paper had been torn from the bottom of a lengthy account book.

'. . . an American medication. Do not carry it. On way to Mincham, so decided add massage salve to my —'

The rest of the note was on another page. On the other side of this torn page was a different message:

'7 May 1985. Sultana missing. Never runs wild. Trying to locate her, saw again the old blue Italian car parked near the weir. Driver crouching. Or small. Meeting Mrs Demian again as she jogs?'

Whatever else McQuarry noted must have been on the upper half of the page, or the upper half of the other side.

She shifted headache medicines, pills for every conceivable pain, and dozens of other items, but there were no daily record books stacked anywhere. Not even the ones McQuarry had told her she could use in looking for evidence of the good works by local tenants. McQuarry had permitted her to use notes of the last ten years but they must be dated after 7 May 1985. This torn piece of his daily record made that clear. The accident involving Veda Demian, Jamie and Sultana obviously occurred after, or perhaps on 7 May.

She spent some fruitless minutes looking for more ledger pages, torn or otherwise, but found none. She gave up finally and tried the public door opening onto the brook path. It was still locked. She turned around and walked back through the little building and went out of the kitchen door.

She walked around the shop, practically in Gordon Brinkby's footsteps and came out again on the brook path; she intended to head for Demian House to help Sheila entertain her boyfriend, Sir Arthur Laidlaw, and doubtless hear from him how she had let down the kindly villagers.

She had barely taken two steps when a stout man in grey uniform called to her from the far end of the village square. He followed this up with a sweeping wave of the arm that might have summoned all of Edenbrook, except that most of the visitors had collected around the pub to make comparisons of each other's newly purchased souvenirs.

While she was trying to identify the man in the uniform, Roberta looked beyond the exuberant fellow and suddenly recognised the big grey Lincoln parked beside the Camberson shop. From an open rear window an elegant hand beckoned to her. Sir Arthur Laidlaw followed this by sticking out his equally elegant head.

She waved back, half expecting the ubiquitous

Mrs Peavis to pop out of the front seat of the car, but except for his chauffeur, Weems, he was alone. Weems called to Roberta, and this time aroused the interest of old Samson Brinkby who had been shuffling into Camberson's tobacconist shop but stopped as he heard the chauffeur's voice.

Even from this distance Roberta could make out the friendly grin which exposed Samson Brinkby's pink gums and a couple of yellow teeth, not yet sacrificed to age or lack of care. Coming up the slope at her usual quick pace, Roberta gave the old man her own friendly nod and smile but for some reason this seemed to startle Samson and he ducked into the shop.

By this time, just as Roberta reached the square, a group around Toby Teague broke up in front of the pub ·entrance and she noticed Toby watching her with interest. She pointed towards the big car and as she passed Toby she called out.

"Must be checking up on me for you tenants."

Toby's eyebrows raised in a question and he shrugged. Then he moved a little closer. "Hope you'll have a report that satisfies Sir Arthur. He's been mighty good to us."

She pretended to be optimistic. "We'll see. Won't be my fault if he's not satisfied."

He nodded. His smile was a mere sketch and she had no doubt he was suspicious, but she wasn't sure yet what he was suspicious of except possibly her close friendship with Nick Demian.

Sometimes she wondered if he had known all along that she would fall for Nick. It was an absurd idea. How would it serve him and his friends? But much of what was happening here seemed senseless. It had also begun to take on a hint of the macabre as if a long-dried stain was gradually coming back to its original bloody life.

These unpleasant thoughts took a good deal away from the smile with which she greeted Sir Arthur as he got out of the car and offered his hand.

His touch was cool, light, like his tall, slender figure and she was grateful. After the last forty-eight hours she enjoyed Sir Arthur's reserve by comparison with the unpleasant doubts she felt now against all those friendly villagers who had been rapidly reduced to suspects, out for all they could get from Nick Demian or anyone else.

For all his pleasant manner, Sir Arthur did not shed his own superior attitude. He never let any-one forget who he was. After all the propaganda he must have received from Toby, the Brinkbys, the Cambersons and their like, he still had changed very little from the charming but superior being she first met the day after Sybille Halloway's death.

And it was Arthur Laidlaw, after all, who had introduced her to Nick Demian.

"Come along, Miss Fisher. Do join me. Weems will take us back to the bridge. It's much nearer Demian House. I abhor useless labour and tiresome hikes."

She laughed, thanked him, and got in. As they seated themselves and Weems started back, retracing his drive over Mincham Lane, she sensed that Sir Arthur was looking her over. The idea made her nervous but she pretended to be preoccupied with the business which had brought her to Edenbrook.

"I'm afraid there is less evidence to use in the Demian tenants' plea than you would expect, sir."

"Oh? That is disappointing." He added lightly, "I hope my friend Nick isn't placing difficulties in your way."

He sounded pompous but she considered the source and decided this language was something that had become a part of him.

"No. I am happy to say Mr Demian has behaved quite reasonably, all things considered. He has a good deal to contend with."

"Really?" It was a remark, not a question. "Somehow, I had the impression —" He broke off. "No matter. What's this that Weems heard a few minutes ago about some woman's body being found in Mincham Lane?"

News travels fast. But she kept that remark to herself.

"Not quite in the Lane. Actually, she was found in the pond beside the Old Mill. They believe it was the French housekeeper at Demian House."

That caught him. "Not Mrs DeVrees! Stunning female, we always thought. Ambitious, of course."

" 'We', you said. I thought no one in the village liked her?"

He shrugged but she was sure he had been embarrassed. "That is to say, she had ambitions. If Nick hadn't been first in line, I always felt that she might have settled for a beaten-up fellow like me." He stiffened anxiously. "For heaven's sake, please don't quote me to Sheila. I didn't actually have designs on the woman. Not my sort, at all."

She wanted to laugh, but didn't. "Don't worry. I'll keep your secret." Just for cussedness, she added, "Sheila Demian says the Frenchwoman got in a huff about something a month or two ago and quit without giving notice. She walked to the square here to catch the Mincham bus."

"But she slipped on the wall and fell into that disgusting muck beside the mill?"

"So I understand. If it was Mrs DeVrees."

"No question of foul play, I hope. That would lower the worth of the area for Nick."

Gossip. Gossip. All that from Toby Teague? She wondered.

She said, "Well, there isn't any way of knowing. The obvious answer is that she stumbled and fell into that muddy water and was caught in the vegetation rotting beneath the surface. Something of that sort."

He didn't argue the matter. "Horrible thought. Such an attractive woman!"

She nodded, even though she hadn't seen the dead woman properly, and was reverting to the original subject of how little she had to justify

Demian's tenants in their complaint, when he sighed and looked out of the window. It was almost humorous to see this man with his aristocratic bearing and cool self-assurance complain.

"I really cannot understand Sheila." He glanced at Roberta, adding unnecessarily, "Miss Demian. What does Sheila want in a husband? We've been — I suppose you could call it friends, since long before my first marriage. She saw me through both my divorces. Yet the annoying creature simply won't give me a straight answer."

Roberta wondered if Sheila's cool elusiveness was her great attraction for the barrister. Roberta would not have laughed for the world but she had an almost irresistable desire to ask him, "What happened before, between and after your various marriages and divorces?"

But he didn't strike her as quite the type to appreciate her making light of his private life or his long 'passion' for Sheila Demian. It struck her as a fantasy image fixed in his mind, of his life as it might have been.

She assured him gently, "Maybe this time you will be in luck. She spoke of you very warmly, I thought. But like most unmarried woman past their first flush of youth, she has made a life for herself and likes it through long habit."

His austere face softened and he thanked her for her encouragement, adding, "You may be right. It is all habit, this living alone. And naturally, she likes it by comparison. I seem to recall she never got on well with Veda."

"No. I don't imagine she would. They couldn't have been the least alike."

His chuckle was soft, not as harsh and abrupt as his words sounded.

"Indeed not. They were entirely different women. Ah! Here is the bridge." He leaned forward. "Weems, stop here. Then take the car in to Mincham, and have it serviced at the garage. And ring down tomorrow morning. I'll probably be driving into town to see what they've got Nick into, poor devil."

"That I will, Sir Arthur."

Arthur Laidlaw did not wait for Weems to offer Roberta his hand but got out and made a gallant gesture of offering his arm. She accepted it but couldn't help thinking with some amusement that the man was of a time past. She preferred Nick Demian's easy, unobtrusive effort.

They followed the brook, gentle and pleasant as it now looked and sounded. Even after last night's wind and rain she thought it much more attractive, less sinister, this afternoon than it had been the night she arrived and had to make her way from the bridge after Sheila, and through a thicket, before she came out into the open and found the little brookside cottages before her. At such a time Sir Arthur's gallantry would have been appreciated very much.

Demian House was older than its neighbours and stood out because of its two-and-a-half storeys but otherwise, architecturally, it fitted in with its wooded surroundings.

Sir Arthur carried a closed umbrella over his free arm and he pointed it at the house.

"If I owned this wretched, blighted area I would tear it all down and build some of those bright, modern tract houses one sees in the States. But I can't get Nick to agree. He sees it all as a sacred heritage. And of course, his bitterness makes him stubborn. Odd, isn't it, on the very steps of a new century?"

Although she thought of herself as fairly modern, she was surprised at his attitude — converse to his old-world courtesy — and pretended not to hear it. Instead, she said brightly as they came to the two front steps, "Well, here we are."

"And none the worse for wear, in spite of that jungle we've just passed through."

To Roberta's amusement Sheila Demian did not meet them at the door. She was obviously giving Sir Arthur very little encouragement.

Merlina opened the door to them, showering the barrister with all the admiration he might have expected from the object of his long, if dilatory pursuit.

Sir Arthur bloomed under the girl's fawning attentions and she coaxed a compliment from him by simpering, "Oh, Sir Arthur, you meet so many really important people. You couldn't remember me."

Ironically enough, while he was assuring Merlina that she was not a young lady easily forgotten, Sheila came down the impressive staircase and out across the lobby to greet Roberta whom she spoke to first.

"Heavens! What a day you've had, finding that body! I know the place well. It should be drained. Have they found out who she is?"

She gave Sir Arthur her hand briefly, interrupting Roberta's reply to dismiss her suitor's warm greeting.

"Yes, I see you, Art. Thanks for coming. But you really weren't needed. They are hardly going to march Nick off to prison quite yet."

"Prison! For what reason, my dear Sheila? You are joking, I devoutly hope." He laughed. "But that is so like you. Mrs Peavis always says — but that's beside the point. How lovely you are looking by the way! No, I simply came to lend a legal aspect to this quarrel between Nick and the Demian tenants." He leaned around the fawning Merlina to kiss Sheila.

Watching the two of them, Roberta noted that his kiss landed somewhere on Sheila's left temple and seemed to have no softening effect on her. Poor Arthur Laidlaw! All his good looks, elegance and title had no effect on the self-sufficient Sheila Demian.

Or perhaps Sheila was in a bad mood. She had resented Sir Arthur's arrival which suggested the Demians needed him. Was the blow to the Demians, and especially Nick, frightening enough to bring a man of Sir Arthur's standing?

Even the fact that Nick's sister herself might admit this terrifying thought haunted Roberta.

She knew nothing, only that which Nick had told her about his wife's death and surely less about the Frenchwoman. He had said he scarcely knew her. The gossip between Toby and Camberson and again, with Will Brinkby, was the wildest kind of talk among men who had reason to spread false stories about their landlord.

And who was the man the Frenchwoman was writing to in that partially finished letter found in the jewelled egg? Roberta couldn't believe that Nick Demian would put up with all that coy, almost childish talk about speaking French and the rest.

No. The explanation was elsewhere.

The paper Roberta carried in her pocket, torn from one of McQuarry's ledgers, had mentioned a small man, 'crouched down', who was waiting to meet Veda Demian as she jogged. McQuarry had seen him waiting before. The only 'small man' Roberta knew reasonably well since this business began was Orin Camberson. McQuarry, Nick, Sir Arthur, Toby and his village cronies, were all tall. Even the women, Sheila Demian and the others were fairly tall, but unlikely to be mistaken for men.

There were the younger set, of course, boys and girls. But at the time of Veda Demian's death they were all children, between four and six perhaps.

Thank God, Sheila changed the subject.

"Jamie wants to see Miss Fisher about his play. Something concerning ancient man in the Alps.

Do I have that right? Merlina, call Master Jamie."

Merlina hesitated with the barrister's topcoat over her arm and his umbrella hanging from her supple wrist.

"I was just tending to Sir Arthur."

"Never mind Sir Arthur. Run along and call Jamie."

Merlina rolled her eyes at Sir Arthur. He seemed a bit startled and avoided her blue eyes, so she shuffled over to the staircase and began to climb without enthusiasm.

Roberta said hurriedly, feeling herself very much in the way of Sir Arthur's romantic pursuit, "No, no. I'll go. I want to talk to him about a camera."

Sheila had no curiosity about 'a camera' or its connection with the villagers. She turned to Sir Arthur. "Come and see what that wind and rain last night did to our trellises. Samson is repairing the rose trellis now. The roses have been gone for some weeks but the roots are all on end, thanks to the wind."

Sir Arthur received his marching orders willingly and they set off through the archway under the staircase and headed for the long French windows where old Samson Brinkby was stringing wire on a trellis.

Roberta took her hostess's departure with Sir Arthur as her own cue and continued up the stairs. At the landing halfway up she swung around the delicate little stand with its illuminated lamp and stepped on a coil of the lamp's cord. She kicked it under the stand and went on.

She was always glad to see Jamie but this time, knowing he had been at school in Mincham with his friends, she hoped he would also bring word of McQuarry's condition. There was the possibility as well that he had learned something from his father about the body of the dead woman, or even about Nick's interview with the old lady who caused yesterday's car accident.

Jamie met her in the doorway of what appeared to be a comfortable bedsitting room. Several of the normal appliances had been provided for his needs, the long bed being low but comfortable; a chaise longue with a cushioned rail for him to stretch his often painful leg; books, maps and globes everywhere; strong handholds on everything, and a great deal of cheerful sunlight that could be shaded by venetian blinds easily reached. The west view out of the window looked over the tops of trees to the left and to thatched roofs straight ahead, until the brook turned at the distant chemist's shop.

Jamie shook her hand warmly, giving her his wide grin, and welcomed her in.

"I could've come down if they'd only called me," he reminded her. "I'm not a cripple. Not really. But come in, I've been working on a treatment."

They went in together. His limp and dragging leg handicapped him surprisingly little. He offered her an old, green-cushioned rocking chair, saying proudly, "Best in the house. Everyone loves it."

She sat down, looking at him with concern. He was right about the comfort of the chair but his mention of treatment suggested more.

"What's this about your treatment?"

"Not that treatment." He slapped his hip scornfully and continued on a note of triumph. "I read all about it. The treatment comes before the first draft. And before the treatment you have to do a kind of little synopsis. They call it something else."

She began to laugh, partly in relief, partly at his precocious study of writing for the screen, television or otherwise.

"Perfect. You'll go far. Maybe I can find you something I did on a television one-shot last year. I brought a couple of scripts over to show Miss Halloway, in case she wasn't sure I could handle her life story. Of course, that's not the same as a biography, but anyway, she didn't want to see them."

She reached out to help him draw up the chair but saw that she wasn't needed.

"She didn't read your scripts? Why not? I would have."

She grinned. "And so you shall. But they weren't exciting enough for Sexy Sybille, I suppose." She changed the subject. "You certainly don't seem the worse for wear after yesterday's crash and last night's rain."

"Me? No. That's because poor Mac got the

jolt that should have been mine."

She didn't want to cramp his enthusiasm for his manuscript but this gave her a chance to satisfy her anxiety about more urgent matters.

"While you were in Mincham today, did you hear anything about the lady who crashed into us?"

"It was a plain accident. It must have been. I saw old Mac at the hospital and I just heard him agree with Father that the lady couldn't help it. Her car was shunted from behind."

Her hands were cold and clammy. She laced her fingers tightly together. "Deliberately?"

His big eyes grew larger as he stared at her.

"Of course not. Nobody in our country would hurt an old lady deliberately would they?"

I'm crazy, Roberta thought. My imagination is really running wild, all because I read more into looks, hints and silences between Nick and McQuarry than I should have.

The thought of the two men put her in mind of Nick's suggestion about the camera. For some reason Nick, and probably McQuarry, wanted instant pictures of the various villagers. If her imagination wasn't too frenzied, did the two men wanted to identify an Edenbrook tenant to some-one else, someone other then Constance Seddley? If so, who? And for what reason?

She started to mention the camera to Jamie who relieved her by saying he knew all about it.

"Father asked me if he could borrow my in-stant camera. Then he had another idea and said 'skip it'. I think he spoke about it to Sister Long-acre; said her brother could do it. Nobody at Edenbrook knew him. He was going to come here right away as if he was a newspaperman, a photographer. About the dead body, you know."

She hoped it would work, but when Toby and his friends heard about it there probably would be trouble. Unless, of course, they liked the idea of having their pictures in the papers about an unexplained death.

Jamie looked out towards the treetops behind the Edenbrook houses. "It'll be sunset in a little while. But tomorrow we're sure to have a London tour in. You know, the lady in the mill pond might bring a whole coachload of tourists."

"I hope your father and Mr McQuarry know what they are doing."

"Oh, Father always does. I wanted to help, but I gave Father my word I wouldn't leave the house until he came back from Mincham." He added, a trifle shyly, "It sounds funny today, about a man's word and all. But with Father, I like to keep it."

"I'm glad you feel that way."

He had a more cheerful idea. "Aunt Sheila and Sir Arthur will have cocktails pretty soon. Maybe Schrammy will have some peach tarts for you and me. She's very good."

"Better than Mrs DeVrees?"

She wished she hadn't said it. It seemed deceptive, like laying a trap. But he took the remark innocently enough.

"Well, I only met her once. When I was home during the holidays. She was . . . you know, formal. Like French ladies are. She looked at me awfully long sometimes." He saw her frown and guessed her critical thought. "No. Not a bad look. Not any awful pity, either. She said she knew a crippled boy. That's what she called it. But it made me feel — well — uncomfortable."

"Of course, it did."

He went on, thoughtfully but not too deeply concerned, as if he merely regretted that this stranger might have been the victim of a horrible death. "I hope it wasn't her that went like that. I mean — do they know it was the French lady?"

"I haven't heard yet."

But she couldn't help wondering if Jamie had suspected the woman of trying to take his mother's place in his father's life. Perhaps it had never occurred to him.

"Let's go down and find Mrs Schramm."

She was about to slow her naturally fast pace but felt he would resent it and they started out together, passing Merlina who puffed up her blonde hair at the sight of him, gave him a seductive look and continued along the top landing.

As they approached the staircase from the windowless upper hall, Sheila Demian and Sir Arthur came in from the garden. Sheila called up, "Wait, Jamie. That damned stair light is out."

Jamie, who had reached the top stair, looked annoyed. "It's not dark yet Aunt Sheila. The sun isn't even down."

Roberta put her hand out but her fingertips barely touched his sleeve. He went on more cheerfully, "Come on. Let me escort you, Miss Fisher."

He moved slowly enough, almost gracefully. Only the drag of his heavily encased leg spoiled the picture. He and Roberta reached the next landing amid an exasperated reminder from Sheila.

"Jamie! I asked you not —"

His good foot had made the descent easily but his dragging leg caught in a coil of cord across the landing carpet. Sir Arthur cried, "Good God!" just as Roberta clutched Jamie's arm, but neither the barrister's shock nor Roberta's hand saved him; the boy saved himself by his hard-as-iron grasp on the banister.

He recovered rapidly as Sir Arthur and Sheila ran up the stairs to him. Only Roberta was obsessed by something else. She herself had kicked the lamp cord back under the stand when she went up fifteen or twenty minutes ago. What was it doing, then, in Jamie's way?

Chapter Twenty

With Roberta's free hand she reached under the lampshade and grasped the light bulb. It was barely warm. Someone must have turned it of as soon as she had passed by before. The bulb seemed loose. She gave it a quick twist. The light came on. With her mind a confusion of thoughts, she managed a falsely bright remark.

"Loose bulb. That's all. Thank heaven Jamie was so quick."

Sheila moistened her lips. She looked pale and shocked.

"Jamie? Are you all right?"

Sir Arthur reached for her anxiously. "The boy is fine. But you look like the devil, my dear. Come and sit down. Where is that chair that used to be on the landing? Ah, here. Sit down a moment. That's my girl."

Sheila surprised Roberta by obeying like a dutiful child. Sir Arthur kissed Sheila's cheek gently, then looked over her head at Roberta.

"Miss Fisher, would you mind getting Miss Demian some water?"

Sheila was recovering. Obviously, she didn't enjoy being treated like an invalid.

"Really, you are behaving absurdly, Art." She looked up at Roberta, smiling a little. She still looked pale in the lamplight, but her blue-grey eyes flashed. "I hate water. Make it a tot of whisky, if you don't mind — Roberta. Mrs Schramm will get it for you."

In spite of the tension Jamie's near miss had caused, Roberta smiled at Sir Arthur's pained expression. He had certainly gone about winning Sheila Demian in the wrong way.

She turned to go down the last flight of stairs, passing Jamie as she went. He had two fingers wedged between his foot and the brace. He pulled his fingers out with something shining in his palm. The lamplight flashed dark as wine on the surface of the stone in a heavy gold ring. He stared at it, speechless. It was Sir Arthur who gave vent to all their feelings.

"Good Lord! It's a ring. Like —" He looked around, then added lamely, "It's your mother's ring, isn't it, my boy?"

"No," Sheila cut in without expression. "It's Sybille Halloway's ring, the one she gave to Miss Fisher . . . How did you get it, Jamie?" The last was said accusingly.

For one terrible moment Jamie blinked back angry and humiliating tears. But they remained on his lashes. Roberta wasn't entirely sure he hadn't taken the ring. He had been fascinated by it, and it belonged to his family in any case. However, she wouldn't give Sheila or her titled boyfriend the pleasure of having the last word.

Roberta snapped, "Why wouldn't he have it? It was his in the first place and given to a stranger. That stranger, Miss Halloway, gave it to me, and I gave it back to its rightful owner, Mrs Demian's son."

"It sounds eminently logical to me," Sir Arthur agreed. "I think we owe young Jamie an apology."

Jamie stood up with the luckless opal in his palm.

"Take it! I don't want it. You never wanted me to have it anyway, Aunt Sheila. It makes you think of my mother." He threw the ring at her.

Sir Arthur looked angry and began pompously, "Now, look here, young man!"

But Roberta could see that Sheila Demian was far more hurt than indignant. She had flinched as the heavy ring grazed her cheek but when Sir Arthur picked it up and presented it to her, she shook her head.

"It belongs to Jamie. I was mistaken. I'm sorry."

No one was more shaken than Roberta when Jamie looked at her, his eyes blazing.

"I hate it! You never gave it to me, and I never stole it. You just said that because you were sorry for me. Well, you needn't be. I wouldn't take it, anyway. It's bad luck."

They all heard Nick Demian's voice in the lobby below as he spoke to the housekeeper. "I suppose so. It's nothing to me. Mrs Schramm!" he raised his voice; evidently, the housekeeper had added something. "If she has no purpose for the stuff, do what you want with it. We'll see about it in a few minutes."

He was not the only one who had spoken loudly. He strolled into the hall and looked up.

"What the devil has happened? I could hear you clear out on the steps."

Roberta felt that a great weight had been lifted. Nick was back again. He would make Jamie feel better. As for the other two, and herself, she didn't care. She and they had all behaved stupidly. Worst of all, they had hurt Jamie unnecessarily.

Sir Arthur was startled, but with his arm still around Sheila's waist, he called down to Nick who was hanging his coat carelessly on the newel post.

"Good evening. Just in time, I see."

Nick looked up. "What is it? A parliamentary debate on the staircase?"

Sir Arthur explained. "A mistake, Nick. Come and settle this. Make my peace with Sheila and your boy."

Jamie started down but Nick met him halfway, cuffing the boy's chin in a friendly way.

"Now, what's this all about?"

"They thought —" Jamie cleared his throat. "It was a mistake."

"What? Even the silver-tongued kingpin of the courts couldn't settle it?"

Nick shook hands with Sir Arthur who looked embarrassed and nodded. "A stupid mistake. On our parts. We all hope the boy will forgive us. Believe me, I never felt less silver-tongued."

Sheila brushed aside politeness, explaining sourly, "Someone's idea of humour. Jamie found an opal ring here on the landing and we thought he had taken it from Miss Fisher." She held out the ring. In the lamplight its deep colours looked like dried blood to Roberta and she was more repulsed than ever at the sight.

Nick took the ring, studying Roberta. He looked as if he understood and, thank God, didn't think she was guilty of accusing Jamie. His eyes were warmer than she remembered. "Miss Fisher has already offered it to Jamie, so she can hardly think he took it now. I refused for him yesterday. Anyway, I should have been here to greet our guest." He put the ring in her hand, leaning over a little, which gave him a chance to mouth the words 'thank you'. This must mean that he believed, or forgave her in this ridiculous mess over an unwanted and unlucky ring.

She shook her head but he refused to take it back. She said, "I hate it. It was never mine. I am a — call me a courier from Miss Halloway to the Demian family. Besides, I'm beginning to believe it is definitely unlucky."

"Oh, come now, Miss Fisher," Sir Arthur scoffed, but with a certain amount of teasing. "A valuable ring can always be sold. The money received surely has no 'unlucky' taint."

Nick grinned at Roberta. "What about some charity? A good influence beyond the reach of curses, and suchlike."

"Anything to be rid of it." She put it into his

hand and he took it back, his fingers lingering over hers until he saw that his action was being observed by his sister and Sir Arthur. He turned away from her at once. She wondered why, but so many things had happened in the last few days that she wasn't going to pry into them now. She was *almost* sure he loved her but apparently didn't want either his sister or his friend to know it.

Nick said suddenly, "Well, what are we doing here on the staircase when I rushed home to be in time for cocktails. While I'm at it, Art, welcome to Demian House, though I expect Sheila has already done the honours."

"Sheila has been enchanting as always," Sir Arthur announced gallantly, though that lady did not look as if she relished exaggerated compliments.

"Never mind that. Nick, what happened about the body? I hope we won't be asked to give evidence or anything. Was the woman from here? Was she Mrs DeVrees?"

Nick shook his head. "No clear proof yet. The death seems to have stirred interest in the City. A London photographer was in the square an hour ago getting pictures of the entire village. We should see Edenbrook in glorious Technicolour any hour."

The fact that he had procured the pictures he wanted thrilled Jamie, but to Roberta's relief he said nothing after glancing at her and nodding.

Since there was no chance for her to speak

with Nick privately, she was glad when Merlina clattered along the upper floor hall and called down to Nick.

"Mrs Schramm says are you coming, Mr Nick? Miss Demian?"

Nick shrugged. "Sheila, this is your department. Schrammy says some women will be here tonight for our contribution. They've put off the play because of the woman's death. But the committee wants to have a sale for the tourists next Tuesday."

From the stairhead Merlina rambled on enthusiastically. "Furniture and bric-a-brac makes the biggest money, Ma'am, as I understand it, but Mrs Schramm says the attic room's all full of pretty clothes. They can be sold as 'used gowns' and all, but some are barely worn. Costumes for the theatre, you know. Amateur dramatics."

"Oh, no," Sheila murmured, rolling her eyes. "Not tonight, not with everything else happening today. As for those cases in the attic, I meant to look into them before summer, but somehow . . ." She made an apologetic *moue* and shrugged.

"Some things are nice, Miss Sheila," Merlina put in. "Ever so."

"Sounds like a worthwhile business," Roberta said. "I'm sorry about what happened to the lady who drowned, but this charity drive, with salable items, surely couldn't offend anyone."

The two men exchanged looks. Not quite boredom yet; reluctant acceptance summed it up better. Nick said, "You ladies aren't going to cheat us out of our drinks. We'll let them accompany this fascinating floor show."

There was general agreement, with Sir Arthur amused and Jamie speaking up for something he called 'lemon shandy' which his father corrected. "An old salt would call that 'shandy gaff'." But he promised to deliver, and Roberta put in like any American tourist for 'Scotch on ice'.

"I won't comment on that," Nick announced to universal cheers.

But not quite universal, Roberta found. Sheila, still moody, objected. "I've better things to do than watch that child in a fashion show. However —" She pushed everyone aside and went down to supervise Mrs Schramm and her blonde model.

The men, with Jamie and Roberta, adjourned to the large library on the ground floor, where Nick settled Roberta and his son. Jamie seemed to be in better spirits now that he was accepted as one of the grown-ups and after a minute or two he went to look out of the south window at the hovering woods. The thickly grown trees and undergrowth looked much closer in the evening twilight. Artistically, Roberta liked them but she had to admit that they gave her a chilling sense of being hemmed in at this hour.

As Nick and Sir Arthur went off to wheel in the glass and gold drinks trolley, Nick remarked to Sir Arthur, "Something tells me there will be a rush for the nearest *Bierstube* very shortly. This promises to be a long parade."

Roberta lingered in the open library door and as Sir Arthur raised his voice in a 'magisterial' scolding, she moved out into the hall to hear more.

"That poor creature managed to ruin your life."

"Veda? Don't be an absolute idiot! She made her feelings — or lack of them — for me pretty clear. The truth is, if it hadn't been for Jamie we'd have been divorced long before she died."

"And you tar all other women with the same brush."

"What women, for God's sake! My trouble with the villagers has nothing to do with women and never did."

There was a little pause, the rattle of glass. Sir Arthur said, "I'm glad to hear you've got over Veda. I really believe she would have fancied my poor tired title if she hadn't had a chance at your millions."

"I don't suppose the fact that you had a wife of your own would have stopped her?"

Sir Arthur laughed. "No. But Meg herself was quite capable. There wasn't much to choose between them. And my second wife seems to have been no better. We never were lucky with women, you and I."

"Until now."

Roberta held her breath, hoping, but not sure. Until Sir Arthur asked in astonishment, "You can't mean to try your luck again!"

"First and last time, I promise you."

Sir Arthur was silent a minute. Roberta listened anxiously as he went on in his quiet way. "Weems says they babble about you and your French housekeeper. And others."

"There are no others. There never were. I hardly knew Mrs DeVrees."

"Very well. Enough said. Weems is an incurable gossip anyway."

"He must be a liar as well. Have you found Jamie's lemon shandy?"

"Right here, dear fellow." There was a pause. Then Sir Arthur said plaintively, "I wish you had a little influence with your sister. Sheila seems to be more set against me than she was two months ago."

"And she will continue to be unless you go for a bed and breakfast set-up near London."

"Good Lord!"

Roberta smiled in sympathy with the barrister as she slipped back into the library just as Jamie turned around. She was afraid he had noticed her eavesdropping. If he had, he gave no indication.

He asked, "Would you mind if I sat there, beside you? It's nice to sit by friends, don't you think?"

Touched and pleased, she agreed. "I certainly do. And you're my first real friend here. Remember? I met you in the Grill Room of the Savoy."

"Sure, I do. You were — well, nice."

"So were you. Now, we're set for your lemon

311

shandy and my Scotch."

"Excuse me, but it's called whisky here."

The two men came in at that minute, Sir Arthur pushing the delicate old drinks trolley, Nick carrying two decanters and a bottle.

From down the hall Mrs Schramm called in her husky voice, "We've got her pinned up, Miss Demian. And a pretty picture she is."

Sheila preceded them to the library. She ordered her brother, "Pour me a drink. I need sustenance after all that twisting and turning. The girl is too plump for most of the things. I think many of them belonged to Veda. Do you care if we get rid of them, Nick?"

Nick handed Roberta her drink, then poured and gave his sister hers. He shrugged.

"Not if it's for charity. They aren't doing any good here."

To Roberta's relief Jamie seemed undisturbed by the possibility of losing his mother's wardrobe. As Mrs Schramm's voice drifted in from the hall, Jamie whispered to Roberta, "I think Father has his instant pictures." He went on in an audible voice, "What do you think he wanted them for?"

But the two men had their attention diverted to the doorway where Mrs Schramm made a sweeping wave with her strong right arm, informing everyone, "The tourists, or the theatre folk, they pay plenty for this one."

Sir Arthur gave a handsome pretence of looking impressed but Roberta saw that Nick's interest was less than complete. He looked at one of the fringed, black, beaded evening dresses of the latest 'mini' length and then took a long swallow of his whisky.

From Roberta's carefully subtle observation he seemed unmoved by any memories aroused by the dress. Sir Arthur nodded approvingly as Merlina strutted around doing full justice to the swinging fringe. Only Sheila spoke her mind, muttering, "How like her!" No one was naive enough to think her comment referred to the young model.

After the second outfit, this time a wildly flowered two-piece silk suit with hem frills that touched somewhat above Merlina's chubby knees, Sheila finished her drink, got up and went to the window. Already, the stars were out. Then she turned and started for the door.

"Don't let me stop the proceedings. I've got to pay Samson Brinkby or he will be out there all night."

Sir Arthur got up and went to the door with her, offering to go with her, but she dismissed him brusquely. She seemed so preoccupied, she had lost all interest in her persistent suitor.

During these moments Roberta asked Nick in a low voice, "Are the French windows always locked?"

Nick was surprised but seemed to understand.

"No. Samson may have gone in and out, although he could have taken the path between the Brinkbys' and our garden."

"Someone rearranged that coil of cord and the

light on the landing. I had kicked the cord out of the way a few minutes earlier. And the light bulb wasn't out. It was simply loosened."

Jamie heard this and watched, wide-eyed but he said nothing. His father's face clouded.

"Damn! I didn't want to think that. I've known old Samson since I was an infant."

Sir Arthur heard the last of this as he returned alone and a trifle dejected. He took his seat but asked, "Hasn't Samson been behaving himself? I know he doesn't do much, but I hope you aren't thinking of turning him off. I'm sure the poor fellow means well."

Nick scowled. "Still worrying about your beloved clients, the villagers?"

"My dear fellow, you have made enough enemies among these primitive people, haven't you? Weems says you are getting a pretty bad name in these parts."

"The hell with Weems! Tell him to mind his own affairs or I will." He raised his voice. "Mrs Schramm, we are ready." A little lower, he went on, "Anything to get this business over."

The barrister sighed. "Nick, you grow more savage every day. Why not soften those rasping edges once in a while. Think of your guest."

"Oh, well, you've heard me before, starting when we were about five years old."

"Not me. I'm referring to Miss Fisher."

"Oh, Roberta." Nick smiled faintly, reached for Roberta's hand and held it a moment. "She's one of the family."

Sir Arthur looked startled.

"Oh. Yes."

Then Merlina stepped in with Mrs Schramm close behind her. The ice-blue sheath gown was stunning in its regal simplicity. Of ankle length it was split up to the knee to make walking easier. The grown-ups watching were forced to admit it was the best of the collection so far.

"Lovely workmanship. I'll bet it's imported," Roberta said, with unintentional offence to the local manufacturers. She could see herself in it and wished her studio friends dressed up more for dinner and social evenings. The girls she knew at the studios either wore outrageous clothes to get on the list of 'worst dressed at the awards' or outfits better suited to wedding cakes.

"Nice," Nick agreed.

It was Jamie who shook up the little group, including Sheila who came into the room at that minute.

Jamie was proudly informative. "It is French. I saw her making it."

"Who?" Sheila asked.

"The French lady. Mrs DeVrees. She was sewing it. She said she knew someone who loved her in blue, like ice."

No one said anything. Only Sir Arthur spoke finally in confusion. "Is she really dead? Sheila, my dear, didn't you say she returned to France without giving notice? You were upset, I remember." He looked around, felt some kind of tension in the room and his voice trailed off. "That is, I must have been mistaken." He laughed in an embarrassed way. "Stupid mistake. I can't imagine how I —"

Ignoring the general atmosphere, Nick said, "Mrs Scramm, while we decide who owned that thing, suppose you let us see whatever else is gathering dust in our attic."

It seemed clear to Roberta. Both she and Nick's sister, and probably Nick as well, believed the dead woman in the mill pond was the Frenchwoman, Mrs DeVrees.

An accident. The woman had slipped and fallen in.

What was she doing down there around the ugly, dangerous pond that evening? Roberta checked herself. No one even knew it had been evening. And why had she left a beautiful dress behind her in a dusty attic? Or was she leaving Edenbrook at all?

A horrifying thought struck her: had she been killed elsewhere and dumped in that awful place?

Mrs Schramm hurried off to change Merlina's gown. She had hardly left the room when Nick got up.

"This is ridiculous. If the clothes belong to the Frenchwoman, I'm going to find out. Schramm mentioned suitcases. They should tell us."

Sheila was already on her feet. Sir Arthur stood up a few seconds later.

"I don't suppose I could add any legal points to the matter, but I am curious. Do you mind?"

Nick made a careless wave of the hand to him,

then said in an unexpectedly gentle voice, "You too, Roberta. Will you?"

"Of course." She tried to let him know he had her full support and belief but the others, the barrister and Sheila Demian, made her uneasy. Still, she was most nervous about Nick.

The others might reason out matters, but did Nick have any inkling of the real fear that gripped her, and possibly his friend, Sir Arthur Laidlaw as well? The hatred and deep resentments of his tenants might be turned against him to a frightening extent. Gossip had, so far, planted suspicions that connected him with the seduction of the Frenchwoman, not to mention hints of 'others'. Even Sir Arthur had fallen for that one, probably because he listened to his garrulous chauffeur, Weems.

But was it just her infatuation with him that made her believe in Nick Demian's innocence?

No. There was more. There was the 'car accident' in Mincham. Roberta had become convinced that it wasn't caused deliberately by Mrs Seddley. Nick's cryptic discussion with McQuarry pointed to another driver who had given Mrs Seddley that nasty jolt, sending her into the side of McQuarry's car. A hit intended for Jamie who would have been sitting there normally?

Roberta could never believe Nick would risk his son's life. The person who drove that unknown car behind Mrs Seddley wanted to further cripple or perhaps kill Jamie, Nick's direct heir to Edenbrook. In Roberta's eyes it always came back to the villagers.

As she walked with the others into the 'Summer Room' which had once been the women's answer to the very masculine library, she remembered the innocent remark from McQuarry's ledger, written sometime just prior to the death of Veda Demian and Sultana, and the crippling of Jamie. She felt the torn piece in her pocket but did not take it out. She knew it by heart.

Someone not too large in an old, blue Italian car, had been waiting for Veda on one of those days as she jogged. She hadn't wanted Jamie along the day she died. The reason would have been obvious if she was meeting someone.

How long had McQuarry stored up his hatred for the person who caused Sultana to be poisoned and ultimately destroyed? His hatred was not for the person or persons who manoeuvred Veda's death. Obviously, he had no use for her. But Sultana was his dearest possession and probably companion.

For ten years had he fed Nick on his hatred? And during that time the villagers' resentment against Nick had grown. Maybe McQuarry was at the back of this. But the idea was absurd. Would he risk his own life in that collision by Mrs Seddley's car and the person in the car behind her?

Impossible.

While Merlina paraded around the room in the French gown, Mrs Schramm pointed out the two suitcases and an old trunk which was full of elbow-length gloves, padded bras and other female necessities.

"That was Mother's trunk," Sheila said. "I remember those pink kid gloves. Yes. And the mink stole underneath."

Neither the barrister nor Nick found it related to the present crisis. Nick turned to one of the suitcases. Not an expensive one, but the brand on the deep brown surface was French and unfamiliar to Roberta. The men realised this too.

Sir Arthur took up a few things and threw them back in the case. "Nothing of yours, I imagine, my dear. Doesn't look like you at all."

Sheila said, "How kind of you to say so, Art!" But there was an edge to the words.

They all recognised that the finely designed garments verged on elegance and were not Sheila's sort at all. Nick found a little square piece of leather that hung by a chain from one handle. He read it aloud.

"Gabrielle Françoise DeVrees."

Chapter Twenty-One

Sir Arthur whistled his surprise. "It seems obvious the lady fell into the pond, and the family assumed she had gone back to France."

"Without any of her luggage?" Sheila asked in a harsh, rasping voice.

Considering her own sympathies, Roberta contradicted her with as much force as she could muster.

"The villagers are very bitter against the Demians. May I remind all of you that they are in and out of Demian House at almost any hour? If the woman didn't die accidentally — and anything is possible — then one of the tenants put her things in the attic, where Mrs Schramm found them."

Mrs Schramm, somewhat agitated, announced to Sheila, "I give my word, Ma'am, I never saw the cases until the girl and I went looking for an old preserving pan, the very thing to prepare some of my special jam recipe in. Neither her nor me saw the tag with her name."

Jamie was staring at the contents of the French case when Nick spoke up for the first time.

"I don't imagine Constable Ackroyd will approve of our rummaging through this. It may constitute evidence."

Everyone looked at Sir Arthur who bit his lip and said after an uncomfortable pause, "I'm afraid you're right." He went on hurriedly, "There is nothing incriminating, so far as we can determine at this point. We haven't even ruled out an accidental death which —" he glanced at Sheila, "I'm much inclined to think is the case."

Though the theory favoured him, Nick, like his sister, seemed determined to put the worst face on the discovery.

"I doubt it. If that gang of would-be conspirators would go this far, they aren't playing with building blocks. A couple of us have suspected for a long time that they were trying to destroy the family, making me sound like a monster, which would benefit them in the courts."

Sir Arthur murmured, "That's pretty strong, old man — but who knows?"

A heavy knocking sound echoing round the hall jarred them all. Jamie, looking understandably troubled, eased himself to the Summer Room door and listened.

"I think they've come for the charity things, Aunt Sheila."

Sheila Demian's strong face was pale but set, as her jaw clenched in hard lines.

"Yes. I'll go. Might as well get this mess out of the way. It's doing no good here."

She went rapidly out into the hall and a couple of minutes later they heard the voice of one of the village women.

"So good of you, Miss Demian. We can do

wonders with some of the old Demian bric-a-brac. You wouldn't have any old furniture to contribute? No. Asking too much, it is. We musn't be greedy."

Another woman, also in the hall, said in her soft voice, "We didn't mean to interrupt you at dinner, Sheila. It was only . . . Orin thought . . ."

From behind the door of the Summer Room, Merlina made a toothy face.

"It's Mama. At least she's not been at the tipple."

Nick looked at the barrister. "What do you think?"

Sir Arthur swept away any demands these people might make when they discovered the owner of the clothing.

"In the first place, the villagers have no legal right to the possessions. Until they do, which is absurd, everything should be left as it was found."

Nick agreed. "And then? Legally, of course."

"First, I should think this fellow Ackroyd, after a little conferring in Mincham, may be ordered by his superiors to bring London into the matter . . . Only my surmise, of course."

"Very likely correct. Meanwhile, someone had better be sent to get Ackroyd himself, or one of his seniors if they are anywhere to be found."

The barrister agreed, adding in his cautious way, "I would suggest — only a suggestion, mind — that all these things be securely locked in your attic. You do have secure locks, I hope?"

"I can find some. I'm wondering if I should equip myself with some good legal protection. Perhaps you can name someone appropriate. I wouldn't even be averse to calling on you."

Sir Arthur laughed at this. The sound should have relieved Roberta but she thought Sir Arthur was much too sure of his friend's safety.

"Don't worry about that yet, Nick. There is no direct evidence. Nothing that ties you to that pond and the unfortunate DeVrees. Anyone might have left the suitcase here. And as Miss Fisher so wisely reminded us, you have made enemies in the village. Remember, I warned you."

"Yes. Damn you. You always were a stickler for law, good or bad. However, I ought to find my old shotgun, just to protect my family, including Miss Fisher here."

Sir Arthur stiffened. "My dear boy, I didn't hear that. I couldn't be a party to anything that could be used against — Never mind. Just keep to the straight and narrow."

Sheila had, meanwhile, been explaining to her visitors that they would have to wait for the Demian charity items. The women, disappointed, gave each other meaningful glances, knowing what would be said in the village of the high and mighty Demians. Sheila promised to speak to the women "Sometime tomorrow. You may count on that."

Orin Camberson, lurking in the background, dismissed this silently as 'female chitchat' and was about to enter the room when he saw Sir Arthur and Nick, both impressively forbidding in the doorway of the Summer Room, and he hesitated. His daughter, Merlina, after pushing her way through the two men, grabbed her father's hand.

"Father, let's go home. I'm hungry. They can talk about it tomorrow when Miss Demian comes to the square."

"Yes. Do let's forget this for tonight," Elly Camberson pleaded.

Her husband paid no attention but spoke to his daughter.

"Yes, you come along, Merlina. You've overstayed your service here by at least an hour. Take off that disgusting thing and join your mother."

"Will you come too, Father? It's after dark, and —"

Orin Camberson studied the barrister and Nick Demian, was duly impressed by the law in the person of Sir Arthur, and apparently thought better of initiating an argument. He grumbled, "I've my women to think of, Sir Arthur. And you, Mr Nick. But I'll be back with the others tomorrow. The Edenbrook charities were promised contributions from Demian house and we mean to have them."

Sheila ended this unpleasant scene by taking Camberson's arm and manoeuvring him into the hall where he called back to Sir Arthur.

"Sorry to disturb you, I'm sure. We never meant that. Didn't know you was still here."

"No harm done," the barrister called to the retreating Camberson and his family. Roberta saw Nick grin at his friend's remark and she wanted to do the same but she was too much shaken by the undercurrents of what had occurred.

Merlina Camberson passed the pale and silent Jamie as she and her father joined the others in the hall and in a voice Roberta could hear, Merlina whispered to Jamie, "You owe me for getting rid of us all, Jamie-boy."

Then they were gone, and Mrs Schramm, followed by Sheila, climbed the stairs to the attic. Nick picked up the trunk while Sir Arthur balanced the suitcases in either hand and started after Sheila.

Passing Roberta, Nick grinned and promised her, "As the fair Merlina says, we owe you one at least. Please don't run away."

Her eyes promised silently. It was wonderful to have him understand her mood and her anxiety for him. Even his grin was reassuring. He had come a long way since she met the sullen, angry Nick Demian a little more than a week ago.

Presently, Sheila Demian came down from the attic alone. She shook her head as she met Roberta standing by the bottom stair of the delicately carved staircase with its archway through to the big lounge on the ground floor.

"Men!" Sheila mouthed the words, and then, seeing Roberta blink at her condemnation, she laughed.

"No. I haven't sworn off men entirely. Only those who seem to surround my life. Can you imagine, with all the trouble we face, partly due to Nick's stubbornness, of course, Art wants to discuss marriage? He must be out of his mind. Either he still thinks I am seventeen — when I confess had a mad crush on him — or he is singularly obtuse."

"But if he loves you?" Roberta suggested, although she appreciated Sheila's desire for independence when it came to Sir Arthur's persistence. He did not seem to be a man who would stand on his own. However, if she gave him a chance . . .

Sheila shrugged. "Wouldn't you know? With Nick worried about that whole DeVrees business, and Art talking about happy marriages he has known — not personally, of course — they've kept Mrs Schramm up there to ferret out any other items that poor woman might have left here. So it looks to me like old reliable Sheila will be responsible for dinner tonight . . . Are you fond of omelettes?"

It sounded normal, almost taking Roberta's mind off the worries up in the attic. "I love them. You wouldn't have a can of mushrooms to go with it?"

"That's about all you'll get tonight. That and a green salad." Starting for the kitchen, Sheila looked back at Roberta. "And the mushrooms are freshly grown in Mincham. Does that tempt your appetite?"

Roberta followed her, feeling definitely more cheerful. "If you've got an apron, I'm your scullery maid for the occasion."

"I suspect you will make an excellent sister-in-law." On the heels of this welcome comment, Sheila added, "If you and Nick don't hang about too much. A little goes a long way with relatives."

It was impossible to be hurt or annoyed at such frankness. Besides, it was very much the way Roberta felt. She promised she wouldn't hang about and, if possible, keep Nick from being too much under foot as well.

"If I get the chance, of course."

"You will," Sheila prophesied as they went into the big, modern, well-equipped kitchen. "Unless, of course, they lock that brother of mine up for murder or some such crime." She ignored Roberta's shudder. "Use this apron. It belongs to Schrammy and will wrap around you at least twice."

Luckily, Sheila talked on through the preparations for dinner, with such complete indifference to the future that some of her self-confidence rubbed off onto Roberta.

When Jamie came in and helped to wash the salad greens Sheila told him, to his horror, that he would make someone a good husband. But at dinner Roberta was relieved to see that he had the full appetite of a healthy teenager and was asking his father endless questions about what he was going to do with the instant photos Sister Longacre's brother had taken.

Somewhat to Roberta's surprise, Nick skirted the subject, going into considerable detail about Longacre's intention of selling an article to a London tabloid in connection with the story of Mrs DeVrees's death. The fact that absolute proof hadn't been obtained, meant nothing, according to Nick.

Roberta knew the whole business about Longacre's supposed article was a lie. She wondered for a minute if he was keeping the truth from his closest friend, Arthur Laidlaw. But Sir Arthur was just marginally interested.

It was only when he mentioned his chauffeur, Weems, hoping the fellow was getting a decent dinner at Toby Teague's pub that Roberta noticed the tightening of Nick's fingers around his cuttery. He was certainly interested in Weems.

Was he actually suspicious of Weems being involved in the criminal activities of the Demian tenants?

But she followed young Jamie's admirable caution and like him, did not pursue the matter. She had very little doubt that Sir Arthur would mention to Weems anything said here tonight. Whatever his gifts in the courts might be, Sir Arthur did not seem to be a man who would keep secrets from those he trusted, or used.

In spite of her vow not to help Mrs Schramm clear up, Sheila hung around the kitchen and larder checking supplies needed for the week.

Jamie disappeared to enjoy a TV programme, leaving Sir Arthur and Nick to discuss the legal aspects of the mounting suspicion against Nick.

"But why must he have legal representation now?" Roberta asked, angry over what she considered the barrister's lack of faith in his friend's word. "Nobody's accused him of anything yet — even though we all know how the villagers have been piling up little things here and there, particularly gossip, just to make him look guilty before there is a case."

"*Was* a case, darling," Nick reminded her. "There may well be one now." They were seated on a worn and somewhat faded sofa while Sir Arthur straddled a chair facing them, looking very unlike the precise, perfectly groomed counsel whom the press liked to sketch.

"I'm afraid that grisly discovery today precludes our dismissing the rumours as mere, mindless gossip," Sir Arthur reminded Roberta. "It is absurd, but despite what we know, juries have a way of fastening on to such stories as the villagers have been circulating. I must say, I wish I'd known what they were about when I let them use me." Obviously, his pride was hurt that he should have been a cat's-paw.

Roberta was increasingly angry at the way that gossip had been built up, and for her benefit. She had been used too.

Looking back, she could almost put together the little digs here and there, gossip supposedly between Toby and Orin Camberson, or Will Brinkby and Toby. Even young Gordon Brinkby, with his damned chewing of liquorice.

She reminded Sir Arthur, "These people who circulated the stories and dirty insinuations — they looked to you, Sir Arthur, when you sent me here. I could swear to it that this was all part of their plan to build me up as another gullible, infatuated woman as witness to Nick's philandering with every woman who ever walked through Edenbrook."

Nick laughed shortly. "Not that bad, surely."

"That bad."

Sir Arthur rubbed his jaw. "You make a passionate case. Not that I don't believe you. I know Nick. It is all perfectly possible, as you tell it." He slapped the arm of his chair. "But I'm damned if I see how we can answer gossip by simple denials. I've asked Weems to move about, talk among them, see if he can find out who is behind it all."

"Weems!" Roberta put in indignantly. "He's the worst of the lot for carrying tales."

She knew she had upset Sir Arthur but he might as well know the truth about his chauffeur.

Nick was looking from one to the other of them but he said nothing. She thought Sir Arthur would explode into a defence of his man but the barrister leaned back, frowning. Then, startling them both, he sat forward abruptly, his eyes lighting with an idea.

"Hinch!"

"Hinch?" Nick repeated. "What's that supposed to mean?"

"Malcolm Hinchcliffe," Sir Arthur explained,

happy as a child with a new toy. "Just the thing. He handled a case very like this some years ago. Pure gossip had been turned into as fine a pile of rubbish as ever passed for evidence . . . Give me the intricate case of a double agent or a traitor who's followed his inclinations over to the bad guys and I'll have him hung out to dry. But country gossip . . . More dangerous, my boy. It festers."

He glanced at the diamond-studded wristwatch presented to him by a generous client and got up.

"There's not much time. The fellow races off to Majorca or Madeira — some such place — after every case. I'd like to catch him just once between cases if I can."

"Not tonight, surely."

"No, no. But quite early in the morning. I'll get Weems to put on speed. Whatever we find out, I'll be back tomorrow afternoon to stand by you in Mincham." He grinned and punched Nick's forearm with his fist. "Unless Weems breaks a leg or the car. What do you say?"

Nick held out a hand. "I say thanks, old chap."

"What are friends for?" Sir Arthur hesitated and looked back at the kitchen. Then he added with renewed enthusiasm, "That ought to impress her if anything will. Dear girl. But they're the only ones worth having."

"You can say that again." Nick smiled at Roberta who was a little more cheerful now, though she dreaded tomorrow.

Chapter Twenty-Two

Roberta could only guess what thoughts Nick had in the night, since they were not yet sleeping together. Too many problems stood between them. Nick escorted her to a guest room on the other side of Jamie's. He insisted that he wouldn't have her risk another night so near Toby Teague, the Cambersons and Will Brinkby. He seemed confident, but her own mind swarmed with doubts that things would go so easily for him.

They were not doubts of his innocence, but of the treacherous liars around him in the village. He had kissed her goodnight, drawing her to him with the strength of tension. She returned his embrace, welcoming his mouth over hers, hot with his desire. Jamie peeked out of his room; he laughed at them and Nick recovered, grinning back.

"You'd better approve, young man."

"I do, Father. I won't look. Goodnight, Miss Fisher, Father."

He ducked his head back and closed his door. They heard his pleasant giggle and looked at each other. She was breathing rapidly. "He approves."

"Did you think he wouldn't?" Nick surprised her by adding, "I'm afraid this is one when he'd better agree with his old father."

Her happy laugh broke off. He looked at her, taking her wrist in a painful grip. "What is it, sweetheart?"

"Does Jamie chew anything anisette-flavoured?"

He was astonished at the question. "Not that I know of. He doesn't drink wine or liqueurs."

"Liquorice. Not anisette," she exclaimed suddenly.

He was more puzzled than ever. "Darling, what is it?"

"Does he get liquorice from any of his friends?"

"I suppose so. Yes. Now I think of it. Gordon Brinkby gives him those things that look like little black whips. Jamie isn't crazy about it but he eats it now and —"

"Ask him."

Without more questions he knocked on Jamie's door. The boy stuck his head out and scoffed, "Father! You don't need my help."

"Are you chewing some liquorice?"

Jamie's eyes widened. "I was. Gordon gave me some this afternoon."

Nick looked at Roberta. "Is that what you wanted to know?"

She was excited but managed to remain outwardly calm until Jamie closed his door again. Nick studied her face.

"What is it? Roberta, tell me."

She took a long breath. "You remember the

night in London when you followed me along the street in a car?"

His features were sober but his eyes seemed to smile.

"Of course. The night I found you so enchanting."

"I accused you of vandalising Miss Halloway's house. It wasn't you."

"I agree, darling." His voice held a teasing sound but he watched her intently.

"When I first came into the house that night I remember smelling what I thought was a form of anisette, a flavour. Something. I smelled it especially in the dresser where someone destroyed my tapes and notes. I thought it might be anisette. It was liquorice."

That did startle him. "Good God! Whoever had broken into the house might have been one of the Brinkbys. What were they doing in London?"

"It was someone youthful. I heard him run through an alley afterwards. You think it's a long shot? A lot of teenagers in London may smell of anisette or liquorice, for all I know. But the Brinkbys, along with half the village, it seems, have been trying to make you look bad. They read the paper. They know you had quarrelled with Sybille, so Will Brinkby sent his son in to tear up things. Just what you might have done if you were angry enough."

"I was angry enough," he agreed, "But I'm not exactly a second-storey man. Climbing in and out of windows is not my style."

She laughed and touched his cheek tenderly.

"No. You'd want immediate personal action. Face to face. No sneaking around."

"That's me." He leaned across and kissed her before adding, "You see? Personal action. Mouth to mouth."

She didn't know whether he took her theory seriously or not, but she did, and when they had said goodnight and she saw him watch her until her door shut, she leaned back against the closed door and thought it all through again.

She knew a mere grain of suspicious activity would mean nothing in court, but it pointed the way. It was one slip-up Nick's enemies had made. But how had they known he would be nearby that night so that hints of his temper and supposed hatred of women — Miss Halloway included? — would add more fuel to whispered accusations?

Roberta bathed in the little private bath on the opposite side of Jamie's room and gratefully wore the tailored nightgown and robe Sheila Demian had loaned her. But through all her actions and her dreams she found herself engrossed in speculation about the sinister knowledge of Nick Demian shown by practically all of his tenants in Edenbrook.

Well, not precisely all. But enough. Quite enough.

By the time the first morning light began to creep over the brook and the thatched cottages that bordered it, Roberta was wide awake and wondering which of those little Hansel and Gretel houses hid people capable of conspiracy and probably murder.

The real horror was that every few hours during the last few days seemed to bring new evidence pointing to Nick Demian. She didn't believe any of that rubbish, but how much further would the conspirators go before they manufactured evidence that really would send Nick to prison for life?

Merlina Camberson brought her breakfast to her looking apprehensive. When Roberta asked her if she was feeling all right, the girl scoffed, "I'm well as can be. It's not me. It's Mama. She's all upset and nervy. Been at the bottle again, I don't doubt."

"I'm awfully sorry about your mother. Is there anything we can do?"

"None, Miss. It's that I'll be needed at home. Schrammy says I can go home and help Father in the shop. If I don't he'll be in a sulk and take it out on Mama. Excuse me."

She ducked out quickly when Nick came in behind her. He looked after the girl, shook his head and came across the room to where Roberta sat at a little vanity table and mirror, eating the delicious toast she had grown fond of.

This was like being a comfortable old married pair, she thought and cheered up just a little at the thought. Could it ever be like this? Why not? All they had to do was clear the interviews with the police today, show the authorities that Nick had nothing to do with this rotten business. She wondered whether Sir Arthur had tracked down his friend, Malcolm Hinchcliffe, and whether he would take on an irascible man like Nick. She must see to it that Nick didn't get impatient and tell Hinchcliffe how to run his business!

"Are you worried about today?" he asked, having kissed her and stolen a piece of toast. "Don't be, darling. I really haven't done anything criminal — not that I know of."

"I know that. I don't think I ever doubted it. I'd like to go with you, Nick. I can't just sit here and bite my nails."

He lifted up her right hand and pretended to examine it. "Such pretty nails, too. But I need you here. And McQuarry is on his way. He'll entertain Jamie. I don't like to leave you with only a boy and an injured man, though. If anything happened —"

"We're not the ones in danger, darling. Stop worrying about us. It's you!"

"I'm not on my way to the moon," he reminded her. "Just jolly old Mincham."

And maybe arrest, she thought, but didn't say it aloud.

"I'll see you downstairs won't I? And Sir Arthur?"

"Not Art. He's in London by now, I'd say, knowing how Weems drives. Art left before sunrise."

"I love you, sweetheart," Roberta told Nick.

"Admirable woman. You took the words out of my mouth. Let's see. Art had coffee with Sheila before he left. She actually thanked him for what she called his services in my favour. I understand she promised not to marry anybody else in the meantime." Roberta was smiling at the barrister's vain hopes. Nick went on. "Yes. He gave me his word. He will be in Mincham with Hinchcliffe, he hopes, soon enough to keep me out of Mincham's deep, dark dungeon to-night. He also says he wants another shot at Sheila."

"More power to him, but I suspect that where Sheila is concerned, he'll always be a bridesmaid, never a bride, so to speak."

"You could be right. I've ordered Jamie to stay home all day. He gets a little bored with just busy women, but he and McQuarry usually have a chess game going. Old Mac should be here any minute." He kissed her and hurried out.

It was admirable of him to seem so self-confi-dent. It certainly helped raise her own spirits. She rushed through a shower, adorned very little make-up, and dressed in yesterday's belted sweater and skirt.

When she reached the lobby downstairs she found Sheila waiting with Nick.

"Roberta, will you please tell my little brother I am quite capable of settling things with those charity women in half an hour, or an hour at the most? Then I'll come back and babysit for a teenager."

Roberta agreed, much amused. "I'll tell him. I promise."

Nick kissed her before saying to his sister, "I merely asked you to hurry back from the village. I'm not sure how long I'll be in Mincham."

"Rubbish. They'll send you home in no time. They've got nothing against you. How could they do anything else? Besides, Merlina told me Elly had asked your friend Constable Ackroyd to come and see her. Probably wants to complain about that nauseating husband of hers. So Ackroyd can't chain you up and take care of Elly too.

By the way, have you shown Roberta those pictures you're so secret about?"

"All safe and sound." He pulled a pack out of his leather jacket and handed them to Roberta.

"Use your woman's intuition and tell me which of these fiendish fellows looks guilty."

Roberta fanned through them with Sheila looking over her shoulder. She saw faces, odd angle shots, youngsters sticking their tongues out at the camera, a woman with a flowered apron sweeping off the cobblestones beneath her cottage porch. Others were equally casual shots, several of men smoking pipes outside Toby Teague's doorway. Only one was of Toby himself. He had knocked his pipe against the corner of the pub wall, evidently saw that he was observed and grimaced almost unrecognisably at the camera.

Will Brinkby stood arguing with his son, Gordon, one of whose heavy jogging shoes was sunk a few inches deep in the brook. Granny Perth posed as prettily as an old lady with two missing teeth could pose, as if she would eat the cameraman up, or *gum* him at any rate.

Even the chauffeur, Weems, had been caught, apparently unawares. His moon-face was obviously doing its best to reassure the stiffened, timid Elly Camberson but he wasn't succeeding. In her hand was a glass, whether full or empty the camera didn't indicate. The setting seemed to be the side of a building, probably her husband's tobacconist-cum-post office. Wherever it was, they were alone.

The teenagers and younger set, seemed to find the camera interesting and several pictures showed them in blurry close-up, trying to examine the camera.

"Interesting," she said, returning them, but she wasn't too hopeful. The identities of several villagers in the pictures could only be guessed at.

Nick had just hoved the pictures back in his breast pocket when the telephone in the hallway rang and after answering it Sheila called to Nick.

"It's Art. Want to talk to him? He's in London. Says he has good news."

"Well, that was quick." Nick came back, reminding Roberta as he reached the telephone stand, "I told you it would go like clockwork . . . Hello? Art? Do we get Hinchcliffe or not?" There was a short silence on Nick's part, then he repeated for the benefit of the two women, "Then you didn't talk to him directly. All right. His clerk. You're sure Hinchcliffe will be with you this afternoon? Nice work. See you in Mincham. Many thanks, Art."

He replaced the receiver and slapped his hands together, pretending to dust off problems. He grinned at his sister and Roberta. "Hinchcliffe's clerk says Hinch will be glad to oblige Art in any way." He winked at Roberta. "Art also says he will expect payment in kind from my tantalising sister. What say, Sheila?"

Sheila pushed him off. "Get along. I'm not letting my future be bartered away, even if it is for my baby brother."

As he went to the front door, waving back to the women, he was looking genuinely light-hearted for once, and Roberta realised how much younger he looked when he felt his troubles were very nearly over.

He met the chemist, McQuarry, on the brook path, explained briefly, and ducked through the thick clump of trees and underbrush to the garage on Mincham Lane where he parked his car when he might need it suddenly. It was the strange, sombre miniature forest Roberta remembered from a few nights ago when the chauffeur, Weems, practically dropped her into the lap of Sheila Demian. She could hardly believe so much had happened between her and Nick since that night.

Among the events, and the thought made her shiver, was the dreadful discovery in the mill pond.

Roberta followed Sheila to welcome McQuarry when he came in with an old-fashioned, snap-top leather bag. She wondered if he expected to change for dinner in the style of a gentleman. She could see that the bag was a bit of a problem. He carried it with an effort in his left hand, obviously avoiding any weight on the arm that was cradled in a sling to protect his right shoulder.

He greeted the two women gravely, showing no enthusiasm and Sheila turned to Roberta.

"Schrammy and I have to get together some of the old Demian treasures for the tabby cats and their precious charity. They will use whatever they have left over for the Christmas bazaar. Would you mind showing Mac to Jamie's room? Not that he doesn't know by now." She addressed the chemist in her casual way, much like his own indifference. "You will certainly make my nephew's day. He's been moaning all morning that he was being kept in solitary confinement."

"Of course." Roberta apparently looked as if she would wrestle his bag away from him because his fingers tightened around the handle and he walked ahead of her up the staircase.

Jamie heard Roberta's voice and that of his friend and came out of his room to greet McQuarry.

"Mac, it's good to see you. The house is deadly when you're a prisoner. Do come in." He looked at Roberta over the greying head of the chemist.

"Miss . . . Roberta, you promised to read the synopsis of my screenplay."

"Of course. I'd love to, Jamie. Can I get anything for you and Mr McQuarry? Have you had breakfast?"

"Whole ages ago," Jamie boasted as he handed her the modest number of pages. "Mac, you aren't hungry, are you?"

The chemist looked drawn and weary. He set his bag down. "Nothing to eat, thank you, but I do need a glass of water. No trouble, Jamie. I know where your bathroom is. I believe I'll take a couple of painkillers for this shoulder." He headed for Jamie's bathroom and then added, "Not that I approve of drugs, Master Jamie. Never did."

Jamie giggled. "That's funny, from a person who works with pills."

"May I help you?" Roberta asked but McQuarry shook his head and held up a little box. "Just water."

While McQuarry was in the bathroom, Jamie whispered to Roberta, "His shoulder must hurt. It's too bad. Mac never complains."

"No. I'm sure not. If I can do anything for either of you, Jamie, just tell me. I'll be in the next room, reading your synopsis. I know it's going to be splendid."

She had made Jamie happy. He beamed.

"Thank you ever so. Oh — and Roberta, I hope Father marries you. Aunt Sheila thinks he might."

She smiled at this, wishing she could be as sure as Jamie and his father that all would go well.

As she opened the door into the corridor, he held out his hand, palm up. She saw the opal ring gleam at her like an all-seeing eye. Looking guilty, Jamie asked, "Is it all right? Father said if I was fool enough to want it, and you let me have it, I could wear it."

"Of course, it's all right. It belongs to your family."

He put it on his little finger. It slipped around, obviously too large. "I have to have it made smaller. Funny. It's too small for my other fingers."

She said, "You do whatever you want with it. Wear it on your little finger and if you lose it — small loss."

"Oh, no, Miss — I mean Roberta. It's my good luck piece. It brought you to Father. He's never been this happy before."

She was so touched she almost felt tears sting her eyelids. She surprised herself by lightly kissing him on the cheek.

"Thank you, Jamie dear."

He was still looking after her with a tenderness that touched her deeply when she opened the door of her room. She gave him a big 'OK' sign with thumb and forefinger. He laughed and she went into her room.

She sat down on the bed and studied the format the boy had given her. It looked almost professional. There were several typos corrected on the first two pages. He had undoubtedly used an electric or manual typewriter. She must remember to ask Nick if she might give Jamie a computer, or certainly, a word processor. Half the time in Hollywood and on location she used a laptop processor and got along perfectly well.

Later, he would get a big thrill out of using disks and add a more professional format to his work.

She was pleased and somewhat surprised at just how vivid a writer Jamie was. He had a fine knack for getting to the colourful, exciting scenes, even at the beginning when he dealt with a Swiss guide, leading an eager American across an alp on foot. The American was the blundering, bossy, bragging character stolen from the British view of Americans early in the century, but Roberta was not offended, having run into a number of tourists during her trips to Europe who were very like Jamie's creation. The Swiss character was accurate too, exaggerated but recognisable. It was these two who discovered an Italian boy standing over the remains of the prehistoric man.

There was somewhat overdone comedy here after what would probably be a scary moment when they first discovered what remained of the long-dead body.

After that, Jamie reverted to pure synopsis and she thought the whole thing showed definite promise. All it needed in this spot was a female, or two, to add pepper to the pot.

Once in a while she heard Jamie's laugh through the wall but after twenty minutes or so there was silence. Probably McQuarry was too tired for Jamie's high spirits to enliven him.

Sheila came by Roberta's room about that time, carrying a couple of suitcases and frowning.

"Well, we're off. Mrs Schramm has left wrapped sandwiches and lunch in the fridge. We'll be back as soon as we can prise ourselves away. You may not credit this but Schrammy is carrying a footstool with a petit point cover. Belonged to Grandmama. It's been in the attic for ages. She's carrying it on her head at the moment. Sure you'll be all right for an hour or so?"

"Perfectly sure. Have a good time with your charity ladies."

"Fat chance," Sheila said, sounding like some of Roberta's fellow Hollywoodians. "If Nick calls, tell him I'll be back in ten minutes. That always annoys him. For some reason, he never believes me. Incidentally, Schrammy has locked up the ground floor and windows. Bye."

"Bye," Roberta echoed, feeling like an Agatha Christie character. She wished she could have Sheila Demian's wonderful indifference to the dangers that beset her family from all directions.

Roberta went back to studying Jamie's script, but there was nothing more to work on without some revisions in the plot lines which did run to melodrama in the latter scenes. Wild shootings that didn't quite suit the anthropology in the first half.

The minutes dragged. Maybe she could be of some help to Jamie with McQuarry who hadn't seemed very well to her. She could use Jamie's work on the screenplay as an excuse.

The house was so quiet she imagined half a dozen catastrophes in the next half hour before the telephone rang and she jumped off the bed nervously. The ringing of the telephone persisted. It sounded too close to be the connection out in the hall. She found it half hidden on the floor under the bedside table.

She reached for it. For a moment she said nothing. It was always possible this was someone trying to find out if she and Jamie were alone, but she couldn't mistake Nick Demian's voice, angry and anxious.

"Hello! Who the — ?"

"It's me."

He seemed to relax. "Well, thank God, sweetheart. I was getting worried. Everything all right?" She didn't know what to say to that. "I'm fine. Jamie's fine. They aren't going to charge you or anything, are they?"

"I haven't seen that damned constable yet. I'm sitting here staring at the walls and the desk officer. Ackroyd was off to see Elly Camberson, minutes before I got here. More marital rows, I suppose . . . Listen, darling, this is important. Mrs Seddley thinks she knows who bumped into us and then took off the other day. Longacre's instant photos triggered her memory. Remember the shot of Elly Camberson and Art's chauffeur, Weems?"

She caught her breath. "Well, it couldn't be Mrs Camberson could it?"

"No, Weems. Mrs Seddley says she remembers the bulging eyes and curly hair. Not much to go on, but there it is. He's been in Art's family since the old gentleman's day, but he seems to have given Seddley that nasty shove. Art's a stubborn fellow about faithful retainers like Weems."

"But why would he do it?" Her head was whirling.

"Weems has been close to Toby Teague and the Brinkbys the last few years. I imagine he syphons off any information he learns from Art's office, from that gabby secretary, Mrs Peavis, and feeds it to our tenants. There might be a deal of money in it if the Demians were out of here and there was no one, like Jamie, to inherit."

"My God! And everyone besides Sir Arthur has trusted him. If Mrs Camberson and her husband were working for Weems, that might explain the instant picture Mr Longacre took."

"Maybe. Look, darling, I'm getting back to the house as soon as I can make it. Meanwhile, keep all the doors locked, inner rooms too. I called Art's office and Mrs Peavis says Weems hasn't been in this morning. He usually hangs about making a nuisance of himself, according to Peavis. I couldn't tell her much about this business. She'd be sure to tell Art, and he's such a fool, he might try to warn his good old retainer."

"Your housekeeper locked everything up downstairs. Sheila said to tell you she'd be back in ten minutes."

"Damn that girl!"

"She said 'good luck'. So do I."

"Got to go, darling."

The phone went dead.

Hoping against hope, she went to Jamie's door and called to him. She heard him limping across the room. When he opened the door he put his finger to his lips, then whispered, "Mac's just closed his eyes, right while I was telling him about my script. He's awfully tired."

Handicapped by the boy's slender young figure, she tried to look into the room. She saw the chemist across the room, leaning back in Jamie's big armchair, probably asleep.

"Is he all right?" She moved gently around Jamie and crossed the room. She tried to feel McQuarry's pulse, but by that time the chemist opened his eyes wearily.

"Sorry, Miss Fisher. Just tired. Shoulder . . . aches a bit. The boy . . . safe?"

Jamie assured McQuarry that he was indeed safe but Roberta said, "Mr Demian called. He asked you to keep this door locked from the inside until he arrives. He is on his way."

McQuarry tried to rise but fell back awkwardly. "I'll see to it, Miss. My word on it."

She left hurriedly. After Jamie closed the door, she rapped on it.

"Lock it!"

She heard the twisting of the key and returned to her room, satisfied, locking her own door behind her.

Trying to take her mind off the long, nerve-racking wait, she took up Jamie's manuscript but there was little more to do with it until they could discuss it together.

She had never been so nervous.

She set aside the papers and went to the window. The entire village must be preparing lunch. She couldn't see anyone along the brook except two young children wading at the turn in front of McQuarry's shop. They appeared to be happy enough, judging by the splashes they made trying to shower each other. She watched them for some time, wishing she would hear Nick's voice calling out as he came in through the hall and up the main staircase to the upper floors.

Minutes must have passed, but her nerves remained alert, expectant.

Just as she turned from the window, deciding to see if Jamie's friend McQuarry was feeling better, she was shaken by a loud, thumping noise in the corridor or beyond.

It sounded like something falling heavily. Please God, it wasn't Jamie! Perhaps it was the poor chemist. Jamie would have a hard time getting him on his feet.

She ran across her room to the locked door.

The key was gone. She had left it in the keyhole, but it was gone now. It was not on the floor, or the carpet, or under the little occasional table. She banged on the door.

"Jamie? Jamie!" There was no answer from across the corridor. The house was full of little whispers, like the wind playing a game with her.

Had there been enough noise earlier for her to miss the sound of a small key falling on the carpet and being drawn under the door? There was room under the door. And at the window she had been distracted.

Whoever was after the Demians was in the house with them now!

Chapter Twenty-Three

Roberta swung around, trying to find another way out. She had no idea whom she could call locally in time to help her and Jamie, but the telephone was here. She reached for it.

No sound. Somebody had disconnected the damned thing!

She went through her bathroom remembering the connecting door to Jamie's bedroom and banged on it as hard as she could. She half expected the door would still be locked and Jamie gone. Instead, after a long minute or two, the key was turned and McQuarry opened it. He looked weary and obviously in as much pain as he was in half an hour ago, but he tried to pull himself together.

"Something hit the door. I roused myself but Jamie had already gone to investigate. Then you knocked."

"Never mind. Can I get out by your door?"

He followed her, trying to make speed for Jamie's sake, but she reached the door first. It was still ajar. Jamie must have hurried out at speed, as Roberta did now. She ran silently along the corridor, stepping out of her shoes in the process, but she was in too much of a hurry to worry about them.

An unearthly screeching noise brought her up short, trembling. It sounded like wood being wrenched away and with it, a second or two afterwards, a boy's scream that she knew was Jamie. Breathing hard and with difficulty, she began to run faster.

She came to an abrupt halt at the top of the staircase, paralysed with horror at the disaster that unfolded itself below her.

Just above the dark midway landing, where the illuminated lamp usually rested on its stand, about three feet of the banister had broken away. Much of Jamie's body, including the leg in its heavy metal brace, was dangling over the side, his feet kicking in the space between the floors. His hands gripped the torn edge of the landing, his knuckles white with the painful pressure and the brace dragging his good leg and his body inevitably downwards.

Hardly aware of what she said, Roberta cried, "Hold on, Jamie. For God's sake, hold on."

She didn't look down. It was a long way to the hall below and it would only terrify her all the more. She ran down the stairs. Just before she reached the landing something very thin caught around her ankles, bringing her down hard on her knees. It was a strong, black thread, one end still tied to the lamp stand.

Simple, but effective enough to trip anyone.

She landed on her knees, very close to his fingers, still trying to keep their grip. She covered his wrists with her hands, trying to relieve the pressure on his fingers.

"Hold on," she begged him again, desperate to transmit some of her own nervous strength.

An easy, liquid voice, not familiar for a second or two, mimicked her from the floor directly below Jamie, where a number of wood splinters had fallen around the chauffeur, Weems. Weems extended his left arm out and up toward Jamie's dangling foot, imprisoned in its brace. Weems's right arm held the lamp from the stair landing, with the bulb lying shattered at his feet.

Obviously, he, or someone giving him his orders, had planned to make Jamie's death look like the result of the banister collapse, with probably the addition of a lamp blow across the head, which would inevitably be disguised by the natural injuries of the fall. All a terrible and unpreventable accident.

Weems was grinning, his lips spread wide. "Come on, boy. Just let the old body fall. Easy does it. It'll be gentle and quiet, so it will. You'll never know what hit you."

Jamie refused to look down. His great, terrified eyes stared up at Roberta's face.

"You won't let go — please don't —"

She kept assuring him, "I'll get you up. Here. Just try." She hardly knew what encouragement she gave. She was too tense, her muscles too strained for her to remember how terrified she was.

"Come, boy," Weems coaxed. "You won't want to live forever. Not in that damned brace

. . . Just drop. Easy-like." He again reached for Jamie's leg, but the teenager thrashed it about so Weems couldn't get a hold.

He kept staring into Roberta's face. "I lost it when I fell. It's gone. Your ring."

"Never you mind. I'm getting you back. Hold on!"

Another man's voice spoke now, near Weems. "Hurry!"

Weems protested, "She got out. She's holding the kid."

"Then they both go. Do hurry!"

Staring down around Jamie's sweating, tense face, Roberta caught a glimpse of Sir Arthur Laidlaw, and was shocked. Weems reached for the broken lamp, the base of which could easily add the death blow.

Roberta cried, "I'll kill you. Touch him and I'll kill you." How she could do this, she had no idea, but she felt fully capable. With Weems involved, who else would he take his orders from but Nick's lifelong friend, Arthur Laidlaw? She should have guessed!

Sir Arthur almost lost his celebrated good temper. "Damn it, Weems! Do as you're told."

Putting all her weight into her hands and arms, Roberta managed to pull Jamie a few inches towards her. It was a little better, but his bad leg still dangled, drawing his body downward.

There was a quick step in the hallway below and then appeared the man who in all the world

Roberta wanted most to hear, Nick Demian.

"Call your dog off, Art. You never were the sporting type. You'll fail."

Jamie, trying to look down between his tired arms, screamed, "Father! It's Father."

Seeing that the attention of Weems and Sir Arthur had been drawn away, Roberta ordered Jamie, "Try again. Another leave."

He tried. His struggles and muscular agony made him cry out. She doubled her effort to give him the extra strength of her hands. Below her, Nick, his dark eyes blazing against his hard features, ordered his friend, "Call it off, Art. You've lost."

Sir Arthur swung around. "Good God, old fellow! The boy stumbled and fell against the banister. When part of it broke, we were trying to get him down. He didn't understand."

Ignoring the last card played by his 'friend', Nick sprinted up the staircase to where the two men stood and reached up to grab his son around the hips and then, very slowly, his hands moved higher, under Jamie's arms. He must know Weems could club him, Roberta thought desperately, wanting to cry out, but afraid of what a sudden yell might do at this moment.

Weems raised the lamp and Sir Arthur said nothing to stop him, but let his chauffeur move toward Nick. At the critical moment Weems stepped on something that rolled under his foot, and he fell back against Sir Arthur.

Roberta wondered if she could hold on a minute more. Rescue was at hand but her arms were being pulled out of their sockets by Jamie's weight. She heard noises in the hallway as two uniformed people came forward.

Then an explosion rocked her. A bullet shot over her head and down into one of the men below. The chauffeur howled out and dropped the lamp. Sir Arthur picked it up by its base and took a step towards Nick. The second shot, aimed above Roberta's head, struck Sir Arthur, and another followed, almost on the sound of the second.

Constable Ackroyd rushed up the stairs but was stopped by Weems who looked suddenly stupified, as if he couldn't understand what had happened. The barrister had let the lamp base fall from his fingers. To Roberta and the constable, Sir Arthur's grimace of pain looked like a horrible smile. He wavered, reached for support from a polished oak table, murmuring, "I'd no idea — such a good — shot."

The table was strong and solid but he lost his grip and slumped to the floor. A thick gout of blood seeped through the barrister's once immaculate topcoat.

Constable Ackroyd knelt to examine the half-conscious barrister who opened his eyes and appeared to make out the officer's young face. He tried to speak. Roberta wondered if the dying man was about to spout more lies. But with an effort Sir Arthur roused himself a few inches and muttered to Ackroyd, "Veda always said — he'd find out. Persistent bastard . . . Pity he had all the money."

His pale eyes were still staring up at Ackroyd, but he was motionless. The constable bent over him, then said, "I'm afraid he's dead. No more confessions there."

Nick's hands, holding his son tightly, brought the boy down against his own body. Jamie clung to Nick's chest and leather jacket as the boy tried to get his breath.

While Roberta rubbed her painful arms and hands, clenching and unclenching her fingers, she looked down, saw the chauffeur's twitching body stretch out and then it, too, was still. She stared up at the still secure top landing of the staircase to see who had rescued them with those short, murderous shots. She saw the chemist McQuarry leaning back against the wall, his good hand frozen on a heavy old-fashioned handgun, too big for any she had seen or handled on a film set.

Constable Ackroyd, having finished his examination of Sir Arthur, turned Weems over with the toe of his shoe. "Well, this one's gone too." He took out his small notebook, sighed and wrote something in it before putting it back. "You people are lucky I came along."

"We are?" Nick asked without looking around at him.

"That is to say, myself and Mrs Camberson. You wouldn't want to explain this massacre yourselves, I hope? You and Mr McQuarry there."

This time Nick did look beyond the constable, toward the fragile, tear-stained woman who had witnessed the shootings, unnoticed by any of the desperate men. She nodded at Nick's questioning expression. She was shaking badly.

"I couldn't let young Jamie be killed. I heard Weems and — and Orin talking about it. Orin thought it was going too far. But —"

"But the fellow did nothing," Ackroyd finished succinctly. "So Mrs Camberson obligingly called me. Sorry I couldn't be in the Mincham office to settle things with you, Mr Demian, but as things turned out, you may find we did right, Mrs Camberson and me."

"Too bad you weren't a little earlier, then none of this would have been necessary," Nick said sharply. "I almost lost my future wife as well as my son."

The constable shrugged. "I'll not say no to that. But there's reason in all things . . . Mr McQuarry, you hadn't ought to be carrying around Lugers like that. You might hurt somebody. It is a Luger, isn't it?"

McQuarry nodded wearily. "Liberated during the clean up in Germany. Never knew it still worked."

Nick was looking up at Roberta. He was gentle with Jamie but asked him, "Think we can get you to the sofa now, Jamie-boy? I want to thank our Roberta in proper style."

Ackroyd glanced at Elly Camberson who began to wipe away her tears and to smile in a watery way. He said, "Quite a heroine, Mr Nick's young lady."

"And Mrs Camberson," Roberta put in loudly, feeling she could afford to be generous.

Jamie tried to make a gesture with his sorely pulled right arm but groaned. "You go, Father. I clutched Roberta like she was my lifeline. And she was. Could you just help me to poor Mac? He's had a bad time of it, too."

"Surest thing." As Roberta watched them hobbling toward her, Jamie assisted by his father's strong arms, she knew that Jamie wouldn't have stood for being carried. She climbed down a few stairs with an effort and went into first Jamie's arms and then his father's.

Nick murmured, "Thank you, my darling. And bless you."

She thought it was worth all the pain and aches in her wrenched body to see that look in his eyes. He edged Jamie past her on the inside of the staircase, away from the broken part of the banister, until Mac reached out and, man-like, tried to shake hands with Jamie. But he saw at once that Jamie's arms would be a long time in getting back their agility. Instead, for the first time in many years, he put his arms around the boy and hugged him. Jamie stifled a few groans.

Meanwhile, Elly Camberson, wiping away tears with her fingers, protested to the constable, "It wasn't Orin or the others that poisoned the poor mare that long time ago, that started it all. It was Weems. Sir Arthur told him to and he did. He bragged about it once in Toby's pub. I was drunk — drinking — and I heard him. Hateful thing he was!"

With Jamie blessedly safe, and feeling Nick's strong but fast heartbeat against her, Roberta and Nick watched McQuarry. Nick said,

"You know how we feel, Mac. We can never thank you enough."

McQuarry was silent a minute. Then he shook his head.

"No need. I didn't do it for the young lady. Or even my friend Jamie, or you, Mr Nick. It was a repayment. Long overdue."

Jamie studied him thoughtfully. Then he told the others staring up at them, "I know. It was Sultana."

Nick caught McQuarry's tired gaze and assured him gently, "Sultana must have known what she meant to you. Even at the end."

"It's been worth the price I'll have to pay now. Prison no doubt."

"I'll get you the best lawyers, Mac. There's mitigating circumstances. They were going to kill Jamie."

McQuarry looked down at the heavy weapon he had dropped when he put an arm around Jamie. He nodded without speaking.

Chapter Twenty-Four

Twenty-four hours after the catastrophe at Demian House, as Nick and Roberta waited for Constable Ackroyd's summons to Mincham, he put his arm around her and drew her to him. From the top of the stairs they studied the broken banister, and he said, "We were lucky, at that." She nodded. The furniture had already been set up again, and the blood from the gunshot wounds cleared up by two girls from the village as best they could. He went on.

"Poor darling, you look like an American footballer with all those padded wrappings around your shoulders."

She smiled, then reminded him, "It's nothing compared to Jamie. He's the most remarkable boy I ever knew. Last night, before we left Casualty, he was boasting that it didn't hurt 'hardly' at all as he put it. All he cared about was coming home and working with me on his script. Bless him."

"You and Jamie," he murmured. "How did I get so lucky, when I've been so blind? You'd think I'd have sensed the falseness of Art. Sheila sensed it. She wouldn't marry him, though he had all the right seductive qualities. But not me. Stout-heart, buddies forever. My only real friend these past years — God, what an idiot I was!"

"What made you come home when you did? Sir Arthur was certainly surprised to see you. So was Weems. He tripped on something and that must have saved you."

He thought back. "A phone call saved me. I called Art's office to warn him about Weems, after all. He had to be told. Anyway, Mrs Peavis chirped brightly, 'Oh no, sir. He's still in Edenbrook with Weems.' He hadn't even gone to London. He lied to me when he called the house earlier. Remember? Why the pointless lie? And after all these years. That did it. A little late, I'd say. I've been more than stupid. Hopelessly blind."

She shook her head, wincing at the effort this caused, as the muscles reminded her that they had been badly treated yesterday.

"You believed in his friendship. It does you credit, darling."

He kissed the top of her head. "If we can just get that body in the mill pond solved decently, maybe then we can get on with our lives. Meanwhile —" He looked around the big room, sniffing. "The place still smells of blood."

As she stiffened he apologised. "I know. I'm sorry."

"The girls did their best, with a good deal of help from Mrs Schramm," she reminded him.

He considered her words and nodded. "I had some time to think last night. If Elly Camberson is right and only two or three of our tenants were actively involved with Art and Weems, I've a notion to sell the cottages to the rest of them. Maybe on some long-term payments they can meet. What do you think?"

She didn't want to overdo her eagerness for the idea so she said simply, "I think it does you credit, and I suspect Sheila would be relieved too. She's been wonderful, helping out in every way during the last few hours. She told me she had put off a dental appointment in Mincham so she could make herself useful."

"Putting off dental appointments doesn't come under the category of sacrifices," he laughed. "Well, at least the rugs are gone for cleaning. And only a few stains came through on the floor. I only hope Merlina isn't mixed up in her father's foulness."

Roberta hurried to reassure him. "No, no. She was on her mother's side. Thank God for poor Elly. But Camberson is Merlina's father, after all. The girls tell me Merlina brought some things to him at the Mincham jail this morning. Everyone in the village is enormously relieved that whatever those men were up to is ended. So not every one of your tenants was involved, Nick. Please don't think that. It's what Sir Arthur would like you to have believed."

Sheila Demian made her way down the staircase behind them, carefully avoiding the broken section of the banister. Nick looked up at her.

"You were way ahead of me, wise old sister that you are. You never fell for Art's famous charm."

Sheila laughed hoarsely. "The truth is, I had a crush on Art when I was seventeen, but I got over that long ago. Only Art didn't seem to know it."

The telephone rang and Sheila and Roberta waited anxiously as Nick picked up the hall extension.

It was Constable Ackroyd telling them he had been delayed by Will Brinkby's confession. He may have heard the "Thank God" of Sheila Demian and Roberta, but business was business and he ended, "We will expect you as soon as you can make it. You and Miss Fisher, of course, are very important witnesses. We will need your statements." He added on a note of pride that "Your boy made an excellent witness. We have had his testimony this morning. Sister Longacre says he is doing well, by the way."

"You questioned my son?" Nick demanded. "After all he went through and without me being present?"

"You misunderstand," the constable assured him brightly. "The boy's all grit. He insisted Sister Longacre call us."

"Damn!" Nick muttered. He looked around at the two women. "All right. We'll be there. Can my boy come home?"

"He's waiting at the hospital, Mr D. Battered but ready, the nurses say. Proud, too. Well then, we'll expect you and Miss Fisher."

"We'll be there." Nick reiterated, and was about to cut the connection when Ackroyd spoke again.

"One more thing. The matter of the woman's body in the mill pond. Mrs Camberson says it was your housekeeper."

"But how — what happened to her?"

Ackroyd was smooth and a little cocky "We're sure you'll weather any little questions that Mrs Camberson hasn't filled in."

There was a click and Nick put the receiver down.

The women looked at each other. Sheila said, "I expect they'll want me then, as well. I knew more about her than either of you could have."

Roberta tried not to let them guess at her inner trembling. "All right. Let's get our coats and be on our way. Besides," she added on an optimistic note, "We'll see Jamie sooner."

They moved hurriedly, even Nick, anxious to get the official business in Mincham over as soon as possible. Roberta didn't know what either of the Demians might be thinking, but she herself was still terrified about any connection they might dream up between Nick and the dead woman.

All the way over to Mincham they passed places that Roberta knew must have sickening memories for the Demians. Nick, like Roberta, had been studying the culvert near the Edenbrook square. The square itself must have held memories she thought as they passed, and then came the long ditch that the brook turned into, until it reached the cluttered weir. He spoke suddenly, startling his sister.

"For some time now, old Mac has been trying to convince me that the man he saw slumped down in the car the morning Veda died was Weems. And like a fool, I denied Mac's own eyesight because it hinted at Art's part in it. And of course, that could never be."

Sheila shook her head. "Veda wouldn't give that slug, Weems, the time of day. To quote my nephew."

"Weems was there to drive Veda to Art, of course."

"God! What a creature!" Sheila muttered and Roberta wondered if she referred to Veda Demian as well.

When Nick spoke he sounded normal. Only the self-contempt for his own blindness remained. "After Veda was gone, and I'll do him the justice to assume he loved her, he must have really hated us. He lived high. He always needed money. What with two divorces, I suppose he began to see me, and Jamie of course, as standing between him and everything we had."

"Marry me, get rid of Jamie, ruin you with scandal and murder. Art would have it all." Sheila treated it lightly, hiding the bitterness she must have felt.

Roberta put in, "The village seemed to fall into Sir Arthur's hands. Fall guys, we'd call them. So he saw to it that Weems used them. Say what you will, darling, he was such a coward, your friend I mean. I'm sorry."

"There is nothing you can say that I haven't

said to myself during these last few hours," he admitted.

They arrived in Mincham before Roberta wanted them to yet she was anxious to have these horrors settled. When Nick pulled up at a little street that crossed the far end of the main road, several official-looking dark cars were parked on both sides of the street, and heads looked out at the Demians' car from every one of them.

"Just the usual press up from London and the provinces," Nick said casually. "Don't let them bother you."

Roberta laughed at the irony of his remark and both Demians stared at her, surprised. She reminded them, "To someone from peaceful Los Angeles where crime is never permitted, the press and photographers are a terror."

"Come to think of it," Sheila told her brother, "We'd better let Roberta handle our public relations."

But in spite of their lighthearted behaviour, all three of them shared the tension as they entered the old stone police building. The narrow, dark halls were forbidding and the atmosphere not lifted by the sight of doors which were all ajar. Obviously, Mincham's secretaries and other denizens of the police fraternity were behind those doors, hoping something exciting would happen.

She was almost glad to see Constable Ackroyd's pompous features as she and the Demians were ushered into a utilitarian office, with room for several other desks, by a middle-aged man in uniform.

Constable Ackroyd, much more official than the uncertain and uneasy witness he had been in yesterday's blood-letting, nodded to the new-comers but made no effort to shake hands. He waved them to three straight-backed chairs. "The latest torrent of confessions was signed and witnessed not an hour ago," he announced. "To the extent that Will Brinkby was a hapless tool of Toby Teague and Bartholomew Weems. Brinkby also admits his son, Gordon, a half-witted creature at best, played a little trick, as he calls it, on Miss Fisher here, by climbing into the late Halloway house in London and causing Miss Fisher a bit of trouble. They were apparently hoping Miss Fisher would blame you, Mr Demian. The idea appears to have been either Weems's, or Sir Arthur's. No one seems sure."

And I nearly did blame Nick, Roberta thought, hating the barrister all over again for having manipulated her so well.

Constable Ackroyd set aside several sheets and turned to another statement.

"Brinkby also named Orin Camberson, and we have that gentleman's cross-complaint against Teague and Weems. With Weems dead we have only one man who makes no confession, but I expect it won't be long before Teague also decides to talk . . . You have been unlucky in your choice of tenants, Mr Demian."

"So I gather. Which of them, may I ask, killed

Mrs DeVrees in the mill pond?"

Constable Ackroyd's lips pursed in a manner which he must have fancied was judicial. It succeeded, as far as Roberta was concerned.

"We rather fear that information may have to be pieced together. Mrs Camberson says her husband saw two men stop the Frenchwoman one evening about a month ago. Mrs DeVrees had taken a short cut behind the mill, perhaps to avoid the villagers. She was headed toward Mincham. They accused her of eavesdropping in the pub. That, at least, is Mrs Camberson's view and mine. It was about nine o'clock at night. The woman cried out, probably for help. Mrs Camberson claims she slipped into the pond and the stout man, this Weems, either pushed her under or let her drown. Perhaps so she couldn't warn you of what she may have heard. You understand the motive is still uncertain."

Roberta felt sick with the horror of it.

Sheila cried out with a sudden thought. "I know how we may find out about the DeVrees woman. I just thought of it."

Nick and the constable ignored this outburst. Nick said, "Then, there is Teague. The fat man who pushed, or didn't push her, was not Teague. It was Weems. But Teague certainly knows the motive."

Sheila leaned over the desk and raised her voice.

"DeVrees went to a dentist in Mincham. McCorkle, I remember. She may have given him her French address. She was always writing to France. Elly told me she bought stamps for mail there on several occasions."

Roberta felt a twinge of excitement and hope. "The unfinished note in the jewelled egg case that they found. Who was the one she wrote that to?"

"A lover in France?" Constable Ackroyd spoke with an official lack of enthusiasm, but he added, "It just may be a clue." He got up, excused himself, and went out of the room.

Nick grinned at his sister. "You may have found — or should I say *recalled* — the situation, my wise sister."

Sheila confided cynically to Roberta, "You'll find it takes a great deal to squeeze a compliment out of him."

But Roberta, anxious as she was, shared Nick's hope that the dentist McCorkle might solve the problem of the unfortunate woman who had died, with or without help, in the stagnant vegetation of the mill pond.

Several minutes later Constable Ackroyd returned, pleased with his own quick thinking.

"Miss Sullivan has obtained the French telephone number given to the dentist by Madame Francoise DeVrees. It is in a village outside Lyon. A lady is on the line now." He added as he returned to his desk, "She apparently speaks good English. The conversation is being recorded and you may hear it if all goes well."

Nick and Roberta said nothing but Sheila

wanted to know, "Then it isn't a lover? A relation, perhaps?"

"As a matter of fact, it is a Madame Barberaux. She is most anxious to know why she hasn't heard the details about Mrs DeVrees." He pressed a buzzer and Sheila jumped as Miss Sullivan's voice filled the room. Even Nick looked a little apprehensive.

The constable's highly official voice answered. "Madame Barberaux, Miss Demian of Demian House in Edenbrook formerly employed Madame DeVrees. I wonder if you could tell us what you know of Madame?"

The woman's voice was sharply to the point and probably elderly. "It is four weeks, Monsieur, since her last letter. I have written several times and received nothing but three words on a piece of paper: 'Deceased', and the cause, 'Brutal'. To the point, you will admit."

Nick and the constable looked at each other. The constable reintroduced himself. "I speak as a member of the police establishment, you understand. It was not generally known here that the lady was dead. We thought she had returned home. How did the note say she died?"

"Drowning. I did not know you were near the Channel. Perhaps a river?"

Constable Ackroyd explained a trifle awkwardly. "We are investigating, Madame. A portion of her last letter has been found. Written perhaps —" He glanced at Nick, then back to the telephone in his hand. "Written to a lover?"

The Frenchwoman snorted. *"C'est impossible, Monsieur.* I would have known. She loved only one male in this world. Louis-Albert. She wrote only to him. I would swear to that. They were in my care."

"And Louis-Albert, he is — ?"

"Her son, but of course. Of eight years."

"We heard nothing of her child," Sheila gasped. "Nothing."

But to Roberta it made sense. The unfinished letter in the decorated egg had always puzzled her with its language, but to a child . . .

Nick put in, "It's strange that she didn't mention him."

The constable repeated this but the woman contradicted him. "No, Monsieur. Louis-Albert is not born — I believe you say legitimate."

"But these things are accepted nowadays, Madame."

"Not in this village. Not even in Lyon, among decent country people."

The constable asked suddenly, "Did your friend ever mention some man with whom she —" He hesitated, avoiding Nick's eyes this time, "She might be said to have had any tender feelings?"

The woman was huffy again. "She said her employer was a handsome man, somewhat indifferent to the females around him. These are her words to me, you understand. It was a bad thing, she said in her last letter."

"Bad?"

"Yes. She did not know the gentleman well. But the people of the village were acting very oddly. Telling lies. She said she had caught them in lies about her employer. Saying he was with the women very much. It was not true. They spread many such stories. She said if they spread more, she would warn the gentleman and go also to the police. That is the last time I heard from Madame DeVrees."

For a long moment the constable was silent, looking down at his desk.

Nick and the women glanced at each other but no one said a word. The room was filled suddenly with the old Frenchwoman's querulous voice.

"Madame owes me two months' pay for my services. I will keep the boy safe. We are old friends, Louis and I. This climate is better for his breathing. But I must know what to expect for his future. You comprehend?"

Constable Ackroyd looked around helplessly and Nick relieved him by speaking up. "I am grateful for Mrs DeVrees's kindness in defending me from the gossip and lies. Tell her, Ackroyd."

Before the constable could say anything they heard the Frenchwoman's anxious, impatient voice. "But what is to become of my little Louis. I am not a rich woman, Monsieur Ackroyds." She had trouble with the name but no one laughed.

The constable shrugged and Nick said, "Tell her arrangements will be made, if the boy is happy with her. But we will come to an agreement. Perhaps my fiancée and I will visit Madame Barberaux and young Louis-Albert on our honeymoon, very soon."

Madame Barberaux softened. She was still assuring the constable of her cooperation when he covered the phone to tell Nick, "You are free to go when you sign the papers on Miss Sullivan's desk. Initial them where Miss Sullivan has indicated . . . Yes, Madame. Quite so, Madame. He is one of our leading citizens. Very well thought of."

Nick stared at the crumbling paper on the wall but Roberta and Sheila exchanged amused glances. Then the three of them got up with one accord, anxious to be rid of all connections with these past few days.

In the next room, even more spartan, they ignored the end of the French conversation and hurried to affix their signatures to the dozen pages on the end of Miss Sullivan's desk. These contained their recollections of yesterday's eye-witness actions at Demian House.

Minutes later the three of them were glad enough to get outside into the freshness of the windy afternoon, ignoring the camera clicks of the waiting press.

Not until they were in the car did any of them speak. They were too afraid other complications would set in. But as they were driving away, Sheila said, "Let's hope Mincham profits from our ambitious friend Ackroyd."

Roberta remarked, "At least, he's been on the

right side in this business."

They all agreed to that, although Sheila added, "I can't help wondering what Ackroyd's superiors will say and do at his neat little takeover of this case."

"Success, my dear Sheila, turns impudent takeovers into future superintendents."

But Roberta was thinking of the boy in France, deprived of his mother in that horrible way.

"Are you really going to help the DeVrees boy?" she asked Nick.

Nick looked surprised. "Why not? The way I'm riding along on this good-hearted business, I may decide the rest of my tenants deserve a break. Hear this, Sheila. You may not believe it but I'm a reasonable man. I just might go along with whatever the tenants can raise in payments. Some sort of monthly scheme. They will probably change their view of me as the devil and I'll rapidly become the good Samaritan."

"Thank God," Sheila told him, to which Roberta added, "Thank God from me too." She kissed him and he gave her the smile she had learned to love, so different from that supercilious and arrogant man she had seen first in Arthur Laidlaw's office. Or had all that arrogance and unpleasantness been painted ever so carefully by Sir Arthur?

Roberta thought of her ride to Demian House with Sir Arthur several days ago and how carefully he had pushed the idea of 'his closest friend' as a womaniser who won all the females from loyal, gentlemanly Arthur Laidlaw!

It was a ride of less than ten minutes before they pulled up at the hospital.

Looking like a bandage-wrapped mummy from the waist up, Jamie waited in a new, electrified wheelchair beside Sister Longacre. For once, he made no objection to the chair.

"It does everything, Father. I could ride to London in it. Look, Roberta, Aunt Sheila. And Sister Longacre says I'll be going up to the City and maybe get my leg cured. No steel. No brace. One of the specialists is a Yank, Roberta."

She started to hug him and caught herself in time, though he laughed as her padded shoulders came into contact with his.

Everyone was talking at once, Sister Longacre assuring them hopefully that it might not be long before Jamie walked better than his father did.

Nick cleared his throat. Roberta knew what an effort it was for him to discuss this possibility without showing an emotion that would upset his son.

"We're going to work toward that, boy, and maybe a few prayers wouldn't hurt along the way."

Jamie looked mischievous. "Then, Father, I've got a big favour to ask."

"Ask away."

"Remember how that fat old Weems slipped on something on the staircase yesterday and couldn't hit you with that lamp?"

"I certainly do. Very well."

377

"Then, can I keep the thing? It did, maybe, save your life." He held out his hand with an effort. "It must have flown off my finger when I was tripped up." In his palm a deeply coloured stone, veined, but dark as wine, gleamed up at everyone. Miss Halloway's opal ring. Everyone was stupified. Nick broke the silence with his laugh.

"If it saved your old father, I'd be ungrateful to refuse. Perhaps opals are lucky after all!"

Jamie looked up at Nick. "It's a pity Mac's not here or I could show him my chair. He will get off, won't he?"

"We'll do our best for him, son," his father assured him.

He wheeled the chair around smartly. "Here I go. I'll race you to the entrance."

Roberta looked at Nick and Sheila and the rapidly departing Jamie. She felt the happiness of her ready-made family, the only complete family she had ever known.

She decided it was impossible to be happier.

We hope you have enjoyed this Large Print book. Other G.K. Hall & Co. or Chivers Press Large Print books are available at your library or directly from the publishers.

For more information about current and upcoming titles, please call or write, without obligation, to:

G.K. Hall & Co.
P.O. Box 159
Thorndike, Maine 04986 USA
Tel. (800) 223-2336

OR

Chivers Press Limited
Windsor Bridge Road
Bath BA2 3AX
England
Tel. (0225) 335336

All our Large Print titles are designed for easy reading, and all our books are made to last.